Central Drive

Central Drive

When There Is No Just in Justice

Regina Neequaye

LIBRARY OF CONGRESS CATALOGING-
IN-PUBLICATION
DATA HAS BEEN APPLIED FOR

ISBN 978-0-9718860-1-8
LCCN 2018902154

Printed in the United States of America

Publisher's Note: This book is a work of fiction. Names, characters, places and incidents either are the product of the author's imagination or are used fictitiously, any resemblance to actual persons, living or dead, business establishments, events or locales are entirely coincidental.

DEDICATION

I would like to give thanks to my creator. To my husband, Lamar Crowell, you are the best and consistently get better with time. I would like to thank my mother, Marjorie Renee Monnigan Reynolds, who gave me the gift of compassion. To my children, Reynolds, Jordan, and Monnighan, you guys have been my inspiration. To my sisters, Denise, Shela, and Vonetta your support is much appreciated.

Chapter 1
Myrtle

It was two gunshots; the seconds in between them felt like hours. The acoustics, so precise, the vibration resonated inside the hollow of my chest. I stand still, holding my breath for what seems like an eternity as I wait for a barrage of return firepower. The silence makes me uneasy. I move away from the windows to the small space under the stairs where the air is thick and musty. I am anxious and fast becoming claustrophobic. I exhale as faint sounds of the police and county rescue sirens become distinct.

The sound of gunfire in the neighborhood is a common occurrence that blends with television, music, and everyday conversations. This was once a vibrant and safe community. Greed and shady political deals changed the demographics from a neighborhood with a healthy mixture of middle-class, upper-class, and generationally wealthy stable households to one with a disproportionate number of income-challenged minorities and first-generation immigrants.

The wealthy households packed up and immediately left the neighborhood at the first sign of the change. Mexican and Blacks gangs moved in and destroyed what was left of our community playing Wild, Wild West games at the ending of the crack cocaine epidemic and the beginning of the opiate pandemic. One week, a rival black gang attacks a Mexican gang; the next week, the Mexican gang retaliates. The violence they brought to the community pushed most of the remaining middle and upper-class households out. With help from the East European immigrants, the gangs have gradually advanced their munitions from nine millimeters to high-power assault weaponry. The East Europeans, relatively new to the community, hide their illegal arms trade, and God only knows what else, behind legitimate businesses.

I lean toward the opening under the stairs and listen for more gunfire. After a few minutes of silence, I move from underneath the stairs and stand in the foyer outside of the kitchen. This does not sound like a typical gang shooting. There is no barrage of bullets followed by tires screeching against the asphalt as the cowards flee the scene.

I used to think about packing my belongings and leaving, but my retirement income is not enough to afford market rent and necessities. My home is paid for, and I am on a fixed income. I have no other choice but to stay. The change in the neighborhood is heartbreaking. The schools used to be award winning. The neighborhood was stable, and home values steadily increased. The 1996 World Games our neighboring city hosted exacerbated an already declining community. People came from all over to enjoy the games and festivities. Many fell in love with the cleanliness and affordability of Atlanta and the surrounding suburbs and did not leave. Some relocated from crime ridden cities with the hope of a better life for their families but neglected to convey their hopes to their offspring who transported the negative behaviors they were fleeing.

The migration created a thriving real estate market never seen before on this side of the Mason Dixon line. The housing market was so lucrative it became catalyst for a nefarious plot between local politicians in the pockets of rich developers. Housing could not be built fast enough to supply the demand. Developers bulldozed parking lots, dilapidated buildings used by the homeless, and old homes in neighborhoods the police would not enter to build luxury living communities to accommodate the new transplants. To Southerners, these new luxury homes were pricey, but for Northerners, who are accustomed to paying exorbitant rent and mortgages, the prices were a steal. Cranes can be found on almost every corner in downtown Atlanta. New construction sites became part of the landscape, but land is finite. Developers eventually began to run out of space. They looked deeper inside the inner city for land, but commercial land was too expensive to meet their profit margins. Prime real estate sitting under public housing became the profitable alternative.

I step into the kitchen, grab a cup from the cabinet, fill it with water, and hold as much water as I can in my mouth. I remove an onion from the bag and begin to peel away the skin. According to my mother, if you hold water in your mouth while cutting onions, it decreases the amount of irritation to the eyes. Just as I was beginning to relax and cut the onion, I heard more sirens and sounds of speeding police cars cutting through the wind.

I distract myself from the uneasiness as more sirens arrive by reminiscing on the old days when one could safely walk the streets in our neighborhood any time of the day or night. The few of us original residents, who still called Central Drive home, could have never imagined this could happen to our neighborhood. We saw it happen in Klaxton, a neighboring county, but did not imagine it would happen to us. As crime increased, Klaxton County schools declined, and the housing values plummeted. Law enforcement decimated the county budget due to overtime paid in a futile attempt to deal with the increasing crime. We erroneously assumed our elected officials would see the disastrous results of our neighbor and take heed, but they did not.

The onion is strong; the water I hold in my mouth does nothing to ease irritation in my eyes. I wipe tears away from my eyes, open the fridge, and remove a slightly frozen chicken for tonight's dinner. Water splashes in my eye, as I drop the chicken in the sink to thaw. I reach for a napkin and notice someone standing outside through a crack in the blinds. I separate the blinds and see Jermaine standing in the middle of the street with a brown paper bag in one hand and a cell phone in the other. A news van, with red and yellow writing, speeds past on route to join the other responders at the corner; this is unusual. Crime in our neighborhood is so common, it is no longer newsworthy.

I peep through the crack in the blinds again. Jermaine has not moved. His head is bent forward; his eyes are glued to his cell phone. He is so still he looks like a mannequin. I close the blinds and assemble herbs and spices on the counter to season the chicken when it thaws then turn on the television. I am surprised and almost shocked to find "Breaking news: Officer Involved Shooting" pans across the breakfast bar in red bold letters at the bottom of the television screen.

Chapter 2
Benazir

"Benazir." His tone is relaxed and perfectly rehearsed. "Dear, I will have the bank deposit ready in a few." He is intentionally cautious with his words. His attempt at kindness is awkward and inauthentic. It feels as if I am engaging with a creepy, sociopathic stranger. I would rather he be himself. Over the years, I have grown comfortable with his cruelty.

My father and I are always at odds. He does not understand me, and I no longer care to understand him. My mother is all I have. My mother is educated and highly accomplished in her field. She is a professor at one of the major universities in Atlanta. She is respected among her peers and sits on many corporate and civic boards. She is well-read and very cultured. The Brute only reads numbers on American currency. I don't understand my mother's reasons for marrying such a backwards man. "Duty and Tradition" are the words she sings when I ask her to expound on the tragedy, I call her life. After she sings "Duty and Tradition," I tune out everything that comes out her mouth. She has the power. She is a citizen. The Brute is not. She could rid herself of him with the swipe of a pen but for this "Duty and Tradition."

His ways are archaic. He is the most self-centered person I have ever met; he believes he is entitled because he is a man. My parents have nothing in common. I am the only good thing that came from their tragic union.

I detest living in the same house with him. He is so toxic that simply looking at him causes me to spiral into a deep depression. My parents spent thousands of dollars on mandated counseling to reveal what I have always known. My father is mentally ill, and he makes the entire family sick.

His assaults on me and my mother started as far back as I can remember. He suffers from a deeply rooted self-hate that afflicts many members of minority cultures living in a Eurocentric society. He unsuccessfully tried to pass the self-hate gene to me. He would often compare me with thin Caucasian girls. He was especially fond of those with blonde hair and blue eyes.

He pushed me to befriend unwelcoming Caucasian classmates. He did not understand the cruelty inflicted on a brown skin girl trying to fit in with white skin and blue-eyed privilege. Befriending people of color felt natural, but Black Americans are the lowest on the totem pole in his opinion. "They are lazy and uncultured," he would say. The fact that ninety percent of his business is with Black Americans does not change his opinion. He also has disdain for Mexicans, but they are slightly higher on his totem pole; he proclaims, "Mexicans are drunks but hard workers." White Americans are the only group he gives a pass. He shows more kindness to the white drug addicts who come into the store begging for handouts than he does to the hard-working Black Americans that patronize his business. Blacks are not genuinely accepted by either of my parents. Pakistanis are too traditional for my liking, so I was forced to navigate toward Caucasian classmates. To be more than a tag along, I starved myself to have the thin, boyish body white boys seem to find attractive. I bleached my hair so much it fell out, forcing me to cut it much shorter than comfortable.

Most of the popular Caucasian kids ignored me. To keep from being alone and totally isolated, I settled for the misfits. Rachel was my misfit Caucasian friend. She was smart and ranked in the top three percent of our class, but she suffered from eating disorders and controlled her weight by purging. I made the tragic mistake of bringing her home for a weekend sleepover. The Brute was so captivated with her she became the new model for my behavior. "Benazir," he would say, "you must exercise harder! Look at your beautiful mother. She has the perfect face but look at her ass." He would turn his nose upward and do quick side to side movements with his head that is normally associated with Indians. "Do you want to be a blubber ass like your mother?" He has no regard for my mother. He is comfortable and holds nothing back in expressing his disdain for the native attributes of the woman he married.

"Look at your friend Rachel. She is a tiny little thing." His bright smile and jovial expression as he spoke of Rachel felt creepy. "You should exercise with her." Rachel does not exercise. She purges. She eats more food in one sitting than I ever thought humanly possible. Watching her eat was an event. She closes her eyes and slowly chews her food, savoring every morsel. If a grain falls out of her mouth, onto her clothing, the table or even the floor, she quickly picks it up, blows it off and puts it back into her mouth. She sits still all of ten minutes after consuming a meal a man four times her size could not ingest, excuses herself to the bathroom, and purges.

I grew tired of the rigorous exercise routine. I was tired of starving myself. I missed the comfort of a full stomach and the taste of food, so I enlisted Rachel for purging lessons. Her regimen was strict. Rule number one, eat as much as you can in ten minutes and move the food all over your tongue to savor the flavor. Rule number two, eat most meals alone, and rule number three, and the most important, place the index finger in the back of the throat before the food begins to digest, so most of what is ingested comes back up through the mouth. After I mastered the art of purging, my friendship with Rachel quickly ran its course. Her obsession with her looks became annoying.

When I entered tenth grade, the Brute's constant nagging began to take a serious toll. I was never thin enough. My hair was too fluffy. I ate too much bread. I should work on my abs. I began to eat less and purge more. The purging began to cause health problems; the acid from my stomach began to damage my esophagus. No matter how much I purged, I could not get thin enough. I began using laxatives in addition to purging to control my weight. I was always hungry. I would go days surviving on lettuce and water or cucumbers soaked in lemon juice.

My body was not getting enough nutrients for basic functioning; I began to pass out in school. The teachers became concerned about my emaciated look. The school counselor called the house to express the staff's belief I should be evaluated for an eating disorder. His response was, "When she gets hungry, she will eat. Paying tens of thousands of dollars for someone to tell a child to eat is crazy." The counselor was persistent and expressed to the Brute her belief that my health and possibly my life was in danger. He is self-righteous. He had no regards for the teachers or counselors. When they called the house, he would pick up the phone after the first ring, wait for a couple of seconds, and slam the handset hard against the cradle. The school counselor became irritated with his response and sent a letter delivered by a Sheriff Deputy that outlined a series of consequences if he continued to refuse to address their concerns. Believing law enforcement interaction could affect his application for citizenship, he reluctantly agreed to meet with the school nurse and counselor. He remained resistant. He yelled at me and my mother in front of the counselor and other staff members while constantly proclaiming, "This would never happen in Pakistan."

After two meetings with the counselor, he decided he was done. In response, the counselor forwarded our case to the Department of Child Services. A middle-aged black woman escorted by the police appeared at our front door and threatened to take me away. I am not certain he was serious, but his response to the Children's Services Worker was, "Take her!" My mother became hysterical, borrowed a backbone, and finally threatened to take me and leave. This was the one and only time I ever witnessed her exercise the power we all know she has.

The Department of Child Services opened a case, and the courts mandated our family to counseling. The counselor barely spoke to my father. She would start each session asking, "Does everyone feel safe?" She would look at my mother intensely. My mother never answered; she locked eyes with the Brute and simply turned away. I ignored the Brute's subtle, menacing looks when the counselor addressed me and asked if I felt safe. I responded, "I don't know." The counselor advised that I keep a log when I do not feel safe and include the names of the people who made me feel unsafe. Initially, the Brute's verbal attacks became harsher and more frequent. However, he quickly changed his disposition, as it became apparent as I walked around with my notepad, I was taking notes and logging every time he was verbally abusive to me or my mother.

Though the counselor did everything within her power to remain biased, it was evident she knew what I have always known; my father is a monster and the source of our family problems. The counselor addressed my log of unsafe feelings in the presence of me, my mother, and the Brute during the weekly sessions. He denied each incident of his abusive actions, past and present. He denied the year he tormented me with exercise I did not want to partake in. He denied referring to me and my mother as "blubber ass." My mother's loyalty to "Duty and Tradition" outweighs her maternal obligations; she co-signed his denial of abuse. It was obvious the counselor did not believe my parents. Finding solidarity with the counselor changed my disposition. I no longer participated in his exercise routines. I stopped purging, and my weight began to stabilize. My prognosis was good. After several months, the counselor ended the sessions with the caveat to call if the Brute's behavior began to deteriorate.

I began to befriend black girls in my classes

because we had more in common. He would often accuse me of behaving too much like Black Americans. My style of clothing, and, in his opinion, less than stellar grades were worrisome. In high school, I sometimes barely made the "A" always 91, 92 or 93, much too many points from 100. I am now a sophomore in college and still a straight "A" student.

He holds strong to his belief that I am unaware of the amazing blessings he bestows on me. He continued on occasions with threats to send me to Pakistan. I used to have bouts of anxiety thinking he would send me away. I would check their credit card statements every month to see if he purchased plane tickets to have adequate time to plan my escape. I developed a habit of saving money in various places in my room in the event I had to leave at a moment's notice.

The Brute is not only emotionally abusive, but he is also a financial abuser. He questions my mother about every penny she spends from her pay. He nagged her and demanded she direct deposits her pay into their joint account. He made himself the financial officer of the family because my brilliant mother with the PhD is not smart enough to manage the money she earns. I work in one of his convenience stores six-hours a day, seven days per week, and my pay is two hundred dollars per week. When I complain my pay is less than minimum wage, he sends invoices demanding immediate payment for rent to live in the house my mother purchased and for the car note he pays out of their joint account where the only deposits are from my mother's earnings.

We fare better than many. We call an eight-bedroom, ten-bathroom house in an exclusive gated community home. My father and I work at one of his stores on the corner of Harrison Road and Central Drive. He has all the money he could ever need, yet it is not enough.

Initially, I did not want to work for him. I dreaded it and even threatened suicide. I ran away to my aunt's home only to return because I felt sorry for my mother. I did not want her to have to bear his cruelty alone. He used to have workers from Pakistan he trusted to work in the stores. Unfortunately, like him, most had expired education VISAs. After September 11, 2001, the government began to crack down on all illegal residents and passed stricter laws that required businesses to verify the legality of their workers. Thus, it became hard to hire undocumented workers. Many people look at our dark skin and hair texture and believe us to be Mexican; the Immigration and Customs Enforcement stings that target Mexicans and Central American immigrants prompted most of his trusted, but undocumented, Pakistani employees to flee to Canada out of fear of deportation.

I detest being in his presence but working for him at the Central Drive store became the best thing that ever happened to me "She is no longer depressed, and she smiles all of the time," he brags to my mother. He credits my new attitude to bonding and spending time with him. Nothing could be further from the truth. I met my best friend while working at his store. His name is Jean-Jacques, but I call him Panther.

I am now an adult, but I would never tell my father about Panther. I often think of sharing my relationship with Panther with my mother, but I know "Duty and Tradition" own her loyalty and takes precedence over mother-daughter secrets. I love my Panther. He helped me heal from years of torment under the Ali Jinnah, also known as the Brute Regime. Unlike the Brute, Panther is strong yet compassionate, and, unlike my mother, he is free and not bound by "Duty and Tradition." Panther is a highly ranked amateur boxer dedicated to his craft. My love for him grew exponentially the first time I saw him in the boxing ring. It was as if he transformed into a god right before my eyes.

"I don't think I can go." We had been dating a couple of months when he invited me to his boxing match against Muhammad the Magnificent, an undefeated boxer in the amateur circuit. Muhammad's stats were high; it seemed everyone in the neighborhood including the Brute placed bets with the Russian restaurant owner against Panther. "I will ask permission, but I doubt he will allow me to go to a boxing match." We were at Kenwood Park, a secluded park in the middle of a subdivision down the street from the store. We carved out every moment we could to spend together. A quick kiss on the side of the store when I took the trash to the dumpster or a meetup for heavy petting and passionate kissing during a lunch break were moments I lived for.

"You are an adult. Right? I want to look out in the crowd and see your beautiful face. Everyone is betting against me. I need a good luck charm." His smile was bright; a tingling sensation ran through my body as he licked his thick lips, stepped closer, and planted light kisses on my forehead. Perspiration glistened like diamonds as the sunlight reflected against his dark, chocolate skin. He stood tall like Goliath next to my five feet, four-inch frame.

"I don't know if I can." Until Panther, I never

saw myself as an adult. I have always seen myself as their child.

"Just come." He passed the ticket. I surprised myself and took it.

I remember the excitement as if it was yesterday. The day of the boxing match I went crazy thinking of excuses to leave the store. "You are an adult" played through my mind all day. Finally, I grabbed my purse and said, "I am leaving for the day." He stood in the front of the register counting money. I did not give the words time to sink in. I grabbed my jacket; left the store, got in my car, and quickly sped out of the parking lot before the words could register in his brain. Instead of going home, I parked at the burger joint down the street, went into the bathroom, and changed clothes.

The parking lot at the Alliance Auditorium was full. Flashing lights from a sea of cameras illuminated the sky like a New Year's Day celebration, as photographers snapped pictures of local and national celebrities stepping out of top-of-the-line luxury cars. Professional scouts looking for the next contender occupied the first two rows of seats in the auditorium. The venue was standing room only. The noise was exhilarating. Women, some dressed in clothing so revealing they could not wear underwear, screamed to the top of their lungs as Panther jogged down the aisle of the small arena behind his stepfather and trainers. The Caucasian man the neighborhood named White Junkie Boy cleaned up well. I almost did not recognize him as he took his seat in the VIP section.

Panther threw his robe off his shoulder, jumped over the boxing ropes from a standing position, and aggressively stepped to Muhammad the Magnificent. The referee raised his hand and slightly pushed Panther away from his opponent. His chest looked like a rising mountain as he inhaled. The darkness of his skin, the deep cuts in his arms, and the hard, curved mounds on his chest mesmerized me. His gentle nature instantly transformed into a Herculean God. It appeared as if his body lengthened an entire foot. His eyes were blank. His normal jovial countenance was flat. The referee stood in the middle of the ring and explained the rules. There was no sign Panther was in tune with his words. He stared straight into his opponent's eyes until the bell rang. The Panther took two quick steps to Muhamad and threw a series of quick punches. The sound of his fist hitting his opponent's face echoed over the noise of the cheering crowd.

I quickly turned my face and closed my eyes when Muhammad's fist made contacted Panther's perfectly chiseled face. The impact was hard. Panther stumbled backwards. His head appeared to turn three hundred and sixty degrees. I opened my eyes and noticed the Russian restaurant owner and the Korean store owner sitting in the second row. They jumped to their feet and grabbed their heads when Panther dodged Muhammad's right fist by a hair and landed two quick left jabs to the side of Muhammad's face followed by a quick right jab to the middle of his forehead. Muhammad the Magnificent hit the canvas hard. His body stiffened like a wooden board, but Panther showed no mercy. He pounded his fists together and circled the opponent as he lay flat on the canvas. The referee pushed Panther in the corner. Muhammad rolled over, grabbed one of the ropes, and tried to prop himself on his knees only to fall forward. The referee began the count; when he yelled, "Ten,"

Muhammad laid still on the canvas. His trainer ran to him, removed something from his pocket, and placed it in front of Muhammad's nose. Muhammad slowly sat up but could not stand. Panther left the corner with both gloved fists in the air and stood on the second rope, receiving accolades from the cheering crowd. He then walked to Muhammad, reached down, pulled him to his feet, and embraced him.

From that day I knew I was in love. I am in love, and I would love to share my happiness with my mother, but I know she would most likely not keep secrets from the Brute. I would never risk Panther's life. My father is in denial; he is a racist. Although I am an adult, he can be angry and almost violent when the black boys attempt to engage me in conversation when they come in the store. He has no worries. I do not like the demeanor of the boys who come in the store with their pants down showing their underwear. They do not have Panther's discipline. I also ran them out of the store. Some are so bold I occasionally have to threaten them with the gun we keep behind the counter. But Panther is different. He is not like the other black boys or the Pakistani boys who speak to my father regarding his plans for my life.

"Benazir." The Brute's tone is soft; it sounds as if he is whispering.

"Yes." I am annoyed with his voice as he interrupts my pleasant travel down memory lane.

"I have the bank deposit ready." He passes the deposit bag. "You must hurry and get to the bank before it closes. Ask the teller for quarters. We are running low." I placed the money bag in my book bag and walked toward the door. I unlock my phone and dial Panther. He does not answer. His voicemail picks up the call. "Don't go the back way through the Nigger Jungle," the Brute warns as I push the door open.

"You sound like the racist whites who always confuse us with Mexicans and terrorists."

"I am many things, but I am not racist, Benazir." He points his finger toward me and shakes his head side to side. I ignore him and dial Panther's number again. He does not answer. "Don't you see I gave that retarded black boy a job cutting the grass and cleaning the grounds?" I ignore him as his chest extends outward with pride; if he were truthful, he would acknowledge the "retarded black boy" was desperate and the only person who would take the job as the wages were below the minimum, and the Brute pays him cash. No one knows anything about his retarded worker other than his name. He is a mysterious member of the neighborhood that goes by the name Jason. He is the last remaining fool on the block who would work for the Brute.

"And what about White Junkie Boy?" he yells as I stand in the threshold at the store entrance. "I gave him free beer, but he wanted more, and I could not afford him." He continues to plead his case as I leave the store. He used to give White Junkie Boy money and beer for emptying the coolers, mopping the floor, and cleaning the bathrooms, but even the junkie refused to continue working for him. He started paying him fifty dollars a week and a case of beer for half of a day's work, four days per week. When he cut the pay to twenty-five dollars and a six pack, White Junkie Boy quit.

I get in my car, back out of the parking space, and push the signal switch upward to take the right turn out of the parking lot to what he calls the

"Nigger Jungle." I look in my rearview mirror; two black males along with a white girl with greasy hair exit a car with North Carolina tags and enter the store. They caught my attention because the girl looks odd wrapped in an oversized, winter coat in spring weather.

I proceed to exit the parking lot when I see Panther running across the busy intersection of Harrison Road and Central Drive toward the store. I panic when he does not stop on the narrow median that divides the four lanes on Harrison Road with fast moving cars traveling in both directions. My heart races, and a wide smile covers my face as he runs full speed toward me. I quickly shifted the transmission to park position. I get out of the car and stretch my arms wide ready to embrace him, but he runs past me toward the path on the side of the store behind the fence the lazy Negros in the adjacent apartments made for quicker access to the corner bus stop. Initially, I did not notice the white detective who patrols the neighborhood running behind Panther, or Detective Chandler, a black police detective popular with the neighborhood residents, running behind them both. As I stand behind the driver's side door, I hear a gunshot. It is so loud I use both hands to cover my ears.

The sound of children screaming over explicit rap music and the panic in adult voices yelling, "Get down! Get the children!" interrupts the few seconds of complete silence before the second gunshot. People fire their guns in this neighborhood all the time. I have never heard a gunshot like this. The two Black American men that entered the store with the white girl run out and fall to their knees. One removes a small handgun and crawls on the ground back to their vehicle as if he is in military combat.

They get into the car and quickly drive away from the scene, leaving the white girl who came with them standing alone in the parking lot.

My heart drops. My stomach begins to turn. Why are the police chasing Panther? Police stings are customary during this time of year. The police occupy Central Drive when they need to meet quotas or need to fund their coffers. They set up roadblocks under the guise of checking identification and proof of insurance, but the true motive is to arrest young black people and force them to pay bond fees and ticket fines. In the last year or so, white people have been caught in the stings as the drug dealers who call Central Drive home are major suppliers to the new opiate market. Occasionally, I see classmates from high school park their fancy European cars in front of the store and wait for the drug dealers to deliver their product. It usually starts the beginning of spring with roadblocks in obscure places or undercover sting operations that target young drug dealers with small quantities of drugs on their persons.

I am paralyzed. I can't move. I want to scream. My mouth is wide open but does not produce sound. Blue spinning lights on top of late model police cruisers make me dizzy as they speed down Central Drive and turn into our parking lot. The Brute stands proud, greeting the officers as they exit their cars. He is so cheap he does not like to give plastic bags to paying customers, but offers the police officers free water, soft drinks, and snacks from the store as they arrive on the scene.

Chapter 3
Myrtle

Helicopters hover over the corner of Central Drive and Harrison Road. Something is terribly wrong. I am uneasy. I sometimes re-think my decision to stay. Most of my friends moved from the neighborhood years ago. I have no place to go; most of my family is deceased. This is my home. No one will force me to leave, not even these misfits that roam the streets with guns terrifying the community. This is my home; I plan to die here. Despite all that goes on around us, we are still a strong community. When I was sick with the flu, my neighbors attended to me more than my family. We have come together on many occasions and pooled financial resources to help pay a mortgage or purchase medicine for a neighbor falling on hard times.

We have endured more than most to maintain a resemblance of community, and we somehow remain strong. The southern migration from the real estate boom eventually slowed down. Greedy developers over estimated demand and over built luxury accommodations. Many of the new developments never reached full capacity, so the Real Estate Developers' Association and the Department of Tourism joined forces and hired the best marketers to create a campaign that courted professionals from neighboring counties to the city with a "Work, Live, Play" campaign.

The virtual tours of the new communities were so alluring, I even considered moving. The college educated dwellers in the luxury apartment communities on Central Drive did not have community ties. Many fell to the allure of the city and left our community to occupy new, state of the art apartment homes built on the land that used to be home to the generational poor.

Right when we thought we were finding stability, our neighborhood was under siege again. If gentrification in the city caused a storm, the resettlement of the Hurricane Katrina victims to Central Drive caused a tsunami. The politicians and Real Estate Developers' Association were not finish; someone in high places decided it was a brilliant idea to settle immigrants from East Europe, Nepal, Sudan, and other refugees from war torn nations into the abundance of vacant apartments and homes in our community. It was a culture shock. Everything quickly changed; women wrapped in cloth walked around with babies tied to their backs. The grocery aisles began to change; products that have occupied shelf space for years were discontinued to create space for imported products that catered to the new residents. I now must drive fifteen miles to purchase a smoked ham or smoked neck bones. Many of the cashiers, supervisors and managers that have worked in our local grocery store for years were transferred to other stores and a multicultural, bilingual staff replaced them.

Many of the remaining homeowners who were unable to adapt to the new demographic left in droves. "For Sale" signs popped up everywhere. Those who could not sell their homes simply abandoned them. Most of the abandoned homes were purchased at pennies on a dollar by slum lords and foreign entities that had no ties to our neighborhood. Some simply sat empty, destroying curb appeal, and dragging down property values around them.

It did not stop there. The economy collapsed in 2008. Unemployment skyrocketed, and right under our nose, a drug trade was created and ran rampant in our community. The underground economy on Central Drive flourished; hell, havoc, and mayhem never seen here before became the norm.

I move closer to the television, increase the volume, and listen to the reporter aboard the news helicopter describe from a bird's-eye view what is happening on the ground. Over the years, I have become an artillery connoisseur. I can with good accuracy attach the sound of a gunshot with the artillery it is fired from. This shot did not come from a nine-millimeter or a magnum, popular weapons with the local urban cowboys. It was powerful like a sonic boom. This was military artillery.

I removed a lemon from the fridge. I grab the chicken from the sink by one leg and begin to wash it with the lemon. The sounds of screeching brakes and doors opening and closing grab my attention. I drop the chicken in the sink, throw the lemon on the counter, peep through the blinds, and notice more of the neighbors congregating in front of their townhomes. I dry my hands, go outside, and join them.

Isla, who never leaves her house unless accompanied by her husband, stands on the threshold of her front door. Half of her face is visible. I almost forget about the gunfire when I see shiny, long, black hair hanging over her shoulder, stopping just above her waist. She, her husband, and three kids moved to our small subdivision of townhomes three years ago. I have never seen her uncovered. Even in the middle of the summer when the heat can exceed one hundred degrees, she is covered from head to toe. She opens the door wider, and in three quick movements, she wraps her long hair that is almost as black as her skin in a scarf. She leaves her house and stands in her walkway on a broken concrete slab.

"What was that? What's going on?" Ms. Geneva, one of the few remaining original homeowners in our small subdivision, stands in front of her door. She is normally impeccably dressed in beautiful jewelry but looks odd and unkempt today. Half of her hair is rolled on pink rollers; the other half is wet and meshed to her head. She walks toward the end of her walkway and stops in front of her mailbox. She ignores the water dripping down her neck and uses both hands to keep her floral housedress closed. Gunfire is not an event that would normally cause a congregation of the neighbors. Breakups, a loved one dying, a couple fighting in the street may generate a neighborhood gathering; we have become numb to gunfire.

Red and blue flashing lights at the corner can be seen through the trees. The muffled sound of police radios mixed with the sound of fast-moving cars stopping to a screeching halt to make room for more official and police vehicles are out of the ordinary. Shooting victims in our neighborhood do not receive this much attention from medical emergency or public safety. First responders, too, have grown accustomed to carnage from the new

Wild, Wild West way of handling disputes on Central Drive. Until Detective Chandler began advocating for change, people could literally lie in the street and die from non-lethal wounds waiting for an ambulance.

At first glance, our neighborhood does not look like the war zone it has become. On the west side, well-constructed, pristine homes surrounded by greenery and immaculately landscaped yards camouflage the results of neighboring gentrification and resettlements. Azalea bushes adorn some the most quality built homes in the state of Georgia. Mature magnolia trees sit comfortably on spacious lawns. Tall oaks stand along broken slabs of sidewalks in desperate need of repair. County workers stopped pruning the trees many years ago, and the roots have pushed through most of the sidewalks. The once level sidewalks many neighbors used to exercise after their evening meals have now become obstacle courses. We pay taxes, yet it seems that a great portion of our tax dollars are appropriated for use in the northern, more affluent part of the county. The median in the middle of Central Drive is the demarcation line that separates chaos from total chaos.

"What the hell is going on?" Jermaine has not left his spot in the middle of the street. He continues to press buttons on his phone, stopping periodically to sip from a can wrapped in a brown paper sack. Jermaine has lived in Central Oaks with his mother for years. He surfs from low paying to very low paying jobs to no job at all. We all expected more from him; he was a very smart kid, graduating high school with honors. When their father abandoned ship, his mother, a public-school teacher, raised him and two siblings alone. He is smart but drinks too much. Drunk or sober, he is always respectful. Every once in a while, he finds employment, hooks up with a neighborhood woman with four or five kids, and moves out of his mother's home for six maybe seven months but never as long as a year. It never fails; the drinking and job instability brings him back to his mother. He staggers toward the middle of the street holding on to the brown paper sack wrapped tightly around a tall can.

"Me can still smell de gun powder." The Jamaican new to the neighborhood walks toward the middle of the street and stands next to Jermaine. She reaches for the can inside of the paper sack. He passes it to her. She does not bother to clean the can before placing it to her mouth. Slowly spectators leave their porches and walkways and gather at the subdivision entrance.

A startling, gut wrenching scream grabs all our attention. The pitch is so high it irritates my inner ear like fingernails scraping against a chalkboard.

Jermaine places his phone in his pocket, limps down the sidewalk, and stops just before he reaches the corner store. A green pickup truck with Henry County tags almost runs him over. He jumps out of the way in a nick of time. He trips over his feet, falls to the ground, and quickly rises with both middle fingers in the air. The paper sack is safely nestled between his forearm and chest. It used to be cars registered in DeKalb and Fulton counties were primarily found in our community. Once in a while, you may spot a Klaxton or Kobb County car tag, but DeKalb and Fulton were dominant. Lately, cars registered in the Northern Georgia counties, North Carolina, and New York frequent Central Drive.

We share neighborhood rumors and engage in speculation while we anxiously await Jermaine's return to share the details. The neighborhood crazy stops in front of Jermaine, extends one of his hands, and obsessively twists his hair with the other. Without saying a word, Jermaine reaches in his pocket, removes a balled-up bill, and passes it to him. We move closer to the scene to get a better look, stopping on the broken sidewalk on the side of the subdivision entrance. Jermaine continues toward the melee, periodically stopping to drink from the can in the paper sack. He converses and fist bumps a couple of neighborhood men standing around. He places the can wrapped in the brown paper sack next to a small bush and walks closer to the yellow caution tape that outlines the side of the store next to the path separated by a black chain link fence that leads to an adjacent apartment complex. A burly white officer aggressively steps in front of him and directs Jermaine and the other onlookers away from the area.

A thin, black woman walks along the yellow tape. She jumps as her thin arms move about the air as if they are made of rubber. She walks on the side of the tape, bends forward, and screams to the top of her lungs before she falls to the ground. She kicks and screams as she flaps her arms back and forth. A hulk like figure picks her up and removes her from the scene. Jermaine leaves the crowd, grabs his can from the side of the bush, and quickly limps back to us where we all stand waiting for his report.

"It is Boxing Boy."

"Boxing Boy?" I have never heard of anyone in the neighborhood called "Boxing Boy."

"Yeah, you know that dude that lives around the street training for the Olympics, Gene Jack?""

"His name is not Gene Jack," the Jamaican corrects Jermaine. "It is Jean-Jacques. "Add the 'sh' and 'j' together to say it properly."

"Yeah." He blows the Jamaican off and places the beer can in a brown paper sack to his mouth, throws his head back, and takes long deliberate swallows." He quickly shakes his head from side to side and throws the can in the bushes. "That is some shit! The guy was so cool."

"What happened?" The Jamaican steps close to Jermaine.

"It will be on the evening news."

"Evening news?" A sarcastic chuckle escapes the Jamaican's mouth.

"Police cars and news vans occupy all of the parking spaces at both corner stores." He takes a deep breath. "Trust, it will be on the news, folk saying that mean white cop that is always fucking with folk shot Boxing Boy after Boxing Boy shot a cop." He shakes his head. "They saying Boxing Boy shot Chandler." Tears form in the well of his eyes but do not flow. "Bullshit!"

"Chandler?" There is a lot of chatter at the mention of Chandler's name. I walk alone back to my house, holding my head down as I attempt to process the solemn news. Chandler? Dead? This is surreal. I was looking at the news just two days ago. Thomas Hensley, a local sports reporter interviewed Chandler in the middle of the football field with a youth team Chandler started made up of children from the neighborhood. Braces on his teeth make him appear youthful despite the gray hair at his temples.

Kids were running around him, some stopping to wrap their small arms around his waist during the interview.

"Chandler, the community has raised almost one hundred thousand dollars for you to run for Sheriff. Are you going to run?"

"I tell you I have not made up my mind." His bright smile was blinding. "I am still discussing this with my wife. Honestly, my work is with these children."

"He is going to run. We need him." A young black woman photobombed the interview with a T-shirt that read, "Chandler Davis for Sheriff. "

"You know Thomas. "He embraced the young woman and kissed her on the forehead. She waved to the camera, pointed to her T-shirt, and left with a bright, child-like smile covering her face. Police sirens and fast cars in the background drown out part of the interview. "We have so much talent here." He looked around the football field where children ran freely, laughing and playing. "Crime overshadows amazing talent in this community. My calling is to mentor as many kids as I can." A serious, sincere look replaced the deep dimpled smile. "Imagine if our kids in the south side of the county had the same resources as those kids in the northern part of the county."

"Let's just say if you did run," the reporter proposed, ignoring Chandler's first response, "What would you do?"

"I would clean up Central Drive. The drugs and crime have taken over the community. The residents are good people. Do you see the number of cars that come here from other counties and other states to purchase drugs?" He points to a black sports utility vehicle slowly driving next to him. "Many and I would say most of the residents here are law abiding citizens caught in the crossfire."

"Can you speak on the drug bust last week

that netted two million dollars in heroin, Oxy, cocaine, and a cache of illegal weapons?"

"I can't speak on that." He smiled. "Other than to say we have fine men and women in blue who really care about this community. We put our lives on the line every day for the people." He smiled. "It is because we care." He laughed as he extended his hand to the reporter. "You know it is not because of the pay." There are no words to describe the sadness I feel from hearing Chandler is dead. If the hoodlums are so heartless, they will kill Chandler, none of us are safe.

The blacks constantly complain of racism but seem to have no problem killing their own.

Chapter 4
Ayanna

"Ayanna Williams please." I answer the phone as soon as I see his name on the Caller ID. His monotone voice is beyond sexy; it is so deep it produces an echo. Though he spends most of his time in South America, a hint of his Grecian accent surfaces when he speaks. Katsaros Galifianakis and I have been spending a lot of time together the last few months. He is different from men I dated before and after my divorce. He is a world-renown technology genius and cyber security expert who looks more Gucci than geek. His olive skin and soft curly hair show his Grecian ancestry, but his mannerism is that of an African American. He works hard and plays just as hard. He brings balance to my hectic life. I work hard and play very little. Unlike Katsa, my play time is usually connected to my work.

My African American colleagues have benefited from generational privilege. Most have fathers who are second and third generation members of the Boule'. They cannot stand next to

Katsa. Like me, Katsaros Galifianakis is self-made. He is a real-life "Trading Places" type of phenome. He is the new guy in town making his way through the political, social, and celebrity scenes.

He started his company in his basement and managed to secure multi-million-dollar contracts with international Fortune 500 companies as well as state and federal governments. His expertise in cyber security is well-known throughout Europe and our friendly allies in the Middle East and Northern Africa. I met him at a political fundraiser last year where the mayor was a keynote speaker. He stood out among familiar faces. He was the topic of conversation among the female attendees, both married and single, yet he appeared unbothered by all the attention.

"Can we make a dinner date tonight?"

"Time and place." I try to maintain my composure. It feels as if a kaleidoscope of butterflies has taken flight inside. I am behaving like a giddy schoolgirl. I try to conceal my excitement, but I am sure he detects it in my voice.

"Stoney's Bar and Grille at six p.m." I hear his television in the background. I press the green button on the remote and turn mine on.

I hear the anchorman in the background and know we are watching the same channel. "I will be leaving town in a couple of weeks. I was hoping we could spend some quality time together before I leave."

"I would like that very much." My smile is wide. My facial muscles stretch beyond what is natural.

"See you in a few."

"I will be there."

Regular scheduled programming has been

interrupted to report an officer involved shooting that concluded with two fatalities on Central Drive. The area is known as a haven for criminals. Shootings on Central Drive are not uncommon. The Mexican gangs have almost taken over the drug market by selling cheap heroin and prescription pills. The black gangs are having a hard time competing. A new clientele of young Caucasian opiate addicts, both male and female, come to Central Drive to score. A turf-like war has been declared as the Mexicans control the opiate market and will not allow the blacks in. The demographic of addicts who call Central Drive home is slowly changing. The area used to be filled with mostly African American, fast walking, crack addicts looking for the next high. They have been replaced by young white men and women driving fancy European cars up and down Central Drive searching for drugs. Unfortunately, the new demographic is slowly setting up permanent residence. It does not take long before they become full blown addicts willing to sell their souls for the next baggie.

"Ma'am, you have a call from the mayor!" Tiffany pushes the door open with a force that creates an air current so strong the papers on my desk rise and fall to the floor. I am caught off guard; she never enters my office without knocking.

"Take a message; I will call him back." I reach for the open bottle of alkaline water on the corner of my desk. I close my eyes and drink half the bottle. When I open my eyes, I find Tiffany still standing in the threshold.

"Ma'am," her voice cracks as she fiddles with her phone, "it sounds like the call is important."

"Thanks, Tiffany." I place the bottle of water

on my desk, remove my nail file from the top drawer, and file the rough edge of my nail on my ring finger. "Tell him I am tied up. I will return his call as soon as I am free."

"Yes, Ma'am." She reluctantly leaves. Most people jump to the mayor's beck and call. I am not like most people. The mayor and the old guard are passé; they are quickly losing leverage with the millennials. The new bloc of voters is more relaxed and sees straight through the pretentiousness of the old guard. They are social media savvy and results driven. Katsaros Galifianakis is part of the new guard. He has the tools and expertise to catapult me among this new bloc of voters. Though he is lowkey, he has over a million tech-savvy followers on his blog. My intent is to finish this term as the district attorney and campaign for state bench. The mayor and those in his circle promised to endorse and lobby for my appointment, but at the last minute, without a discussion, they decided to back the Caucasian District Attorney of a neighboring county.

I never place all my eggs in the same basket. Politics is a tricky game. The players are fickle, self-centered, and narcissistic. After the mayor refused to endorse me, I moved on. The mayor was surprised and salty when he learned I left their political clique and formed an alliance with independents who are growing astronomically. The mayor and I have been estranged ever since.

I increase the volume on the television. The news camera scans the parking lots of the corner gas stations. Reporters, store employees, and nosey bystanders gather in the small parking lot. I am surprised a shooting on Central Drive made the news until a photo of Chandler Davis appears on the screen. My heart drops at the mention of his name. I turn up the volume and lean closer to the television. Chandler Davis was very popular in the community. Many reached out to Chandler for help with their children.

Chandler is also easy on the eyes; many women in my circle have literally thrown themselves at him. He is a devoted father and husband. To my knowledge, he has never bitten the bait. His chiseled face is a better match for modeling than a police badge. He is beyond handsome, yet very approachable. His honesty and respect built a solid trust with the community on Central Drive. He is responsible for creating a free after-school program to keep children out of trouble. He organized little league baseball, football, and basketball teams that won state championships five consecutive years. He is an all-around great guy. I grab my phone and scroll through the contacts. I tap the mayor's number and press dial.

"We may have a problem, Ms. Williams." He begins conversing before greeting me. He pauses. "Chandler Davis has been shot. He is dead. The perpetrator is an eighteen-year-old black kid."

"I am looking at news coverage as we speak."

"This could go south quickly. We do not need the bad publicity." It is election season, and the mayor is up for reelection. He barely won the last election. He received forty-nine percent of the votes. He won the run-off election by less than one thousand votes. To this day, many questioned the validity of the votes. Accusations of voter fraud are rampant.

The police have been in the news too often across the nation for shooting unarmed black men. How this is handled can make or break the mayor.

"Chandler was killed by a neighborhood misfit. One of our officers on the scene responded with justifiable force and killed the perpetrator." He pauses. "The community will be up in arms."

"I am on it, Sir. I will have my assistant get in touch with the detective assigned to the case. Hopefully, the officer's body cameras recorded everything."

"Yes, Ms. Williams, that is a problem." He lowers his volume to slightly above a whisper. "The Southern Precinct has not been issued body cameras. We ran out of funds. We are putting funds for body cameras in the next fiscal budget." He talks as if he is on the campaign trail. I was happy when he finished his tired speech about the decrease in tax revenue that prevented funding to purchase cameras for the South Precinct and was happy to end the call. I picked up the phone and make an early morning appointment with my nail technician. I turn off my computer and grab my bag.

"Tiffany." I stand in front of her desk.

"Yes, Ma'am." She stands as she shuts down her computer.

"Please contact the store owners and request access to the footage from the cameras of all three convenience stores that sit on the intersection of Central Drive and Harrison Road."

"Ma'am, should we request a subpoena?"

"Yes." My eyes are glued to my hangnail. Tiffany stands still in front of her desk. She glances at the clock and locks eyes with mine. "Anything else?"

"No, Ma'am. I am on it."

"Since you will be working late, feel free to come in a little late tomorrow morning." She removes her purse from her shoulders and allows it to drop on the floor.

Central Drive is a melting pot of immigrants and many ethnic groups. It is a microcosm with its own set of laws. Much of the action, both legal and illegal, take place at the convenience stores on the corners of Harrison Road and Central Drive. The Korean store owner is a naturalized citizen. According to one of our informants, the Korean rents the back of the store for illegal activities. He is a key player in the drug market but also engages in credit card fraud, identity theft, and trading stolen merchandise. The East European is Russian; he owns a seafood restaurant next to the Korean store and is relatively new to the neighborhood. Sources report he is part of a sophisticated gun smuggling ring and runs a high stakes gambling operation. The Pakistani owns the convenience store across the street. He is our patsy. He turns on anyone including those in his circle for a brownie point believing we can assist in his quest to become a citizen. The shooting took place on the side of his store.

I cancel my evening appointments to make time for Katsaros Galifianakis. I habitually navigate to the polished type with money, those with tailored suits, fancy cars, and exclusive zip codes. Katsa, as he likes to be called, is like a breath of fresh air. Unlike members of my social network, he is not a member of the local political network. His company is obscure but well known in cyber security circles. It took a few encounters for me to catch his eye, and I want his undivided attention. I walk across the street to the employee gym to pass time. I do my usual work out that normally takes an hour, but because I am excited about spending time with Katsa, I work out super-fast to have time to shower and spruce up before our date.

It is six p.m., and instead of changing back into career clothing, I slide in tight form-fitting jeans. I keep clothes for every occasion in my office closet in the event I do not go home after work. My phone vibrates in my pocket; believing it to be Katsa, I answer before looking at the Caller ID.

"Are you avoiding me?" My mood quickly changes.

"Of course not, why would you say that?" I lie; I am avoiding his needy ass like the plague.

"I have been calling you all week." His tone is aggressive.

"I have been very busy." I want to shout a few obscenities but remain calm. His neediness is overwhelming and way past annoying, "Can I call you back? I am in the middle of something." I do not allow him time to respond; I end the call and place the phone back in my pocket. Trevor is becoming a nuisance; he is a member of an outdated political class fast losing generational privilege. He has outgrown his usefulness. Spending time with him has become a chore. Trevor's season is over.

Katsa, on the other hand, brings a new kind of energy. Spending time with him almost feels like a privilege. Our first date was beyond fantastic.

"Do you like rock climbing?" he asked when he called the night after our first meeting.

"Never did it."

"We can start with a little rock to get started."

"I don't know. What about snakes? What if I fall?"

"Meet me at the Peachtree airport in an hour."

"Airport?" I smiled. "I have been to that airport, but I did not see any mountains."

"I have not seen any either." He chuckled. "Pack two days of clothes. I will have you back in time for work Monday morning."

I drove to the airport so ecstatic about spending time with Katsa I did not bother to ask where we were going. He stood at the entrance of the airport when I arrived. His smile was wide. He appeared as excited to see me as I was to see him. He placed a soft kiss on my cheek while removing my bag from my shoulder. We walked the tarmac to a private jet with a large KG painted on each wing.

"Katsa!" A middle-aged male with olive skin and salt and pepper curly hair greeted him with a kiss on each cheek as we boarded the plane.

"John!"

"Who is the lovely lady?" John looked over his shoulder at me suspiciously.

"This is my friend Ayanna."

"Friend?" His smile was wide. "I thought all of your friends were gadgets." He lightly tapped Katsa on the cheek as we walked into the cabin. "Where are we going?"

"Honduras."

"Honduras? I did not bring my passport."

"You won't need one." He passed John a stack of papers; he left us in the cabin and went to the cockpit. Katsa went to the bar where he made one martini and passed it to me before pouring juice in a second glass for himself. We were in the air for almost four hours. I waited for him to make a move, a kiss on the lips, a hug, or even a conversation with subtle sexual overtones. To my surprise, we engaged in general conversation like two buddies on a mini vacation.

I fell asleep halfway through the flight. I woke up to John announcing the plane would be landing and instructing us to fasten our seatbelts. The plane landed and parked in his private hangar on a spacious estate. Two Range Rovers were parked on the tarmac in front of the hangar. John left in one. Katsa and I left in the other. I was beyond impressed. Katsa was a different kind of experience. His four-bedroom five bath home was spacious, but I somehow expected a mansion.

The drive from the hangar to his home was ten minutes. We were greeted by a petite, olive skinned woman dress in rugged jeans and a white, starched, button down shirt. Her shoulder length hair was slightly curly like Katsa's.

"Katsa, you came home early. I was not expecting you." They kiss one another on the lips and embrace. Initially, I thought the olive-skinned woman with beautiful jet-black hair was a love interest. Their exchange was uncomfortable and made me uneasy. "You finished your business fast."

"Theresa," he turns and looks in my direction, "this is my friend Ayanna."

"Ayanna, this is my assistant Theresa." She embraces me. I noticed a long scar on the left side of her face. It looks as if it was placed there intentionally as it was red and slightly raised, but the right makeup could easily cover it. It was almost a perfect line that connected the corner of her eye to the corner of her mouth. She stepped back and away from me. Her embrace did not feel genuine.

"Theresa, por favor, prepare un dormitorio para Ayanna." My Spanish was not good, but I understood he instructed Theresa to prepare a room for me. I was surprised we would not be sharing the same room. I expected this trip to be an opportunity to act on the energy I thought we shared. To my dismay, he spent a lot of time in his room the evening we arrived.

The next morning, I was up at seven a.m. He and Theresa were sitting at the table holding tight to a cup of coffee when I came downstairs.

"There is coffee if you would like a cup." Theresa looked much younger today. Her hair was pulled to the top of her head in a messy bun. If you are the assistant, I thought to myself, why are you not moving from the table to the coffee pot? "There are fresh croissants in the bread box." She smiled. I ignored her, made a cup of coffee, and took a seat next to Katsa.

"Are you ready for your rock-climbing lesson?" His smile was contagious.

"I was ready when I arrived." My attempt to bait him into sexual flirtation fell on deaf ears.

After I finished my coffee, he took my hand and led me to a five-car garage in the back of the house. He removed a harness from the closet and passed it to me along with a pair of hiking boots.

"I guess you to be a size 8 medium." He smiled.

"Good guess." I chuckled and removed my shoes, set them to the side, and slid my feet in the leather hiking boots. We climbed into a late model Jeep with dried mud on both sides and left the gated estate. We traveled about ten miles through a rocky terrain with sporadic vegetation.

"How long has Theresa been your maid?"

"Maid?" He frowned. "She is not my maid. She runs my affairs and takes care of my house when I travel." I detected a slight bit of anger in his voice as if Theresa was more than an employee. "She is the best coder on the planet and one of the smartest people I have ever met." I wanted to explore his relationship with Theresa but decided against it believing if they were more than business partners, he would not invite me to his home for the weekend with her present. We traveled for thirty minutes before we arrived at what he called a small rock that looked like a mountain. We parked the Jeep at the bottom.

"Surely you don't expect me to climb this on my first try. This is my first lesson."

"Of course, I do." He smiled and rubbed his hands up and down my arms. "You work out. Look at these arms. Surely you want to push yourself. You seem very competitive." He buckled the harness around my thighs and through my legs. He attached one end of a long cable to me and the other end to the bottom of his harness.

"What are you doing?"

"Don't worry. You are in good hands." He laughed. "I am making sure you don't fall, but I am going to need you to pull your own weight." He cupped my hips and gently squeezed as he took in all my curves. We made eye contact, and it seemed as if this was the first time he noticed my attributes. "Your body is strong. This should be a breeze. I will unhook the harness from my harness and attach it to a rock as we climb."

I wanted to stop climbing the moment I grabbed the first rock and broke my nail, but I continued up what he called a small rock.

"Can we rest?"

"We are just getting started." He laughed. "You have to push your body. Push your mind. By the time we reach the top, you will have used every muscle in your body."

I kept climbing; he was right, every muscle in my body began to ache.

It took over an hour to get to the top. Once

we reached the top, we looked around at nature's landscape. "It is beautiful up here, isn't it?"

"If you say so. I am a city girl, but I am enjoying the experience." We sat at the top, making small talk, and enjoying the view. "How are we going to get down?"

"The same way we got up." He laughed.

"You are fucking kidding me."

"No, but we better get going." He extended his hand. I grabbed hold to it, and he pulled me to my feet.

"Can't you call a helicopter or somebody to pick us up?"

"Nope, we are going down the same way we came up."

"I need to take a break."

"Let me know when you are ready." I walked to a grassy area and lay down. He lay beside me. Before I knew it, we were both asleep.

I was deep into my sleep when he woke me. I looked into the sky; the sun was beginning to set. "We had better get started. Coyotes come out at night."

"I can't believe you let me sleep for so long." I stand and wipe the dirt off my backside. "A snake or bug could have crawled on me and now you say there are Coyotes here?"

"Yes."

"You mean the dogs that look like wolves?"

He laughed. We put on the climbing gear and scaled down the rock. He was right. Going down was much easier. We stood at the bottom and removed our gear. His shirt inadvertently rose to his chest as he removed his harness. I pretended not to notice the long scar that extended from his chest past his navel. He grabbed the gear and threw it in the back of the Jeep. The drive back was relaxing. I was hopeful when he reached over the console and placed his hand on my knee. His smile was sensuous. He looked like a male model with his hair pulled back in a ponytail. I was thinking surely, he wants to kiss me now, but he remained focused on the drive home.

"Damn!" I was beginning to doze off when the car began to shake and lose pressure.

"What is wrong?"

"I think we have run out of gas." He smiled. "Good thing we are only a mile from the gate."

"A mile? You have got to be kidding me."

"It is not that bad." He took my hand. "This will give us time to talk." We walked back to the house, hand in hand, but did very little talking.

We walked thirty minutes before we finally reached the house. The lights were off inside. The only illumination came from the moon. We reached the gate, and he pressed a series of numbers then placed his hand on the display. The sound of the lock disengaging was smooth and almost inaudible. We walked through the gate to the front door. Katsa turned the doorknob. His leg almost hit me in the head as he flipped in the air. A strong arm quickly wrapped around my neck. I felt my skin begin to tare as cold metal was pressed against my throat.

"Theresa!" Katsa quickly stood and flipped on the light. Her other arm was extended with a gun pointed at Katsa's head.

"Katsa! Katsa! Where is the car?"

"Apologies, Theresa." I became almost enraged when he apologized to the scarface with her arm still tight around my neck holding a knife at my throat.

"I thought you were an intruder." She

released me, threw the knife on the floor, tucked the odd shaped handgun in the back of her pants, and walked away. He no longer had to explain Theresa's role in his life. Theresa made me uncomfortable the rest of my stay. She was cold and unengaging. The morning we left I heard her moving about upstairs, but she did not come down and bid us farewell. I was happy to leave Honduras.

I did not see him again for a week or so after we returned from the mini vacation when he called for another date. Each date was better than the last. Our relationship seems to be growing but slowly. I look forward to meeting him at Stoney's tonight.

I was finger-combing my hair when the phone rang again.

"What? I said I would…"

"Ayanna. Did I catch you at a bad time? Are you okay?"

"I am fine." I look at the Caller ID. A wide smile beams across my face.

"Can you come to my place as opposed to meeting at Stoney's? The homeowner's association is sponsoring a jazz concert on the roof.

"Sure, I am on my way." I applied a fresh coat of lipstick to my lips. I don't want to look obviously made up. Katsa is very laid back and unpretentious. His face has been on the cover of every local magazine and many of the tech magazines, yet his popularity has not gone to his head. He is the new kid on the block in the circles I frequent. Everyone wants a piece of him, but somehow, he manages to remain humble. While in America, he lives in the heart of Buckhead in a swanky penthouse condominium not too far from the one I purchased after my divorce.

People are surprised with my ability to keep

it together after my divorce. My mother was exceptionally kind. My father carved out time every Sunday to spend with me the first six months after the divorce. I went through the motions and did my best rendition of the wounded wife in public settings, but I am very happily divorced. Marriage is stagnating. My ex-husband did me a huge favor when he left the country with the kids. The lack of baggage has allowed me to solidify myself with the crème de la crème. Katsa is actually the crème but different from what I am accustomed to. I have never been attracted to non-black men, but there is something different about Katsa. He has a soulful swag. I drive to the gate and enter his security code on the keypad. A picture of him pops up on the display. The look on his face is playful. He greets me and presses the buzzer. I enter the garage and drive up the ramp to the top. I exit and take the elevator to the 22nd floor.

He opens the door, greets me with a soft kiss on my cheek and a champagne glass filled to the rim with Cristal. I toast with my glass of champagne to his glass filled with orange juice. Katsa is the only male I know over 21 who does not drink alcohol.

He is a gentleman. His moves are slow and calculating. I am patient but would not mind if he moved faster and solidified our relationship with a title of some sort. He turns the television on. The evening news was interrupted by a "Collect call from…" He immediately turned the television off.

"Is that a call from prison?" I didn't mean to sound judgmental, but I am surprised he knows someone in prison.

"There is one in every family." He laughs, but his laughter is not jovial. "A cousin who can't stay out of trouble." He takes a sip of his orange juice and escorts me to his oversize designer sofa. He flips the television back on and was going to change the channel but stopped.

"Hold on! Don't turn just yet. This is going to be a mess. I am surprised at the continued news coverage."

"I really don't like the news. It is too depressing. I want to relax." He presses the off button on the remote.

"You seem to relax a lot."

"I work hard, and I play harder. I need to hire more software engineers. This business moves like the speed of light. If you snooze, you lose."

"I imagine." I rub my hand up and down his arm and trace the contour of his defined muscles.

"Technology is very competitive and at times overwhelming. I plan to retire at 50."

"And do what?"

"Whatever I want to do." He leans closer and kisses me. The wine relaxes me. He gently pushes me down on the sofa with one hand. With the other, he lifts my shirt and unsnaps my bra. His moist tongue feels good against my naked breast. He is finally moving at a pace I like, but to keep his interest, it is my time to slow the pace.

"I can't stay very long."

"Why?" The dampness in the crotch of my underwear is uncomfortable. My cell rings as he unbuttons my jeans. "Don't answer." I ignored the phone. I placed the phone next to me. I allow him to go a little further to make him want more. I have no intention of giving him the entire cake, just a taste of the icing.

The phone rings again with a bird chirping ringtone. "It is the mayor; I have to respond." He rolls off me. He gathers a mass of dark black curly hair and secures it with a rubber band. I scanned over the message. "I have to go. The mayor has called an emergency meeting. We have to get ready for the press." I lightly pushed him away and point to the television. "Can we turn the television back on to the channel where the news covers the shooting on Central Drive?" He turns the television on still holding tight to the remote. "I will need to view the stores footage of the shooting."

"Do you have the phone numbers to the stores? Most everyone is using wi-fi. I may be able to find their IP address using the business numbers." He turns off the television and reaches for his laptop. "You can view footage from here." I provide the phone numbers knowing this is against the law. Within a couple of minutes, he locates all the IP addresses except for the one from the Pakistani store.

"The shooting happened at the Pakistani store. I really want to view footage from the store."

"He probably still uses in-house cameras. The footage is recorded on tapes or DVDs and cannot be downloaded." He places a device in the laptop's USB port and quickly begins to type. A video instantly displays on the monitor. He presses the play button, and we view the video from the Korean store. The footage is grainy, but visible: a black male wearing a gray or dark colored hoodie runs at rapid speed on Central Drive toward the Pakistani store. At one point, it seems as if the male intentionally slows down, turns around, and trots backwards. His mouth moves as he raises his hands in the air. He quickly turns around and sprints faster than an Olympic runner. Detective Whitley, a white cop in street clothes is close behind but begins to lose ground. Chandler runs behind them. They run through the Pakistani store parking lot to the side of the store where the footage of the chase is no longer visible on the camera.

"That's it? What about body cameras from the police?"

"The South Precinct does not have cameras yet."

"Seems like this is where they need cameras the most." He presses a few buttons on his laptop. "What about audio? Are the recordings in the police cars digital?"

"I don't know. You are speaking another language." The footage is still displayed on the monitor. About fifteen minutes later, news reporters arrive on the scene. With cameras and microphones intact, they walk behind the store to the crime scene. "I'll tap into the news footage." Our eyes meet. "Hackers do it all of the time for tabloid news." He opens a briefcase and removes several wires and other devices.

Broken branches, some totally uprooted lay about the scene. One expensive athletic shoe lies haphazardly in the overgrown field between the convenience store and the apartments. Detective Whitley sits on the ground leaning over Chandler Davis' long, lifeless body with one hand over the other quickly pressing down on his chest then covering his mouth, desperately trying to breathe life back into an apparent dead body. A thick muscular black male in his late teens or early twenties, with black weights strapped around his ankles, lies on his back. Blood pours out of the holes in his body. He raises his head off the ground and looks in Detective Whitley's direction for several seconds before his head hits the ground. A red stream leaves his body, filling the cracks in sun baked Georgia clay. Detective Whitley pumps rapidly up and down on Chandler Davis' chest. "Call the bus!" I look at his lifeless body from the reporter's footage and know immediately it is too late for Chandler. Several officers arrived. One of the officers walk close to the reporter with his hands on his weapon and shouts, "Turn that camera off and get the fuck out of here!"

"Officer, it is our first amendment right..." The reporter removes her press credentials and presents it to the officer.

"I don't give one cat's ass about amendments and rights! Can't you see this is an active crime scene?" The officer's hand touches his revolver. "You have three seconds to get away from here, or I will arrest you!" The news reporter walks away from the crime scene. The reporter squeezes through a small opening in the black chained link fence on the side of the store that separates it from the neighboring apartments. The cameraman passes the camera to the reporter, squeezes through the opening, and joins her. They continue filming as if there are not two dead bodies lying on the ground.

Chandler and I ran in different circles, but he was very popular in the political scene. He was an advocate for the Central Drive neighborhood. He was behind the community policing initiative formed to create better relationships between the residents and police. He lived in this very community until his wife threatened divorce if he did not move the family from Central Drive. He was so comfortable he rarely carried his revolver on his persons. He often claimed that he needed no protection; he regarded the ratchet, good for nothing misfits in this community as his people.

He was so popular that residents began

raising money for a campaign for Sheriff though he had not decided to run. I must admit he was good for the community. He spoke at Parent Teacher Association meetings and with the help of school administrators, formed a program where volunteer police officers attended parent-teacher meetings in place of parents who could not or would not attend.

Forensics arrived on the scene unusually fast and cordoned the parking lot in front of the store as well as the side and rear with yellow police tape. The reporters stationed on the apartment property continued to film the scene. A large automatic weapon lies on the right side of the teen's black muscular body. Detective Whitley quickly stands, runs next to the body, and begins to kick the lifeless body with such force it raises off the ground. Another officer grabs him and tackles him to the ground. He wraps his arms tight around Detective Whitley who appears overwhelmed with grief.

Detectives Whitley and Chandler worked together when they first graduated from the police academy. They recently re-united when Chandler was transferred back to Central Drive from the Northern precinct to advocate for the community and assist in eradicating the opiate epidemic after the son of a wealthy socialite was found dead at a bus stop with a syringe stuck in his arm. He volunteered to return to the community to fight the crime and violence that escalated with the rise of the opiate market.

The footage captures the sound of several feet rapidly hitting the ground. The officers on the scene are startled and brand their weapons as a thin black woman followed by several neighbors and the Pakistani store owner's daughter arrive on the scene.

"Get up, Jean-Jacques! Jean-Jacques, get up!" A loud, piercing scream that disturbs my inner equilibrium comes from the mouth of the thin female with a head full of wild hair. I turn the television volume down. The Pakistani girl and the woman, both screaming, wrap their arms tight around one another.

"What the fuck happened?" An African American male so muscular he looks as if he just left the penitentiary walks toward Detective Whitley. He stops in his tracks when Detective Whitley places his hand on his revolver. He is jumpy and behaves as if it is taking every atom in his body to restrain from charging Detective Whitley.

"You better calm your ass down!" Detective Whitley commands. His demeanor quickly changes from the grief-stricken officer who lost a friend to cop on the beat. The hulk looking figure does not flex. He stands still; his body is rigid, face contorted, brows raised so high they almost touch in the middle.

"What the fuck happened to my boy?"

Detective Whitley who has a street cred reputation surprisingly and almost cowardly walks away. The woman and the Pakistani girl still hold tight to one another rocking back and forth. The woman leaves the Pakistani girl, walks to the crime scene tape, and begins the ear-piercing screaming before falling to the ground. The black male picks her up dodging her wildly swinging arms and carries her away.

Katsa's face is flushed. He pours a large glass of orange juice and drinks it in three hard swallows. "Damn, this is crazy!"

"I hate to leave." I placed the empty glass in his hand. "I will need to get with the mayor. This situation can go south fast."

"What about the party? Will you come back later?"

"We will see." I look at my watch, peck him on the lips, grab my purse, and leave.

Chapter 5
Jefferson Thomas

I sit at the table behind two stacks of books in the community area among fifty noisy inmates. I have completed seventy-five percent of my five-year prison sentence. If this was state time, I would be out. The feds want it all. No time off for good behavior, no chance of early parole. My only option is to continue to look for mistakes in the prosecution of my case, find loopholes, and search for possible violations of my civil rights. I spend every hour in this place searching for reasons to file motions for an appeal. My lawyer suggests I give up and do the time. We sat side by side every day for three months during the state's trial where he earned more money representing me than he probably made all year. I would think if he learned anything about me, he should know I never give up.

The situation could have been worse. If the power hungry, fame seeking prosecutor bitch had her way, I would be doing a life sentence. She thought she had me. She was cocky. She forgot who Jefferson Thomas had become. I had long left street hustling; taking high risk chances for a few million dollars was beneath me. It must have slipped her mind that I was her Ivy League equal.

Honestly, I also underestimated Ayanna and how far she would go to make a name for herself.

She found a weak link in my operation, exploited it, and used it to her advantage. I admit I did not see it coming. Stacy, my confidante, was the weak link. She was my chick as well as business partner. We made a lot of money together. Our business was solid. She left our partnership for what she believed to be a better situation. Stacy knew me better than anyone. She knew almost every detail of my high stakes international business. She also knew if she left, there was no safe place on earth for her. She mistakenly believed she offered Ayanna a slam dunk case against me in exchange for her freedom. Our business was unique with voluntary as well as involuntary members. The wealthiest of the wealthy paid big bucks to satisfy peculiar sexual appetites. Stacy provided documents, disks with business contacts, and financial data to Ayanna, the assistant district attorney at the time.

What Stacy did not know is her digital signature was on all the evidence she gave the District Attorney's office. There were no paper documents that could connect me to our special business. All data files regarding my business are stored in data centers outside of the continental United States and have back door after back door and revolving passwords. Stacy's was the only constant. Where Stacy thought she was simply the face, she became the business every time she accessed our data files. I was always one step ahead. I purposely placed documents in my safe in Stacy's presence believing, but hoping she would not, one day turn on me. I was prepared when she did.

Ayanna and I were inadvertently part of the same political circle. I financed most of the campaigns of the elected officials currently in office. Those powers, with my blessing, were grooming her to replace the outgoing District Attorney, but she was impatient. She was not a team player. She wanted to quickly make a name for herself. I became a pawn in her vicious game of chess. She was envious of my position and political connections. She believed destroying me would quickly catapult her rankings amongst the powers that be. The bitch thought she had me but could not prove a connection between me and the evidence Stacy provided.

My businesses were layered. I spared no expense in securing the best experts to secure my businesses and ensure no questionable transactions could lead to me. She and the state hired the best forensic computer scientists to unravel my encrypted computer files, but my money was longer than the District Attorney's budget. There are people whose lives depended on all aspects of my businesses remaining encrypted. I don't blame Stacy for leaving through the back door. I am not very good at losing but aligning with this enemy was nothing shy of a declaration of war. I rest well every night knowing Stacy may not be behind bars, but she is far from free. Knowing she lives in constant fear and is always looking over her shoulder makes doing this time like a walk on the beach. She does not know the place or time I will strike, but she knows I am coming.

My defense attorney tore the prosecution's case to shreds. The judge released me and ordered the State to investigate prosecuting Stacy Lincoln, but she could not be found. I am in prison because I made a careless mistake; one offshore account that held deposits from legitimate real estate holdings was traced directly to me. I forgot about the account and never filed taxes on the income.

Ayanna has never been a graceful loser. After the judge ordered my release, the calm look on her face made me uneasy. The smirk on her face made me uncomfortable. I wanted to run out of the courtroom. I reached to hug my attorney after the judge's decision to dismiss the state's case. Out of nowhere, federal agents approached, locked silver cuffs on my wrist, and placed a federal warrant in my attorney's hand for tax evasion. I was remanded in federal custody without bond. I got sloppy, and it cost my freedom. Her federal colleagues were unwilling to make a deal. I had no choice but to take a plea, pay the taxes, and do the time.

I look up from the stack of books and hear, "The regularly scheduled programming has been interrupted to bring breaking news of an officer involved shooting." Reporters are trained to be biased in their reporting. It never fails, their voices elevate and fill with emotion when reporting the details in officer involved shootings. A picture of the alleged killer pans on the right of the murdered officer's photograph. I step closer to the television. His eyes are angelic. Life still lived in this young man's eyes. I know killers; this young man is not one. Lately, there has been a murder of unarmed black men by the police every other day.

The camera pans from the news anchor desk to a picture of a decorated officer with the name "Chandler Davis" under the picture. The reporter stands at the crime scene in front of the parking lot full of onlookers and reporters, "Two are deceased." Initially, I ignore the news and go back to reading the law books until coverage pans to the justice center, and a reporter places a microphone in front of the mayor's mouth. The District Attorney extraordinaire stands next to him like the seasoned politician she has become. Her hair is different. The notorious French roll has been replaced with a short pixie. She looks a tad bit masculine. The cuts in her forearm are too pronounced for a woman for my liking.

"Fuck this shit!" Deez Hands is what he calls himself. Supposedly, he is a world-renowned rapper and music producer also doing a bid for tax evasion. I don't listen to rap music, so I would not know. He leaves his chair, walks to the television, and turns the channel.

"Hey," I stand, "I was looking at that. Turn back for a few."

"Fuck you, niggah!" Deez Hands walks away from the television and stands in the middle of his make-believe entourage.

I walk to the television and turn back to the news. Deez Hands and his minions leave their chairs and surround me. I pay them no attention and continue to stand in front of the television with my hand on the power button.

"Man, let's fuck this niggah up!" I continue to ignore the minions. It is as if I am in a trance. The reporter passes the microphone from the mayor to the District Attorney. Her lips are moving. However, I am filled with so much rage I cannot process the words coming from her mouth.

Deez Hands and his minions encircle me like a hungry pride. The menacing looks on their faces are for show, a mask that can be wiped away with the waving of my hand. I do not move. I ignore the theatrics and continue looking at the television, observing my enemy in my peripheral vision.

"Niggah." He walks to me, and using both hands, shoves me in my chest. I stand firm. He propels backwards, loses his footing, and falls to the concrete floor. He quickly rises and advances toward me again. I look around to ensure no guards are present, ball my fist, and jab him in the throat. His eyes bulge outwards as he stumbles backwards with both hands tight around his throat. His minions back away; they all go separate ways as Deez Hands rolls around on the floor trying to catch his breath.

I step over Deez Hands, leave the television room, and stand in the long line of inmates waiting to use the phone. I grow tired of listening to "I will be home soon" or "Don't give my pussy away" from inmates with life sentences. I want to interrupt their conversations and say, "Dude, you will be in here for life. She probably fucking while you talking to her," but I remain cool. I am grateful there is no one waiting for me on the outside. My children are well cared for by their mother. She is smart; she moved on before Ayanna could pull her into her vicious web.

I finally got my turn to use the phone.

"Hello." His voice relaxes me.

"KG, it's me, Jefferson."

"It is good to finally hear your voice."

"I called you a few days ago."

"I know. Someone has a bone to pick with you. She is ready for me to come home."

"Not so fast, don't go underground just yet. I think I am about to set my trap."

"It's about time. I was beginning to think you were going to let her slide." KG laughs.

"You know me better than that." A chuckle escapes my mouth. "I never let my enemies slide. They all pay."

Chapter 6
Josh

There is a mean, obsessive, and compulsive Gorilla riding my back twenty-four hours, seven days per week. I call it Monster. He is powerful, relentless, and rarely sleeps. He wants what he wants when he wants it and will do anything to get it. I am Monster's bitch. To support Monster, I do odd jobs at the seafood kitchen owned by a Russian. The restaurant is in a small strip mall home to three other businesses. The Koreans own the strip mall and operate the convenience store that is a mainstay for the community but also a front for several illegal enterprises. I run errands for the store owners and hustle money any way I can. I usually work alone, but occasionally, I hustle with my girl Simone.

I work for anyone on Central Drive for money except for the Pakistani. I tried working for him; it did not work out. I worked sixteen hours a week for a case of beer and fifty bucks. The Pakistani got slick and thought he would take advantage of my situation. After working all week, I placed my case of beer on the counter and held out my hand for the fifty dollars.

"Six pack." He pulled the case of beer away from me, placed it behind the counter, removed twenty-five dollars from the register, and passed it to me. "Business is slow this week."

"Hold up." I pushed the money back to him.

"This is not what we agreed too."

"Take it or leave it." I am a junkie not a slave. He is disrespectful and cheap. People believe southern whites to be prejudice and racist. In some cases, the stereotype is true, but the most racist whites have nothing on racist, class-conscious Pakistanis. They open their stores in black neighborhoods and treat the customers worse than unwelcome guests.

On the side of town I am from, the behavior is quite the opposite. Pakistani store owners are engaging. They do not follow patrons around the store. Their tone is not hostile. I was in shock when I landed on Central Drive and found myself subjected to the Pakistani in the hood. The Pakistani in the hood seems to hate everyone except for whites with money which are few on Central Drive.

There is nothing special about Central Drive. There are no sites to visit on national registries. I am trapped here because this is where I found my medicine. How someone from across the world lands here is a mystery. I can only ascertain there is a directory of some sort with location listings for shady entrepreneurs looking for sites for their shady businesses. The business owners on Central are the shadiest of the shady. I started working for Vladimir, the Russian, when he first landed on Central Drive a few weeks before he opened his restaurant. In my other world, I never had an occasion to meet these types. He is a hustler. He is a smart businessman but a hustler just the same.

Vladimir parked his van in front of the empty space next to the Korean store. The first day, he covered all the windows with Kraft paper. I waited all day for two days for him to come out, but he did not surface. Finally, I was looking to score one morning when I saw him standing outside the restaurant in front of the door. He was dressed in the same shirt he wore the day he arrived.

"You need some help?"

"Nah." He scanned me from head to toe. "I am good." He appeared comfortable around blacks and junkies like me.

"I work cheap." Monster was on my back and riding hard. I could barely keep still. My entire body itched. My sweat glands were working overtime. I removed my T-shirt to wipe away perspiration. He stared at me as if I was an alien, stepped away, and walked back toward his storefront.

"Hey." He turned and tilted his head sideways and scanned me from head to toe. "A dumpster will be delivered in about an hour." He opened the door. Sheetrock, plyboard, and wood were scattered all over the floor. "I'll pay 200.00 if you remove the shit on the floor and place it in the dumpster."

"Hell yes!" Visions of the many sacks I could purchase danced in my head. I was happy Kraft paper covered the window so I could hide from Simone. If she saw me working, she would demand a cut. Vladimir lived in the storefront while renovating it. We worked all day and night removing the debris and placing it in the dumpster. He shared that people thought he lost his mind when he opened a cash business on Central Drive. Admittedly, I thought he was a sucker, but his street smarts made him a solid member of the Central Drive family. There is a certain personality type that conducts business in places like Central Drive. There is a lot of money to be made but doing business here could be a dangerous endeavor.

Traditional business etiquette does not apply.

People from his native country tried to discourage him, warning him of the frequent robberies, conspicuous drug sales, and in your face prostitution on the three-mile strip. The neighborhood can be deceiving. Central Drive looks and functions like a typical suburb by day, but the night covers a seedy world I knew nothing of in my other life. There are many that participate in the underground economy, but there are just as many who go to work for an honest day's pay. A diverse work force calls Central Drive home. Every day, people working in the fast-food industry wearing food-stained uniforms to office workers wearing freshly steamed suits navigate around the druggies and hustlers to the bus stop to catch the number 321 to the train station. This balance is the only reason Central Drive is not a total war zone.

Vladimir is from Chicago by way of Georgia, the country not the state. It is all the same to me; he is Russian. It was pure chance that he made it to Georgia, the state. He is a professional dollar chaser. He traveled to the State of Georgia to place a bet on an amateur boxing tournament. These tournaments do not make mainstream news, but in the underground economy, gamblers wage hundreds of thousands of dollars which makes it a multi-million dollar, unregulated and illegal industry. The fight was sold out; it was so popular, street hustlers sold copies of the fight for fifty bucks. Vladimir placed a bet on a young Mexican kid, well known in the boxing community. His opponent was an undefeated Jean-Jacques, a young black kid new to the boxing world known for his killer left punch. Vladimir had a lot invested in the fight. As a matter of fact, everything he had was invested in the

Mexican beating the new kid. His restaurant in Chicago was not doing well. He needed the funds to cover expenses and to pay an unorthodox, defaulted loan to a dangerous, unconventional, unregulated lender. He bet ten thousand bucks on the Mexican. The opponent Jean-Jacques was unknown in the Chicago area.

Vladimir lost the bet but became enamored with Jean-Jacques. He was so obsessed with him that he constantly watched footage of the first time he saw Jean-Jacques in the boxing ring. At the end of almost every work week, Vladimir sits in the office in the back of the restaurant with his kitchen staff where they wind down with beer and cocktails. The night never ends without Vladimir expressing his dream of managing Jean-Jacques, also known to the community as Boxing Boy. "This is the ticket." He shows the film clips we have all seen fifty times of the first time he witnessed Jean-Jacques' boxing skills.

The boxing match started before the first punch was thrown. Vladimir narrates he knew he was in trouble when the black kid hopped over the ropes with ease. "His legs were strong like iron. His boyish face immediately lost its affect once his feet touched the canvas." Vladimir's voice was elevated; his pitch so high with excitement he sounded like a soprano in an Italian opera. He was animated; his hands moved up and down as he spoke. "The black kid is like the Incredible Hulk in ballerina shoes. He was quick with his hands!" Vladimir balled his fist and sparred with the air. "The Mexican would miss making contact with his face by a hair. Jean-Jacques was gracious and would only throw a punch or two every now and then. One was good enough. The sound when his left fist made contact with the opponent was so precise it echoed through the auditorium." He shook his head and took a deep breath. "This boy is the ticket."

When Vladimir lost his bet against Jean-Jacques, he did not return to Chicago. He would have been a dead man had he returned. He called his wife and instructed her to leave everything that could not fit in a suitcase and catch the first flight to Atlanta. He claimed he left everything and never looked back.

His move was a win win. The businesses on Central Drive have a loyal clientele. It is a demographic, cultural thing. Blacks spend money. Vladimir, the Korean next door, and the Pakistani across the street take very good care of their families from the money blacks seem to throw away. Laundry detergent, sugar, milk, and eggs can be purchased at the local supermarket, less than a half of a mile down the street at least seventy-five percent cheaper, yet for some reason, these items are sold in the corner convenience store. Though the store owners make a lot of money, they rarely give anything back to the community.

There are several streams of income generated from businesses on Central Drive. The receipts from legal sales of merchandise recorded on the cash registers and illegal cold cash generated from high interest, illegal loans, trading in stolen merchandise, high stakes gambling, and a lucrative drug market. The illegal businesses generate a fortune. It is easy to transact illegal business on Central Drive. People don't complain like they do in other demographics. These businesses would not last a week in my neighborhood. People in my neighborhood would notice and respond to excessive loitering and the weekend crowd that disrupts traffic with frequent phone calls to law enforcement.

The back of the Korean convenience store also serves as a mini-Vegas like gambling house. Every Friday night, the parking lots of the surrounding apartments are filled to capacity as people converge on Central Drive for gambling and unorthodox business deals. A couple of the locals created illegal valet parking in the apartment building across the street to earn money.

During the day, the stores look like any other neighborhood corner store in the hood, but when the streetlights come on, the scene drastically changes. Clouds of smoke hover over tables covered with money and shot glasses. Young women from the neighborhood wearing skirts so short half of their bottoms hang below the hem, supplement government benefits serving guests lines of cocaine and shots of alcohol. Every now and then, a serious fight erupts. Opponents brandish knives and heavy fire power, yet if someone gets shot or stabbed, no one dares call the police, not even the victim. No one complains. The community seems to go along with it.

I was helping Vladimir stock the kitchen when I saw Jean-Jacques run pass with lightning speed. There was nothing abnormal about that. He was always running up and down the street sparring with the air. He was a loner, and for some reason, people left him alone. Vladimir stood next to me in front of the window and proclaimed, "One day, I will manage that boy."

I was much older than Jean-Jacques, but I admired him. A few months ago, one of the neighborhood drug dealers was roughing me up on the side of the Pakistani store. I was bent over, holding tight to two bruised ribs. The beating was so severe my teeth were knocked loose. Others passed by and did nothing as I was getting pummeled to death, but Jean-Jacques walked to the melee and stood between me and the three young guys roughing me up. No words were exchanged. The thugs simply backed away. He grabbed me, threw my arm over his shoulder, and helped me to the front of the store.

"Aren't you too old to be hanging out here?" I did not respond. I could not talk. My jaw was dislocated, and my gums ached as my teeth shifted in my mouth. I simply nodded in total agreement. "Where do you live? I will help you home."

"Dunwoody." I had been on Central Drive so long I had made it my home, but somehow Dunwoody came out of my mouth.

"Dunwoody? Where the rich white people live?" He stopped and tilted his head to the side. "I see you around here every day."

"Stay away from drugs." I managed to stand and limp away. That was the beginning of our friendship. The word on the street was that he finally found a corporate sponsor. He lives with his mother, stepfather, and older sister. The mother is strange. I believed her to be Haitian most likely second generation; she spoke with an African American dialect with a hint of Haitian Patois. Every once in a while, she purchased phone cards from the convenience store and uses the only pay phone in the neighborhood where she loudly speaks French or Haitian Creole. She was a proud woman with a strong personality.

Vladimir came up with a brilliant idea that he would venture into another legitimate investment and sponsor Jean-Jacques. Everyone around the neighborhood had watched Jean-Jacques devour his opponents in the ring, but outside of the ring, he had a humility so contagious even gang members respected him.

The townhome community where he lived with his family was out of place. Most of the yards were immaculately landscaped. There were a few with overgrown lawns with debris scattered about. Modern cars were parked in front of mostly well-maintained homes. I knocked on the door. She opened the door without asking who was on the other side. I did not expect such a petite woman to have so much fire. A mass of hair extended from her head like Medusa. The whites of her eyes were bright and stood out against unblemished dark skin.

"What is this?" Vladimir gave me an envelope with a three thousand dollar check inside. I passed her the envelope. She opened it, sucked perfect teeth, and turned up her nose.

"Vladimir, the restaurant owner on the corner, would like to request a meeting to discuss your son's boxing future." I smiled in a futile attempt to break her disapproving stare. "This is a token of what will come if you decide to move forward."

"Are you crazy?" She threw the check at me. "Don't bring yourself to this place again." Her eyes were fiery. A mixture of Haitian patois and broken English flowed from her mouth with a poetic rhythm as she cursed me to hell and slammed the door in my face. A hulking figure opened the door as I turned to leave. He did not speak, but it was my cue to leave and a not so subliminal suggestion that I do not return.

Rumor was she moved here to get away from the gangsters in Florida. The kid's stepdad trained him. The stepdad was a large fellow himself with defined muscular physique. He trained Jean-Jacques at a gym he owns on Memorial Drive. The boy was known for his killer punch, and thus far, won all his amateur fights. He was known throughout the South, and many people made mad money betting on him.

I finished helping Vladimir stock the kitchen and had begun cleaning the tables when the sound of a gunshot so loud it was like an atomic explosion startled me.

I drop the tray of cheap glasses onto the floor. A second gunshot equally as powerful follows; all movement in the restaurant comes to a screeching halt. The kitchen traffic is always noisy, but for about two maybe three seconds there is total silence. After a few more seconds, the sound of children screaming interrupted the silence. Minutes later, loud police and ambulance sirens vibrated my inner ear. I look out of the window and see people beginning to congregate in the parking lot in front of the Pakistani store. I pick the glass off the floor then walk across the street to the sidewalk. Jermaine, a local weed head and alcoholic in denial, stands with his camera extended, capturing the event on video.

"What's up?" We bump fists. "What happened?"

"They say Boxing Boy got shot." He looks solemn and out of place without his brown paper bag. I have never seen him without it.

"Jean-Jacques?"

"Yeah."

I grab my head because I can barely fathom the news. Cars move slowly in both directions on Harrison Road. The scene creates a bottle neck. I turn my head away from the scene to gather my thoughts when I see Jean-Jacques' parents driving north on Harrison Road right before Central Drive. I flag them down. I walk to their car and lightly tap on the window. His mother quickly locks the passenger side door. I ignore the judgmental scowl on her face. Traffic is slow, so I run in front of the car to the driver's side and bang on the stepfather's window. He looks confused, but he presses the automatic button, and the window comes down.

"Pull over, it's Jean-Jacques!" He drives onto the sidewalk and quickly gets out of the car, leaving the engine running.

The stepfather walks past me to the crime scene tape, immediately demanding answers. I stand behind him as he stares down at the trigger-happy cops occupying the parking lot. I hold my breath and pray the police do not shoot him. The aggression in his posture is intimidating. I want to walk to the crime scene for a better view, but the restaurant is filled with patrons, and the neighborhood bus boy did not show up for work today. I go back inside the restaurant and continue to clean the tables. I work alone today, so I get to keep all the tips. The jingle from the change and the roughness of the wrinkled dollar bills in my pocket make me anxious. To distract myself from the happenings across the street, I dream of sacks I will purchase when I finish work.

I place dirty dishes in the dishpan, clean off the table with water mixed with off brand bleach. A solemn feeling creep inside. I pass the window on route to the kitchen and hear a loud, piercing scream. A few minutes later, Jean-Jacques' stepfather carries his mother to the car. She throws her hands wildly in the air then falls to the ground.

The stepfather, the Pakistani store owner's daughter, and neighbors try to console the grieving mother. Her eyes roll to the back of her head as if she is in a catatonic state. She screams, "I am sorry, Michel." The sorrow on her face is uncomfortable to witness. Even Julio and Donovan, neighborhood rivals, put aside their differences to help the stepfather manage Jean-Jacques' mother.

Everyone in the neighborhood, from the minister of the big church on the corner to the drug dealers, the gangbangers, and gangbangers in training to the little old ladies that pass out Christian literature at the bus stop admired Jean-Jacques. He was the Great Black Hope to the community. He was the neighborhood golden child respected by all, me included. I have not felt anything in a while, but a cloud of melancholy hovers over me as I remember his million-dollar smile and slightly off-centered nose he bragged was his badge of honor from his first fight. He used to say, "I win fights because I never want to feel the pain I felt when my opponent caught me off guard and moved my nose."

Chapter 7
Myrtle

I sit in my car at the intersection of Central Drive and Harrison Road waiting for the traffic light to change; yellow, fluorescent tape cordons the shooting scene from the rest of the Pakistani store parking lot. Things are slowly getting back to normal. The corner is bustling with activity. Day laborers, mostly Hispanics, but a few blacks and a speck of white drug addicts new to the community, sit on empty paint buckets under a crepe myrtle in desperate need of pruning. They drink beer while waiting for construction and landscape contractors to pick them up for work as if there is no open container law prohibiting it. The bums appear oblivious to the empty beer cans, bottles, and discarded paper scattered around them. The yellow tape is the only reminder that someone was killed yesterday.

I turn into my neighborhood, admiring the freshly cut lawn until I turn on my street and see Isla's overgrown yard. It sticks out like a sore thumb. She and her husband rarely cut their grass. I don't know if goats kept their grass low in Africa, but this is America. They need to maintain their lawn. I call code enforcement on them at least once per month during spring and summer. They often complain to me in broken English about nosey neighbors unaware I am the one who reports them.

I back my car into the driveway to make it easy to unpack my purchases, press the button to open the trunk, and walk to the rear of the car. I bend my knees like the physical therapist instructed and remove the heavy bags of dirt I purchased to get my flowerbed ready for spring. Next spring, I will hire a professional landscaper. I am getting too old to maintain a yard.

"Let me get that for you beautiful." Officer Whitley startles me. My open trunk obscures the view of his car parked directly in front of mine.

"Thank you, Officer." He towers over me. His muscular body is a pleasant sight for the eyes. "You came just in time. These bags of dirt are heavy. I'll be soaking in a tub of Epson salt tonight." I look away; his smile is almost flirtatious. "I am getting my flower garden ready for the spring."

"Your yard is beautiful." He pulls a daisy from the ground and brings it to his nose. "It is nice to see people take pride in their community."

"Oh, this neighborhood used to be beautiful. I know it's hard to believe." We stand next to one another and canvass the surrounding lawns, admiring the many who still keep their lawns tidy. I walk back to the car and remove trays of begonias. He takes the tray from my hand and aligns the begonias next to the dirt. I reach in the car, remove two bottles of water, and pass one to Detective Whitley.

"Thank you." Chills ripple from the top to the bottom of my spine as he lightly rubs his hand across my arm.

"This community needs neighbors like you, Myrtle." I look away. His blue eyes are penetrating. He embraces my hand as two young black males walk across my lawn.

"Hey." He quickly releases my hand, takes a couple of steps forward, opens his jacket, and displays an oversized gray metal gun in a leather holder under his forearm. "Use the fucking sidewalk!" He walks back to me. "We are going to get this neighborhood back in order after we get rid of all of the thugs."

"Yes," I manage a fake smile, "wouldn't that be great? I hope I am still alive to see it." I don't want to discourage him, but we did everything we could to save our community. He is relatively new to the area and unfamiliar with the history. We saw what happened in Klaxton County. That county was the test county to dump the poor from the city of Atlanta after the land grab. It did not take long to feel the effect. The Klaxton County residents fought back by lobbying their county commissioners to pass legislation enacting a moratorium on homes that could be rented with the government vouchers; they were backed by elected officials who voted to shut down the public transportation system many of the transplants depended on to get to minimum wage jobs. Unfortunately for us, the voucher holders left Klaxton County and moved to DeKalb County where public transportation operated regularly and frequently in many neighborhoods. Many set up camp on Central Drive where there was an abundance of available rental properties.

I use my hand as a visor to block the bright sun as Jermaine passes my house. We make eye contact, but he does not speak.

"Jermaine, what's wrong with you?" He looks at me then at Officer Whitley and continues down the hill toward his home.

"Is he causing you trouble?"

"Jermaine?" I smile and feel a little giddy at Officer Whitley's chivalry. "Of course not. Jermaine is harmless."

"You let me know if anyone causes you trouble." He takes my hand, softly weaves his fingers into mine, and places a soft kiss on the back of my hand. "Are you sure he is not causing trouble?"

"God no." I smile. "I have known him since he was a baby." Officer Whitley is committed to getting our neighborhood back on track. A couple of drug dealers I made known to him are no longer on the corner, but there are so many. The two he locked up will not make a dent.

He escorts me to my front door. We are startled by an older model Cadillac with a Louisiana license plate blasting music so loud I feel the vibration in my feet. This is the type of madness that changed our neighborhood. I shudder every time I see a Louisiana license plate in the neighborhood. Resettling the poor from Atlanta is just one of many cataclysmic events. Nothing was more detrimental than that big storm in New Orleans. The videos of people on rooftops waving signs pleading for help pulled on many heartstrings. Our local politicians with high aspirations began to bow to the needs of politicians in Washington who were embarrassed by the government's response to Hurricane Katrina. Our neighborhood was used as an olive branch. The number of renters using government housing vouchers tripled, and homeowners who long left the community allowed their greed to become more important than the well-being of the neighborhood they left behind by preferring to rent to voucher holders as opposed to renting to hard workers with earnings.

We must take some of the blame, as we inadvertently provided the infrastructure for the greedy to carry out their plan. The East side of Central Drive has more multi-family housing units in a five-mile block than any other place in the state. I was one of the founding members of the hated and now defunct board that formed a non-profit to attempt to stop the construction of the apartments before they were built. I could see the tragedy years before it happened. Ten different apartment communities occupy five square miles. In the beginning, the apartments catered to a luxury demographic of middle-class college graduates that wanted suburban living with easy access to the city. The apartment owners kept their promise for several years and were able to maintain the standard, but in time, this too changed.

Leasing agents now have no requirements for renters occupying what used to be luxury apartments. Employment and background checks became a thing of the past. Those that remained protested and conveyed their concerns at city council meetings. The community concerns went unheard. The council members were more concerned with the agendas of those who made large financial contributions to their campaigns and playing kissy face to officials in Washington DC in hopes of advancing political careers. If I had the time, I would give Officer Whitley a true to life history lesson.

Officer Whitley holds the screen door open. I step inside. He stands between the open screen door as I stand on the threshold. He looks at me the way men used to look at me forty years ago. His head is slightly tilted to the side with his eyes looking upward and his mouth spread in a half of a smile.

"Ms. Myrtle, there may be people who want to stir trouble. They may stop by and ask questions about me."

"Oh..." A look of concern covers his face. "Is everything all right?" I feel funny between my thighs as I caress his shoulder to comfort him.

"Everything is fine. I am sure you heard about the shooting. One of my close friends was shot by one of the drug dealers you pointed out a couple of weeks ago." He lowers his head and wipes his eyes. His face is contorted like he is about to cry, but he manages to hold the tears inside.

"Yes, I heard Chandler was killed. We all loved him. He was one of the best things that came from this community."

"Yes, he was a great guy." He looks away. "If anyone approaches you with questions about me, you will let me know. Right?"

"Of course, I will." He steps close, kisses me on the cheek, and leaves. I walk to the kitchen like a giddy schoolgirl, stand in front of the sink, and pour a glass of water. I peep through the blinds and see blue lettering on a local news van as it speeds to the corner.

My heart is torn into a million pieces when I think of what has become of this community. We used to live a good life. There used to be one store on the corner surrounded by woods. It was family owned and operated by the Swansons, who lived in the neighborhood down the street. When I first moved here, I would often see him, and his wife walk to work. Not too long after our townhome subdivision was built, he sold the store to foreigners. At first, we thought they were Mexican but later learned they were from Pakistan. The Swansons immediately packed up and left, but not before selling twenty acres on the three corners across from the store to a real estate developer. The land went undeveloped for years. Then one day, tractors arrived and bulldozed trees to the ground. Within a couple of months, a small strip mall replaced the forestry. I thought the owners were Chinese, but some say they are from Korea. I honestly cannot tell the difference.

Later, two gas stations were built on two corners across the street from the Pakistani. A few months later, a drug store was built on the fourth and remaining undeveloped corner. The gas stations were welcomed in the beginning. People were happy about the convenience. However, the demographic changed. The corner store where we used to get gas became a spot where the criminals congregate and engage in illegal activities.

Officer Whitley has no idea how our paradise became hell. I am grateful he is here to straighten things out.

Chapter 8
Ayanna

I lift my head, look over my shoulder, and slowly lay back on my fluffy feather pillow. Sharp pain cuts through both temples. It feels as if the room is spinning. Acid slowly flows from my stomach to my esophagus. I swallow hard to push it back down. I look over my shoulder again and glance at the clock. It is 9:30. I'm ready to start my day. This spooning thing Trevor does is beyond annoying. He lies behind me nude from the waist down. His arm is haphazardly draped over my hips. The pillow comfortably cradles his head. His breathing is light and soft. He is getting too comfortable again. It was not my intention for him to spend the night, but we were inebriated. He was in no shape for the thirty-minute drive to his estate in South Atlanta.

The last time Trevor spent the night, Mrs. Bordeaux stood outside of my condominium building in ninety-degree weather in an unbuttoned floor length mink with nothing underneath. Thank God the concierge recognized her from a prior altercation and contacted me. Trevor left out the back stairwell and drove around to the front of the building under the pretention he received a call from a friend that his wife was standing outside in a mink coat in the heat of summer.

I am not in the mood for Mrs. Bordeaux to

get out of line again. This is all business to me. She has no worries; this relationship with her husband has run its course. When one must get drunk to be with someone, it is past time to move on. I slide from beneath his arm, remove the covers, throw my legs over the mattress, and place my feet on the floor. I contemplate my next move to rush his departure as I slide my perfectly manicured feet inside warm furry slippers.

"Ayanna." He grabs my arms and pulls me back onto the bed. "I love you." His grip is tight, not tight enough to feel alarmed but tight enough for concern.

"No." I pull away from him, walk around to the other side of the bed, grab his clothes from the chair, and pass them to him. I want to throw them at him and ask him to leave, but I keep my cool. "You must stay focused." He covers his face with the pillow. "Love has nothing to do with this relationship." I smile, but truthfully, I want to curse his ass to hell. "We are political partners." I want to remind him that he has not kept his part of the bargain. I should be on my way to the state bench. He and the mayor are colleagues. He should have been more persuasive when the mayor changed his mind about endorsing me.

My cell phone rings before he responds. The sound of an elephant roaring is the special ringtone for my children. "I have to take this call." It has been four years now, and my ex-husband finally has come to his senses and allows the children to call. After experiencing episodes of both children severely acting out, he finally listened to their British therapist and has agreed to co-parenting.

"Hi Che'." I walk away from Trevor who is paying extra attention to my conversation. He became annoyed last night when my phone continued to ring, and I did not answer but responded by text instead.

"Hi, Mother." Her accent is Ghanaian with a British twist she acquired from attending boarding school in London. She is very formal. Osei' sent her to etiquette school and acting classes to keep her busy to control some of the acting out. "Are we still on for summer? I am finalizing my itinerary. Will you host OJ and me?"

"Of course." I changed my tone to match hers. She has taken her role of African Princess, heir to the Badu-Bonsu throne very seriously. "Your father has scheduled an appointment to meet with me next week to discuss the particulars."

"Yes, he will be visiting on business in the states next week. I am aware of my father's schedule." She makes no effort to hide the contention in her voice, and as usual, she must be assured, where her father is concerned, I know she is in charge.

"How are your studies, Che'?" I changed the subject.

"You well know, Mother, they are nothing shy of perfect." She chuckles. "Nothing shy of excellent."

"As I expect." Trevor's eyes are glued to mine. I cover the phone. "It is my daughter." I step further away from Trevor and continue my call with Che'. Her conversation gravitates from the sophisticated seasoned socialite to the twelve-year-old girl she is. After several minutes of expressing her refined qualities, she ends the call.

"Where were we?" He wraps his arm around my waist.

"I was headed to the shower, and you for the

door to go home to Mrs. Bordeaux." I grab his coat and pass it to him. He reluctantly steps in his trousers. He slides his arms in his shirt but does not button it.

"You are a strange woman, Ayanna. Is this all you want?" His facial expression is serious. "Most women would die for a man like me. I am willing to leave it all for you." He opens the door and stops in the middle of the threshold. "She can have the cars, beach property, and our family home. I will give all of that up for you." His tone is serious. His eyes are penetrating, almost threatening.

"You sound like a woman. You are too emotional."

He steps back inside my condo and walks so close to me that I feel threatened. "I saw the pictures from the Convention Ball."

"Oh?"

"You were all over Katsaros Galifianakis. What is Galifianakis promising you?" He rubs his hands across my face. "He has new money and no real connections. He is rich, but he is not part of the circle." He turns his nose upwards. "New money but no connections. Wasn't he raised in foster care at some point in his life? He is basic poor white trailer trash."

"He is not American. I am not sure they have trailers in Greece." I smile. The look on his face is menacing. "The world as we know it is changing. Katsa is a member of the new political class." Trevor's anger boils as I speak fondly of Katsa. "He was raised in an orphanage and has done very well for himself."

"It is not a good idea to forget those who help you along the way." He caresses my shoulder. His touch is not gentle. "You need more than that." I ignore Trevor. He is old school part of the old guard. The rules in the political arena are changing. The new generation of voters detests old money and their good old boy connections; they are looking for change. Katsaros Galifianakis is hip. He is a tech genius, an innovative specialist in cyber security, and the new flavor in the political circle. His money is new, but new billionaire money is just as good or better than, old millionaire money.

I turn on the television to find more news coverage of police involved shooting.

"This madness needs to stop." His eyes are glued to the television. "Sometimes, I am ashamed of being Black." He stares at me four seconds too long for comfort. He turns the doorknob, looks around my condo, and says, "I don't like feeling used." His tone is flat. He makes me uncomfortable. I am relieved when he crosses the threshold and finally leaves.

I grabbed my phone and find Katsa has called three times since last night. I call him as I walk to the bathroom.

"Hi, guy." He answers on the second ring. His voice sounds as if he is in a jovial mood. I take it he is as happy to hear my voice as I am to hear his.

"I called you a thousand times yesterday."

"Your math is off. When I looked at the call log, I counted three." I laugh. "You mean a techno guru can't count?"

"What are your plans for the day?"

"I have none."

"Would you like to take a three-day trip to St. Kitts? My pilot can have my plane ready in an hour."

"Let me check my calendar for the next three days, and I will get back with you in a few."

Chapter 9
Josh

It is fucked up what happened to Jean-Jacques. He was the kind of kid that at the mention of his name, a father would proudly extend his chest and the kind of kid that a mother protects with all of her being. In the community, he was affectionately known as Boxing Boy. I proudly called him friend. No one, me included, believes he killed a cop. Sure, he was a beast in the boxing ring. I have never seen anyone transform the way he did once he stepped on the boxing canvas. His face transformed; the contours became more defined. His body appeared to expand, and his eyes so fierce, it seemed as if they emitted fire. He looked like the epitome of power in the boxing ring, but he was a gentle giant. His contagious smile was quite the opposite of the intimidating effect he projected in the ring.

Conversations about Boxing Boy, threats of revenge and conspiracy theories can be heard on every corner from Ponce de Leon to Memorial Drive. The entire neighborhood is up in arms. Young men can be seen openly carrying weapons. Most, more than likely, have no gun permit. God forbid if they are caught and found to be convicted felons. The cops, even the mean, red neck, racists are lying low.

I am angry. I am uncomfortable feeling the

feelings Jean-Jacques' death triggers inside. I lost the ability to feel anything a while ago. I can only imagine what others feel who have known him for a much longer time. This is a high crime neighborhood. Shootings, rapes, and muggings are common, but it seemed as if all the low life agreed to let Jean-Jacques be. He ran through the neighborhood every day, and no one bothered him. The Mexicans and Blacks hate one another. They have created arbitrary lines in the community, they have no land titles too, that each knows not to cross. Jean-Jacques could run through Black and Mexican boundaries at will. The Mexicans loved him just as much as the Blacks. I admired him. He was raw talent, something I wish I could have been. In my heyday, I was an athlete held in high esteem. Unlike Jean-Jacques, I had a team of people who created hype to make up for the raw talent that did not come naturally.

When I was not high or hungover, I would wait for Jean-Jacques on the corner of Harrison Road and Central Drive. He was like clockwork. One could tell time using Jean- Jacques' workout sessions. He turned the corner on Harrison Road to Central Drive every morning at 9:47 during his morning jog. I would have to sprint to catch up with him. I could make it past the Pakistani store and the two apartment complexes next to it. I would lose my stamina by the time he turned right on Memorial Drive. He would never slow his pace to accommodate me. By the time I walked back the half mile trip to Central Drive and Harrison Road, he would have completed his three-mile route.

In the beginning, we did not engage in conversation. I would simply run along the side of him. One day, I was sitting on the corner wanting to get a sack but could not get enough money and did not feel like running. He motioned for me to join him. Reluctantly, I joined. The feeling of my chest tightening and my face getting flushed as blood pumped hard through my body ignited that competitive edge all athletes have in common. I fought hard to control my breathing. My heart rate increased. Perspiration dripped down my face. By the time we reached Memorial Drive, my chest felt as if it would explode. I could not continue.

"Tired old man?" He ran backwards around me. "You are an athlete?" He pointed to my toned, muscular legs and arms. So far, the drugs had not taken away my muscle.

"Played college football." I smiled, bent forward, and rested my hands on my knees to keep my balance. "I was the starting quarterback in high school and college." I boasted with pride. I no longer allow myself to think about those days of glory when strangers screamed my name to the top of their lungs. I tucked the memories away of the thousands of people in stadiums across the South, many with my jersey number and my name in bold capital letters on their backs, rooting for me as I threw passes half the way across the football field.

"Leave the drugs alone, and you can get your stamina back. You should not have given out so soon." He removed a stopwatch from his pocket, still jogging in place. "We have not run an entire mile." He continued West on Memorial and left me bent forward still trying to catch my breath. Those brief words of encouragement from Jean-Jacques gave me life, not enough to make me stop using, but a glimmer of hope.

I have been stuck on this shit hole called Central Drive for six months this time. I have been frequenting the area for well over a year, but now I am stuck. No person or entity is holding me against my will, but Monster will not allow me to leave. The medicine I need to stay alive is here. The pain of withdrawal and the thought of facing my family after another fuck up is more than I can handle. The medicine momentarily shuts off feelings of despair and shame for being the loser I have allowed myself to become. I have burned all my bridges. I could have never imagined Mother would toss in the towel, but even she has finally given up on me and with good reason. Nine months ago, my mother purchased another new car after I pawned the one she purchased six months prior. She had no idea one could get cash for a car with a bank lien. Hell, I didn't know it was possible until I did it. The underground crime network on Central Drive is incredible. My girl and get high partner hooked me up with a Turkish small car dealership owner with an office in the back of the Korean store.

I should have known better. All my life I was taught if something sounds too good to be true, it probably is, but when Monster calls, all rational thought disappears. We walked into the store. Simone asked to speak to Jack. The Korean clerk ignored us and continued to check out the small line of customers purchasing overpriced goods. After all the customers left, the store clerk spoke into his mouthpiece then motioned for us to follow him. I noticed a barrel of an AK47 under the cash register as we walked behind the counter. We passed a line of grocery store carts with items in plastic bags from various stores. We reached the back and stood in the front of a steel door. The Korean tapped on the door and waited about thirty seconds and tapped again before using a key to open it.   An oddly shaped middle-aged man with olive colored skin and dark, curly hair stood on the other side of the door. He and the clerk locked eyes. The clerk left as the olive-skinned man walked in front of a solid wood mahogany desk that looked out of place in the makeshift office. He and Simone met in front of a brown leather sofa that fit snug between the desk and a long conference table. They hugged and kissed one another on the cheek. He grabbed her ass, squeezed it, and pulled her close, totally oblivious to my presence.

"Come on, Jack, this is not the right time." She peeled his fingers away from her jiggly backside and sat on the sofa.

"I know what will change your mind." He removed a plastic envelope from his pocket and spread two lines of white powder on the desk. He passed a rolled-up dollar bill to Simone. She leaned forward, placed the rolled-up dollar close to his nostril, and deeply inhaled the powder. She quickly moved her head side to side and passed the rolled-up bill to Jack. "I am working late tonight." He grabbed his crotch and smiled with no concern of the two missing teeth at the bottom of his mouth.

"My friend here," she ignored Jack and motioned for me to come closer, "he needs a little loan on his car." Jack walked to his desk and focused on the monitor with my car on display.

"Do you have the title?"

"No, it is not paid for." I glanced at Simone then back to Jack. "Simone tells me the title is not necessary."

"He comes from a good family." Simone intervened and smiled at Jack.

"No worries. Simone vouches for you. Bring me the current registration." My body temperature began to rise as the amount of medicine I could purchase danced in my head. I immediately began calculating in my head. The car was worth over thirty-grand. I would not be greedy. I'd ask for five grand.

I am always in awe with the amount of money the dealers have folded in their pockets from drug sales. Some dealers offer discounts if you purchase large quantities. A brilliant idea popped in my head. I will buy enough medicine to sell. I could use some for myself and sell some to pay the loan. I quickly left Jack and Simone, sprinted to the car, unlocked the door, and rambled through the glove compartment to find the registration and ran back to the store.

"Wait!" The clerk stopped me from entering the back of the store that led to the office. A thin female with pimples covering most of her face stood behind a thinner male. They both had oily hair and appeared as if they had not seen soap and water in a very long time. They stood patiently in line holding plastic grocery bags filled with diapers, toothpaste, bath soap, and dish washing liquid most likely stolen from the grocery store down the street.

The Korean clerk pushed items on the counter aside to make room for the items the drugged-out couple came to sell. They removed items from their grocery bags and placed them on the counter as the Korean assigned a price. The clerk passed each a ten-dollar bill for their items that would cost at least a hundred in the store.

"Hey, dude," my voice was filled with frustration mixed with an equal amount of anxiety and anger. "Can you let me in?" The clerk ignored me, left the counter, and began stocking the shelves with the items the drugged-out couple sold.

"Hey," He yelled to the couple as they were exiting the store. "Bring washing powder!" He made circles with his hands to compensate for his limited English. "Next time bring baby formula. The powder kind I pay double."

"I am here to conduct business." The store clerk continued to act as if I was invisible. "Jack is waiting on me. My girl is in the back waiting with him." The clerk continued stocking the shelves. Two minutes turned into five minutes then ten.

"You go now." The clerk adjusted his earpiece and pointed toward the back of the counter. I entered the makeshift office; the funky smell of blended body fluids hit me so hard the nasal hairs tickled the inside of my nose. Simone was sitting back and deep into the sofa. Her eyes were rolled to the back of her head. The top button on her pants was unfastened. The first button was in the third hole of her shirt and made her shoulders appear lopsided. Her eyes were glazed. He left Simone on the sofa and returned to his desk. He adjusted the waist band of his polyester pants around his enlarged abdomen. I passed the registration, and he passed a stack of papers for me to sign. I did not bother reading the papers, believing none of this was legal and could not possibly be binding.

"How much do you need?"

"Five thousand."

"Three thousand is as high as I can go."

"This car is less than a year old."

"Three thousand!" We locked our eyes. My dissatisfaction with the deal showed all over my face. "Take it or leave it." He placed his pen on the desk, folded his arm around his rotund midsection, and leaned back in his chair. "Find a business that will give you a loan on a car you do not own." Thinking of the medicine I could cop, I signed the papers.

I felt less than zero for taking the deal, but the dope would soon make those feelings disappear. Jack removed a pistol from the drawer. I felt uneasy when he pointed it in my direction. He opened a lower cabinet never taking his eyes off me and removed three one thousand-dollar stacks of one hundred-dollar bills. I took the money and quickly left the back office and almost sprinted through the hall that leads to the convenience store. Simone was close behind. I peeled one hundred dollars from one of the stacks and gave it to Simone. She cursed me to hell and back. She somehow believed she was entitled to half. I left her standing in the middle of the parking lot where she continued to curse me.

I purchased small baggies from the beauty supply store and scooped small quantities of the dope I purchased from Donovan in the plastic baggies. I purchased a liter bottle of cognac and set up camp in the cheap hotel on Memorial Drive where many addicts and those almost homeless pay rent by the day. I had it all planned out, but nothing in life works for me as planned.

The medicine went faster than I suspected. I used all the medicine I put aside to sell. I spent most the money in less than three weeks, and I missed the first payment when the loan became due. I was not worried, believing the contract to be unenforceable.

The rapid, powerful knocks on the door startle me. I quickly placed my gear out of sight, opened the door, and found Simone standing behind Jack with an *I got you look* on her face. She escorted Jack to my hotel room out of spite. She was still angry I did not give her half of the money.

"I need your payment." I laughed in his face. "You can pay a $500 fee for another 30-day extension, or I need the full amount of the loan plus all interest and late charges." I was amazed by the authority in his tone.

"I ain't giving you shit! Fuck you!" I slammed the door in his face and continued my private party until the last baggie was empty. My mind told me to let this be the last one, but my body craved one more. I left the hotel room with the intent to replenish the drugs and buy more booze. I parked in front of the liquor store and left the car running. I left the liquor store, drove out of the parking lot, and noticed a car following. I turned off Harrison Road onto Central Drive. I drove three blocks then turned off Central Drive into the duplex subdivision they called China Town that has no Chinese residents. The blue flashing lights startled me. I parked on the side of one of the duplexes. I rolled the window down and waited for the officer to approach.

"What is the problem, officer?"

"Driver's license and registration please."

"Sure." I reached into the glove box, removed my driver's license, and passed it to the officer. "I don't have the registration." He removed the license from my hand, walked to his car, and sat inside. He did not use the laptop computer attached to his dash. Instead, he placed his cell phone to his ear. After five or six minutes, he returned to my car.

"Sir, please step out of the car. You are under arrest."

"Arrest?"

"Step out of the vehicle!" He reached in the car and aggressively pulled me from the seat. "You have the right to remain silent. If you give up that right..." He handcuffed me to the door of the car and quickly went through my pockets. He removed two folded twenty-dollar bills and stuffed them into his pockets.

He escorted me to the back seat of his unmarked car. Instead of going to the county jail, he turned right onto Harrison Road. He parked his car in the corner of the Korean store parking lot, went inside, and stayed about twenty minutes. He returned to the car with a scowl on his face and sped out of the parking lot. I was so afraid I thought I would shit my pants when we stopped in front of the oversized, steel garage door at the county jail. My knees became weak. I almost fell as he assisted me out of the car.

"You should pay your bills!" I was charged with fraudulent obstruction and theft by deception for fraudulently using property I did not own as collateral.

"Should we process him in, Detective?"

"No." He looked at me eye to eye. "He will probably make bail." I was shoved into a holding cell with what appeared to be over one hundred men crammed into a space designed to accommodate fifty. I joined several inmates and waited in the long line to use the payphone.

"Josh, you are in jail?" It was a statement and a question. Panic shook her voice; it was hard to understand her. "Are you in there with the blacks?"

"Yes." I played into her fear. "Please come and get me." I lowered my voice as if I were under surveillance. "These guys are crazy. I just saw someone get stabbed over a small bag of chips." I intentionally made my voice tremble and surprised myself at how easy lying had become.

"Oh my God!" Within two hours, mother

paid Jack the entire loan plus interest and penalties for the charges to be dropped. I had to agree to a stint in rehab, but the truth was she would have paid to get me out of jail regardless.

I left the jail with a bondsman and our family lawyer, forgetting about the promise I made to my mother to enter rehab. He offered to take me home where mother and Rebecca were together waiting for my release. I declined, walked to the corner, and caught a bus back to Central Drive.

I have no anger or resentment with my mother. Unlike Jean-Jacques, I am the worse son on the planet.

People in the neighborhood are still on shock over Jean-Jacques' death; it's the subject of almost every conversation. I walk inside of the Korean store. I wait in line hoping Choi is in a good mood.

"What's up, man?" I placed a bottle of beer on the counter.

"One dollar seven." I place my hand in my pockets, remove two quarters, and place them on the counter.

"I will bring you fifty-seven cents in a few."

"One dollar seven!" He is stern.

"You for real, man?" I step back and make my shoulders jump as if I am challenging him to a fight. "I will bring you fifty-seven cents in a few!"

"One dollar seven!" The aggression in his voice escalates and catches the attention of everyone in the store. "Out!" He points towards the door. I pick up the two quarters, throw them at him, and leave. My sweat glands are working overtime. My stomach is beginning to boil. I need a sack to get straight so I can think of my next move. I walk to the bus stop with my sign in tow and beg for change from people exiting the bus. The look of disgust on some of the people's faces makes me feel less than zero. Some people offer half eaten burgers or leftovers in Styrofoam boxes. I have no interest in food, but too polite to turn the offerings away. Others offer spare change.

"What you doing, white boy?" Jermaine steps off the 321 Eastbound bus only it does not look like Jermaine. His hair is cut short; the unkempt braids are gone. The baggy jeans that sit below his hips are replaced with neat slacks and a dress shirt.

"Jermaine?" We bump fists.

"Yes, it's me, white boy." Jermaine is a character. On an occasion or two, he has thrown me a few dollars to get the monkey off my back or given me weed on credit to help with the cravings when I couldn't get the medicine. "Trying to do better. Has anyone said anything about the funeral since I been gone?"

"Where you been? I have not seen you in a few days."

"Somewhere to get my mind right." He laughs.

"Naw, I ain't heard nothing yet."

"We can't let this shit go. No one believes Boxing Boy killed a cop period. Everyone loved Chandler. Everyone loved Boxing Boy, so ain't nobody on Central down with that lie." He shakes his head. "There is a flame ignited in me. I am not going to let this one go. Ain't no way am I going to let this one go. Boxing Boy deserves better than this."

"I feel you." I put my hands in my pocket and pulled the insides out. "You got anything you can let me hold?" He removes five dollars from his pocket. "You got some green?"

"No, white boy, I let that life go."

"For real?"

"I am for real with it. I was wasting my life away. It's time for a change." He leaves the bus stop, walks past the corner store where he is known to frequent and down the sidewalk on Central toward his house.

I stayed at the bus stop and collected more coins to add to my medicine fund. After several hours, I collected enough for a sack. I walk past China Town; there is a new black dealer that has arrived on the scene. His sacks are slightly bigger. It is a trick. As soon as his clients become dependent, he will increase the price while decreasing the amount of product and potency. He set up shop at the apartments across from China Town where most of the residents are working class. I knock on the door. A young white, blond haired, blue eyed female answers. She could not have been older than sixteen.

"What's up?" Her body language and tone of her voice were identical to Simone's.

"Is Quan here?"

"What you need?" She sticks her lips out like a duck. "My old man ain't here. "What you need?"

"I need a ten-dollar sack." We stare at each other too long for comfort.

"What you looking at? Give me the money, niggah!" I pass the money; she passes the sack and slams the door.

I walk to the abandominium Simone occupies. I knock on the door, but she does not answer. I turned the doorknob and was ready to remove my stash so I can beam up. I cross the threshold and find Simone bent forward performing fellatio on Miguel while some dude I have never seen before humps her like a jack rabbit from the rear. She turns her face to me and continues the threesome as if it is normal behavior. The room smells like unwashed ass. I cover my nose with one hand and raise the other with a peace sign. I step over a couple of passed out bodies as I make my way to one of the rooms in the back.

I found a spot and remove my gear. I am not at ease. I feel odd watching Simone turn a trick for money to feed her monster. I think of my mother and what should we think of me aligning myself with Simone and this lifestyle. Feelings rise in me from out of the blue. I put the gear to the side. I sit with my back against the wall and allow the tears to flow. I am overwhelmed with so many feelings I can't single out one in particular. I finally managed to stop crying and tie the tourniquet on my arm. I melt the medicine on a spoon, syphon it in the syringe, and inject it in my arms. Instead of feelings of self-loathing disappearing, they intensify.

I untie the tourniquet, throw the needle and the empty bag on the floor and walk to the front of the abandonminium. Miguel and the Jack Rabbit are gone. Simone is now alone. She holds her pipe in one hand and the lighter in the other, totally oblivious to me and her surroundings. I walk past her and leave.

I walk to the bus stop, catch the bus to the train station, and catch the train with no destination. This is the first time I willingly left Central Drive in a long time. I board the North bound train to the end of the line then cross the platform to the Southbound train. I ride for an hour before transferring to the Eastbound, Westbound platforms and do the same. I lock eyes with a police officer patrolling the trains and exit at the next stop. I find an empty bench under a covered bus stop. I am consumed with grief and shame. Thoughts of suicide occupy my mind. I surrender to the idea I may need help. I don't go to the posh rehab my mother would have gladly financed. Instead, I go to the County Crisis Center.

The line to speak with the intake worker extends out into the hall. From where I stand, there is no end in sight. I look bad. My face is sunken. My eyes are glazed, and my lids are so inflamed they appear fire red. Compared to some of the people waiting, I look like a GQ model. An unbearable funk fills the lobby. Some of the people appear to have not washed in months. The workers appear unbothered by the smell. I wait patiently for my turn to speak with the intake worker. I use my sleeve to wipe away sweat that drips down my face as the worker interviews me. She appears to not notice the beginning of my withdrawal symptoms. A nurse drags a mobile diagnostic station to the intake desk and begins to take my vital signs as I sit at the desk and answer questions. My blood pressure is through the roof. I was immediately admitted, given a bed, and placed on meds to help detox the drugs from my body.

Initially, I had planned on staying in rehab for a day or two. I simply need a break, but after the withdrawals kick in, I'm too sick to leave. The stomach cramps are the worse. If giving birth is anything like this, I applaud women. After the second day, the cramps subside, and I think about leaving the center again, but the diarrhea and muscle spasms are paralyzing. I am too weak to move. My body begins to shut down, and my legs are so heavy they feel like a ton of steel. When my heartrate goes ballistic, I panic and begin throwing chairs. I beat my fists so hard against the window the frame loosens.

The orderlies enter my room in what appears to be full riot gear and tackle me to the hard floor. I scream to the top of my lungs when I feel a sharp pinch in my left buttock. My body instantly goes limp; my muscles begin to feel like rubber. The faces of the orderlies are blurry. The room begins to rapidly spin; suddenly, everything is pitch black.

I woke up two days later. The nurse enters the room, and I cover my eyes to adjust to the light as she opens the curtains in one quick move.

"Rise and shine." The nurse's jovial disposition is annoying. I want to sleep. She walks to the bed and places the earpiece in her ear. I jump as she places the cold drum of the stethoscope on my chest. I am uncomfortable speaking as my breath smells as if I have a dead dragon in my mouth. The chipper nurse grabs the blood pressure monitor, removes the cuff, and wraps it around my arm. "Are you hungry, dear?"

"Yes, ma'am."

"The doctor will have to order a special diet. Your blood pressure is through the roof." She smiles as she pats my hand. "I am Nurse Veronica. Press this red button if you need anything." After the fourth day, I was able to sleep. I forgot the relaxing feel of natural sleep. Passing out or blacking out is not sleep. I call my mother on the fifth day. Initially, she's angry and hangs up the phone after she hears my voice. I waited for an hour and call again. She allows the phone to ring twenty times before answering.

"Mom, I don't want anything." She does not respond. I can hear light breathing and muffled sniffles in the phone. "I am in a treatment facility. I am getting help."

"I don't believe you!"

"It is okay, you don't have to believe me, but I am getting help. I am going to get better."

"God, you have put this family through hell!" She hung up the phone. I make my way to the recreation room and watch a few television shows sitting next to a guy with two missing fingers engaging in a full conversation with himself. After a couple of hours, I leave and go to the phone again.

"Hello."

I gather my nerves and call again. "Mom?"

"Yes?"

"I am still at the center getting help."

"Good." I hear compassion in her voice. "Your children need you to get better. God only knows how they will turn out if they are raised by a single parent."

"I am going to do better." Her faith in me quickly returns. The next day, she comes to visit with a new wardrobe I did not need. She purchases meals for the staff and presents gift cards to all the staff assigned to my floor. Again, she becomes my personal publicist. She makes sure the staff knows that I was not to be treated like other patients. She advocates on my behalf to my wife. Rebecca was ready to turn in the towel. She had had enough. The days, weeks, and months away from the family and never-ending lies were too much, but my personal publicist is at work. She somehow manipulates Rebecca into giving me another chance.

To seal the deal, Mother purchased a brand-new BMW to replace the one I allowed a dealer to use in exchange for a couple of sacks about a month after I landed on Central Drive. This addiction took me low from the onset. I was feigning bad; I did not have cash and could not find my bank card. I loaned the car to the dealer for a few sacks. I did not bother to get a full name, nor did I check to see if he had a driver's license. The dealer took the car and was gone for three weeks. I stayed away as long. Rebecca reported me missing and the car stolen. The police spotted the car. The dealer led the police on a high-speed chase through three counties before crashing into the median on Interstate 20 hitting three cars in the process. Miraculously, no one was seriously injured. The dealer was arrested on several felonies.

His girlfriend begged me to tell the police I loaned him the car. Initially, I agreed, but she was not offering enough medicine. Luckily for Rebecca and Mother, she refused to give me the amount of medicine I wanted. She offered twenty-five sacks promising more when her boyfriend is released from jail. Even a dope fiend like me can go deep inside occasionally, and stumble on a principle. Her guy was looking at five years. That prison time is worth much more than two hundred and forty bucks in smack. It is a good thing because the car was in Rebecca's name. Because it was reported stolen, the insurance company covered the damages and paid the car loan. Rebecca loves the life being married to me affords her. Life would be perfect if it were not for Monster. Rebecca is a good wife and mother and deserves a better husband.

When I started leaving for consecutive days, she worried about me so much she developed ulcers. She would have panic attacks every time I left the house. Something as simple as going to the convenience store would lead to a lengthy interrogation. I was the one shooting dope in my veins, but I made everyone around me sick. My drug binges created severe anxiety issues for

Rebecca. She is currently taking anti-depressant and anxiety medication and under the care of a psychiatrist. It is crazy. I am the drug addict, but she needs a psychiatrist. When I would leave for a mission, she would call every other hour trying to make contact. I ignored most of her calls. When I answered, I promised to come home, always saying I was thirty minutes away but would show up three days later. I could not come home. I had to stay close to Central Drive to get what I needed. I was addicted to heroin, and I was also addicted to the new lifestyle.

Initially, Rebecca was clueless about my addiction. She would blame herself for losing money, jewelry, or expensive purses. It took a while for her to make the connection that things went missing when I came home. Sometimes when I finally made it home, she was so happy to see me that she would forget about her anger. Other times, she was so angry she would get physical sometimes hitting me so hard I walked around with black eyes and deep scratches in my face for days. My visits home became brief and infrequent. I tried to stay home but by the second day, I would become restless and irritable. The withdrawals became unbearable. I started the cycle all over again, and I would end up back on Central Drive with Simone and the crew. Once I started the cycle, it was hard to stop. Except for Jean-Jacques, my new associates reinforced my addiction.

I enjoyed Jean-Jacques' company. He was a reminder of my old life. I was not always a junkie. I left a comfortable privileged lily-white life in Dunwoody. I had everything any man could want. A wife from a good family my mother handpicked for me. Rebecca is beautiful. She has the prettiest, toned, long legs I have ever seen. Thick, long, blond hair enhances chiseled cheekbones women spend thousands of dollars in plastic surgery to duplicate. Her eyes are ocean blue with a hint of green. On the exterior, she exemplifies southern grace, but she has a wild side. Mother knew nothing about that makes her the perfect confidante.

Rebecca has always known I smoked marijuana and enjoyed a strong alcoholic cocktail. She did not know about my special medicine. My world changed forever the day she found out. I was wasted, but somehow managed to navigate the car home and ease the car inside the garage. Her side of the garage was empty. I was so excited I was about to remove my stash in the car. I came to my senses when I realized I would be exposed if Rebecca and the children came home and found me. The house was quiet. I made it to the top of the stairs. I could not go any further; the five steps to the bathroom were too long. My stomach began to turn at the thought of the warm liquid going through my veins. I wrapped the tourniquet tight around my arm, warmed my medicine, syphoned it through the syringe, and stuck it in my vein. The world immediately slowed down; I sat on the floor with my back against the wall upstairs in the foyer next to the baby's room enjoying the euphoria. My neck muscles felt like Jell-O; it was hard to steady my head. A hard hit against the wall brought me back to consciousness. I felt an immediate rise on the back of my head. The sound of the garage door opening startled me. I wanted to move, but my feet were too heavy. I rolled my body to the baby's room, used the bed rails to pull myself to my feet, and quickly tucked my stash under the covers.

"Josh, we are home. Where are you?"

I managed to stand, leave the baby's nursery, tiptoe across the hall, and stumble to our bedroom. I removed a blunt from the nightstand, and I quickly lit it. She instructed my son to go to bed. The baby fretted as Rebecca climbed the stairs. I turned my head and looked at the clock. It was seven, time for the baby's feeding. I heard Rebecca fumbling around in the nursery, most likely trying to get comfortable so the baby could latch to her breast. The baby quieted down. Several minutes passed. The rusty hinges on the nursery door squeaked like a crying baby. I promised to oil them weeks ago. I heard her feet touch the carpet as she walked toward our bedroom.

"What are you doing?" She opened our bedroom door. "Are you starting the party without me?" She quickly twisted her hair in bun and stepped out of her jeans and thong underwear at the same time. She stood in front of me. Milk dripped from her hardened nipples. She walked closer and straddled me. The musk from her privates turned me on. I raised my arms, and she pulled my shirt over my shoulders. I lightly pushed her away to take three steps to the closet and remove a bottle of cognac. I didn't have a glass, so I took hard swallows from the bottle and passed it to her. She turned up the bottle, took a few swallows, and pushed me back to the chair. She took the blunt from my hand, wrapped her thin lips around it, and inhaled. She held her breath, placed her face close to mine, and opened her mouth, allowing the smoke to form clouds as it escaped. I placed my face close to hers and inhaled deeply, pulling the smoke from her mouth into my nostrils.

I took the blunt from her, and she dropped to her knees like a seasoned stripper. With one hand, she unzipped my pants, and with the other, she loosened her hair. She gave head so good it was as if she had taken lessons. I subconsciously compared her to Simone and thought Rebecca's head game was better. She shifted in fifth gear and did something like a cartwheel and landed with her legs open with her goods in my face. She was so wet her juices dripped down my chin. Initially, I thought the wail came from Rebecca until she kicked away from me and landed on her bottom. She quickly grabbed a T-shirt and ran to the baby's room.

"What the fuck, Josh!" I quickly slid into my jeans, ran to the nursery, and stopped in the threshold. Rebecca had the baby in one hand and the used, empty syringe in the other. The baby wailed to the top of her lungs as blood dripped down the side of her face. "Dude! What the fuck..." The words were stuck in her mouth. Her eyes were wide. Her face was red as a beet. "You are shooting heroin?" It was an announcement and a question all wrapped in one. Tears flowed from of her eyes. "How?" She threw the needle down.

"Oh my God! I am so sorry." I reached for the baby, Rebecca turned around, went to our bedroom, slammed the door, and locked it just as I turned the doorknob.

"Rebecca! Rebecca! I am sorry! I swear I am sorry!" She did not respond. I twisted the doorknob, trying to break it off so I could get in the bedroom. The baby's crying softened. I was overwhelmed with sorrow. I slipped on my shoes and went downstairs. I grabbed my wallet from the table and reached for the doorknob that led to the garage. As I stepped across the threshold, I noticed Rebecca's purse. I rummaged through her purse and looked for money, so I didn't have to stop by the ATM. I stuffed the four one-hundred dollar bills I found in my pocket and left.

I did not intend to get stuck on Central Drive. The population of Caucasian middle-class young adults on Central Drive is growing. None of us came here to stay. The medicine trapped us.

Life has been sucked out of me. One of the reasons I gravitated to Jean-Jacques was he was like a breath of fresh air. I was attracted to his innocence. Jean-Jacques reminded me of happier times in my life. When I first came to Central Drive, I had an endless supply of money. I was treated like a celebrity. The dealers provided private rooms in their apartments for me to get high. Sometimes, violent encounters would break out because I spent more money with one dealer and the others would become inflamed with rage. Miguel was my favorite dealer. He was a family man, and like many in this neighborhood, he was an illegal immigrant regulated to jobs that pay under the table which most often paid minimum wages or less. He sold drugs to support his family.

I was leaving the Korean store one day when I first met him. He stood on the corner under a tree with a crowd of Hispanics and a few blacks waiting for contractors to drive by in search of day laborers He stood out among men who appeared hungover and unclean. His jeans were clean and freshly ironed. His work boots were fresh and appeared new. He stood holding a hardhat covered with stickers under his arm. His nails appear freshly manicured. His hands appeared as if he had never seen a hard day of work.

"Hey, white boy, they let you out for air?" I guessed news traveled fast. I had been at Donovan's for a week. "You going hard, Pale Face." He laughed, letting me know what could be considered as a racist insult was just a phrase to break the ice. "You should try some real shit. They cutting that shit too much that's why you look like that." He looked around to make sure no one was looking and passed a twenty-dollar sack. "This one is on me. Try it. You won't come down so hard; you won't be on the chase all day, and all that nodding will go away."

"If this is as good as you say it is, I will be back."

"Trust, Pale Face, you will be back. You can find me here every morning after I drop the bambinos off at school." I took the baggie and rushed back to Donovan's apartment.

The apartment was filled with people. I went back to the room he reserved for me and fixed my stuff. I syphoned the melted heroin and slowly pressed the needle into my vein. I was feeling the affect, but it was gradual and smooth. I placed the yellow wax paper baggie next to the pile of blue bags in the ash tray next to a makeshift bed of a mattress and box spring. I was feeling what I needed to feel, and the wax paper sack was still half full.

"What the fuck!" I was still high when Donovan barged into my reserved room. "Where you get this shit?" He picked up the wax paper baggie and examined it with his eyes then stuck his tongue in the bag.

"What?" I heard him, but I was still high and couldn't respond. "What's up, Bro?"

"I am good to you. I give you complete access to my home, and you sell me out to that no-good motherfucker Miguel." It did not register that he and his homies were throwing punches until the tip of their work boots, that never seen a day's work, made contact to my face. I am a junkie, but I am not a wimp. I grabbed a boot, not sure who it belonged to, and twisted it around, flipping the owner and kicking him in the groin. Donovan, at least one foot shorter than me, threw a punch and missed. I ducked and hit him so hard in his stomach blood flew out of his mouth. I grabbed my jacket and dashed toward the door.

My ribs hurt when I breathed. I took a few solid punches to the right side of my face and could barely see out of my right eye. I somehow made my way to the Korean store.

"Hey, dude. You can't come in here like that. Look at you." The store clerk rushed to the front of the counter and grabbed a mop. "You are dripping blood on my floor." He continued his tirade in broken English. "You dumb white kids come down here, buy drugs, and hang with these people. You are out of your league. Take your ass home!"

I left the store but did not go home. I was not ready. I told myself one more sack and I would go. One more always turned into one more.

Leaving Central Drive is not an easy task. Another drug dealer was waiting outside when I left the store. When I first landed on Central Drive, my popularity was one hundred, but all good things come to an end. After the fight with Donovan, I walked around the neighborhood in a fog. I had not eaten a real meal in days. The hunger pangs made it hard for me to concentrate. I spent most of my cash with Donovan. I removed my teller card and walked to the ATM inside of the Pakistani store. I inserted the card, entered my PIN, and pressed $200. I waited for the sound of the machine counting the money. Instead of money, *"Insufficient Funds"* blinked on the ATM display two times followed by a slip of paper that slid through the thin receipt slot and fell to the floor. I snatched the receipt off the floor. It read, "Balance $00.00." The day before, I had over fifteen grand in my account. I removed my phone from my pocket.

"Rebecca! What the fuck!" She did not respond. I hung up and dialed the number again. "Are you there? Rebecca? Rebecca?"

"Yes, I am here."

"Where is my fucking money?"

"It is our money." I did not give a shit about anything she was saying.

"Rebecca," I lowered my tone. "I need you to put the money back in the account."

"Fuck you!"

"Baby, just put one hundred dollars in. I really need that money. Deposit one hundred dollars back in the account, and I will be home in a little bit."

"I told your mother what happened. I told her your careless ass placed the baby at risk and just like always, the bitch acts as if you can do no wrong. I told her I was filing for divorce; she promised if I file, she will cut me and the kids off. She is fully aware that I do not have a job. I guess I should be grateful for a roof over our heads. She agrees to pay the mortgage and utilities because they are in your name." Empathy crept in but only briefly. "I took the baby to the doctor. The blood test comes back tomorrow. She had best be okay, or I will kill you myself!" The anger in her voice was real.

"Please deposit some money in the account."

"The nerve of your mother to cut us off because you are a fuck up!"

"Please." The pain in my stomach is intense.

"Please, I need money."

"I will be using what money we have to take care of our children until I can get a job. That bitch mother of yours may control you, but it stops now with me."

Mother handpicked Rebecca to be my wife when we were twelve years old. She manipulated opportunities for Rebecca and me to spend time together. She hosted pool parties, and Rebecca would be the only girl my age attending except for my sisters. Rebecca's family was invited to many of our summer vacations. Her family is influential but not as influential as mine. Mother and Christina, Rebecca's mother, are both members of High Society Social Club, but Christina does not descend from an influential, generational wealthy family like Mother, but somehow married into one when she married Rebecca's father. Rebecca is right. Mother uses money to cover my many shortcomings and as long as Rebecca stays in line and plays the role, Mother keeps the money flowing.

Mother did not know I was battling a heroin addiction. She thought I was seeing another woman when I first started staying out all night. She hired the best interior designer to soften Rebecca's heart to convince her to stay in the marriage. When that did not work, she purchased expensive luxury cars. Rebecca was okay with the weed and every once in a while, we bought small quantities of cocaine, but when she found out about the heroin, all bets were off.

"Rebecca," I totally blocked out the update on the baby, "I need two hundred dollars. That is all I need. You can have the rest." She did not respond. I was getting sicker. I needed a sack. My stomach began to rumble. I stood holding the phone to my ear listening to a dial tone for several minutes. I looked across the street and saw Miguel. A ray of hope crept in. I ran across the four-lane street, stopping on the medium in the middle then dodging fast moving cars to get to Miguel.

"What's up, my friend?" He stood among the group of day workers waiting for work. "I knew it would not be long. I told you, you would be back. The "My Niggahs" cut their shit too much. They are cheap and know nothing about customer service." His eyes focused on my face. "What happened, Pale Face?" I almost forgot about the scuffle earlier.

"Had to show some folk who is boss." I beat my chest with a closed fist. "Hey, do you have more of that good stuff?"

"How much do you want? I have a twenty-dollar sack and a fifty-dollar sack right now, but I can get more."

"Yea." I smiled. "I need a credit for a few hours. My wife has to transfer money back into my account."

"Pale face," he placed the sacks back into his pockets, "We don't do credit. We have a one-time sample policy."

"Hey, I am good for it."

"No way, Pale Face, check me when you have the cash."

Defeated and feigning, I walked away. My ego was wounded, and Monster was acting up. The stomach pangs were killing me. I set up camp at the bus stop in front of the Pakistani store and begged for change from people waiting to board or exit the bus. After three hours, I had twenty dollars. I spotted Miguel crossing Harrison Road with two kids, one on each side of him.

"Miguel, I still need that sack."

"Pale Face!" The scowl on his face was somewhat intimidating. He motioned for the kids to continue walking. "What the fuck is wrong with you? Have some respect. You see my kids?" He pointed to two small children walking down the sidewalk with book bags strapped to their backs.

"Sorry, man." I reached in my pocket and removed a pocket full of coins mixed with a couple of balled-up bills.

"Fuck out of here." He pushed my hand away. "I don't have a piggy bank, Pale Face." He walked away as I picked up the coins from the ground. I could barely stand straight. I walked bent forward as I removed my phone from my pocket.

"Rebecca, please transfer fifty bucks back to my account. I am begging you, baby, please just this one time."

"This is the last time." She hung up the phone. I walked around until I did not have the energy. I walked to the Korean store and sat under the tree with the day laborers. I checked my account every five minutes for hours until I finally gave up and realized she was not going to deposit money in the account.

I should have gone home months ago, but I was too afraid to leave Central Drive. After I was officially cut off from my family, I resorted to living in abandominium after abandominium. I hooked up with Simone and Chris. They charged seventy-five dollars per week for an abandoned apartment they broke into, changed the locks, and made keys. It was an okay spot. It had electricity. Chris is an electrician. He drilled a hole through the neighbor's house, connected a circuit, and stole electricity. The residents probably argued with the power company every month about the amount of the bill. Simone,

Chris, and I come from different worlds. If it were not for the drugs, we would have nothing in common. Our common denominator was we are all drug addicts with a plethora of burnt bridges and disappointed loved ones left behind.

The fun had long gone. This was a dangerous lifestyle. If Jean-Jacques, the Boxing Boy, whom everyone loved and respected could end up dead, it could happen to anyone, me included.

Chapter 10
Marie

I call the police department; the receptionist transfers me ten times before I finally reach someone who provides instructions on contacting the medical examiner. The funeral home has been trying to take custody of the body for a week. I demand they release his body so I can put him to rest. It has been ten days since my son was murdered. The neighborhood boy, who walks around going nowhere and is always taking pictures and videos of himself with his cell phone in one hand and a paper bag in the other knocks on the door. I leave the living room sofa to answer. Jikki steps in front of me as I open the door.

"Hello, Sir." The young man stands in the threshold. His hair is neatly cut close to his head. He passes a box of chicken and a six-pack of soft drinks. "I want to offer my condolences." His mouth moves, but I can't understand his words. His transformation from the neighborhood bum to the neatly dressed, polite, young man standing at my door is mind boggling.

"Thank you, son." Jikki takes the food from his hand. He passes the food to me, and we lock eyes, both confused at the transformed young man standing in the threshold of the front door.

"Have you made funeral arrangements?"

"No, they have not released the body."

"I live around the street." He points toward his house. "Please let me know. I would very much like to attend and pay my respect." He looks down. "Boxing Boy, excuse me, Gene Jack was a great kid. Everyone looked up to him, including me." I am consumed with pain but almost found myself laughing at his pronunciation of Jean-Jacques' name. Most people mispronounce his name. I can see frustration on my boy's face right now to the reaction of people never getting his name right.

Laughter quickly turns to tears. Jean-Jacques Baptiste Gomez is all I had of Michel Baptiste. Jean-Jacques is my everything. From the time I laid eyes on him, I knew he was special. He fought with his entire being to take his first breath when I pushed him out my body. He was so slippery he almost fell through the doctor's gloved hands. I lay back waiting for the introductory loud wail after the first breath. In Haiti, I had witnessed the Doula assist in bringing life in the world on several occasions. The slap on the behind echoed through the room. I waited a few seconds, but there was no crying to follow. I raised my head off the pillow to see the doctor rush a lifeless tiny body to the back of the delivery room. The nurses and doctors surrounded him, blocking my view. I snatched the IV out of my arm and threw my legs over the bed. The loud wail bellowed from the tiny brown body stopped me in my tracks. The nurses and doctors exhaled in unison as they gave one another high fives.

"What are you doing out of bed?" I did not respond. I extended my arms.

"Mon bébé s'il te plait." I heard Michel's voice in my head say, "Speak English." I cleared my throat. "My baby please."

"Honey, I will bring him to you. We need

you to lie down."

He was a tiny baby and was most likely premature. I was in the detention center during the early stages of the pregnancy. My nutrients came from processed food. I barely ate. I was not accustomed to the flavor and texture of the food. If I were in my home country, my Maman and Matants would have taken proper care of me. They would have given me proper herbs to nourish me and the baby. Yet, he appeared healthy; his eyes were bright. He was alert. He looked at me as if he could see straight through me. It was as if he was saying, "I am here in my father's stead. I will never leave you."

The detention center was crowded mostly with Mexicans and immigrants from Central America. I was terrified of catching diseases either from other detainees, or from the many injections we were forced to accept to prevent bringing diseases to America.

Despite the obstacles, Jean-Jacques grew big and strong. By the time he was six, he was almost five feet. He was six feet tall at 14 years old with the body of Hercules, and he was quick. He could catch a fly with his hands before it welcomed itself inside the house. I would scream, "Kill it!" In his baritone voice, he would say, "Mommy, everything wants to live and be free. The fly apologizes for mistakenly coming into your house." He would open the door and set it free.

His massive size caused many problems. School boys became emboldened enough to test him but never challenged him one on one. It would be two on one, three on one and sometimes four, but Jean-Jacques always won, and the challengers were defeated with much regret. I was occasionally summoned to his school to meet with one parent other times two with doctor bills in hand requesting immediate payment. I laughed in their faces as the school administrators played back tapes of boys initiating violence against Jean-Jacques.

Eventually, the boldness of these idiots became too much. I removed him from school and homeschooled him. The harassment did not end with his removal from school. The police constantly stopped him for no reason. And the girls and women were pathetic. Many older women approached him. I would say, "This is a young boy! You need to find yourself a big man." By the time he was 17, he had grown into a man. His interest in the opposite sex was apparent, but his focus was boxing. To keep him busy and out of trouble, my man trained him. We had no idea he would excel in the sport. We were simply trying to keep him busy. Initially, I did not want Jean-Jacques involved with boxing. The first time he came home with a black eye, I demanded the training cease, but Jean-Jacques and Jikki were relentless. My man saw Jean-Jacques's greatness and was determined to develop it.

I am thankful for Jikki; he took us in and helped me create a beautiful world for my two children. One I plucked from the ocean. One I pushed through my body made from the blessed union with Michel. Jean-Jacques showed me the light in the darkest of times. When I lost Michel to the fury of the ocean, God soothed me with Jean-Jacques. I would never have been able to survive losing Michel had I not found out I was with child.

As a tot, people would say I had a sparkle in my eye. Everyone in my parish saw my strength before it became apparent to me. We were poor and education was not a priority, but I wanted education. I knew education was key to a good life in the future. In my house, money, when we had it, was spent to educate my brothers. When they placed their schoolbooks down, I would pick them up. I learned to read at three. I was a poor girl from the slums of Port-au-Prince but managed to complete my studies and pass college entrance exams.

My parents, like many, were unable to sustain their marriage under the weight of poverty. By the time I was ten, they ended their union. My father left Port-au-Prince and started a new life with his new family in Genevous. He provided little to no support to my mother. The only time in the year my mother could depend on a package from him was at Christmas. The other 364 days, she was on her own. For her, marriage to a wage earner was a way out. My mother wanted me to marry a young man who landed a job on one of the cruise ships. I wanted more. I refused to marry. She could no longer feed me, so I had to provide for myself. My only income was a mango stand in the city. I worked twelve sometimes thirteen-hour days, yet I did not make enough money to pay boarding fees, and my work hours left little time for my studies. I dropped out of school and got a job in an American owned sewing factory. The conditions were beyond terrible, but I was able to make ends meet with my weekly pay and clothing pieces I managed to slip underneath my shirt or stuff in my oversized pants to sell in the city.

I am from a land of proud people so hated by the peoples on the earth because we did not ask for our freedom. We shed the blood of our oppressors and took it. We have been punished by the world till this day. Many of us live in our own country in the shadow of the Blan, foreigners usually white but a few blacks that take advantage of our resources and exploit our desperation. They live in good housing with electricity 24 hours a day while we live in shanties and lucky to get two hours of electricity a day. Those of us lucky to work have to provide sustenance for several people. Those who cannot find employment and have no working relatives are beyond destitute.

I was miserable with my work. The conditions in the American factory were deplorable. Summers were the worst; the only cooling came from large fans that circulated hot air. The labor laws state workers were entitled to two breaks and one lunch. We were allotted two fifteen-minute breaks and no lunch. There were many people desperate for employment, so the supervisors exploited the employees and treated us like animals. I resigned to this abhorrent life until I met Michel. I was walking from my work to the small room I rented in Port-au-Prince. He was leaving his second job as a ground's boy for the Etienne family. I sat on the side of the concrete street picking glass out of my feet, as he passed.

"Etes-vous d'accord?" He leaned close, looking at the blood dripping from my foot and asked if I was okay.

"Oui." I look into slanted eyes set deep into a dark chocolate flawless face. "Je vais bien." I assured him I was fine, slowly stood up, and hobbled to the Tap Tap. He followed holding onto pants that were two sizes too big with one hand and a folded American magazine in the other.

"Madame, you do not look okay to me."

"You speak English?"

"Oui," he answered slowly, "Madame, I do."
I was slightly impressed. Most people in my
immediate circle spoke French and Spanish. I
enjoyed engaging in English. I rolled my eyes and
continued hobbling to my destination, leaving him
behind. I saw him the next day as I ran to the Tap
Tap stop. I waved my hand back and forth, but the
Tap Tap did not stop. I missed it by two seconds.

"Why are you standing here? You let the Tap
Tap leave."

"I was waiting on you." He places his hands
in his pockets kept together with a row of safety
pins. "I missed it on purpose. Would you like to get
a coffee?"

"Coffee?"

"Oui" I am impressed. It feels as if he was
asking me to a fancy restaurant in Petioan Ville,
where the rich, mostly foreigners and local
politicians dine, and people like me serve. Most of
us blessed to find work save all our money. Coffee
at a café is a luxury for special occasions.

Michel was not as formally learned. He
dropped out of school to work, but he reads all the
time. He was smarter than most. He spent much of
his time reading magazines the tourists threw into
the hotel garbage and books they left behind. When
he came up with the plan to leave Haiti, I was
initially skeptical.

None of my family members escaped to
America. Some managed to travel and live in the
hostility of the Dominican Republic. A couple
relatives married tourists from Europe to escape
poverty. I had heard of many who left Haiti for
America only to be turned around and escorted
away from the American waters. I studied Michel's
plan for months. I was skeptical but could find no

glitch in it. I made it to America, but my Michel did not, but he planted a gladiator inside of me with the spirit of Jean- Jacques Dessalines.

I close my eyes. I see Michel standing next to Jean-Jacques. They have the same eyes. Jean-Jacques is a toddler asleep in his makeshift bed; he rolls over and disappears. I open my eyes and close them again. I see Michel and reminisce on our life in Haiti.

"Michel." The sun was blazing hot. I was surprised he was home. I usually arrived before him. "Comment a été votre journée?" An agitated frown stretched across his face when I asked about his day.

"Speak English or Spanish! No more French or Creole. Speak English or Spanish!" He balled his fist. "We will leave in two weeks. If customs stop us, we will say we are Cuban."

"Je comprends." I hit the side of my thigh. "Apologies, excuse my French." We both smiled. "I meant to say I know. I understand."

"I am serious, Marie." His expression was a mixture of empathy and annoyance. I was fluent in French and Spanish. I learned English two years before meeting Michel. Michel had been trilingual since birth. "We have to leave this place. Things are getting worse. The Etiennes are rejoicing that the army has taken Aristide out of the country." I did not wrestle with politics, but Michel was very astute on political matters. "Things will be bad."

"Things are always bad." I laughed, but he was serious. "Si." I leave our makeshift bed in the one room shanty we have called home for three years. "He took my arm and pulled me back to him.

"Apologies. I am not vexed, but this is our chance for a good life. Not just for us but for our families as well. We cannot mess it up." He looked around. "We will leave this place for a good life in America."

We took two steps to our bed from a small space we called a kitchen that consisted of a propane tank connected to a portable stove. There was no basin just a bucket with water we gathered daily from the community pump. We sat on our straw bed and removed the magazine from under the pillow. It had become almost as sacred as the Bible. The pages were filled with pictures of beautiful American women dressed in stylish clothes. Bright smiles covered soft faces. Everything on the pages appeared taut.

"We will eat chicken and good meat," he whispered to ensure our neighbors did not hear, and our conversation remained covert. He smiled as he turned the worn, wrinkled pages and pointed to the pictures of a couple sitting at a bistro outside in the bright sun in an advertisement for sunglasses. He placed the magazine to the side, removed the woven straw rug, and used his hand to lift the wood from the floor. He removed our glass jar from the hole. I removed my wages from my purse and passed them to him.

"How much?"

"Six thousand US dollars plus your pay."

"I have five hundred gourdes."

"I will convert them to dollars tomorrow at the hotel."

"Is that enough?"

"It will be enough. We will spend two thousand to travel to Cuba and America. My cousin will house us. She has a job for you in her sewing factory."

"She does not like me." I frowned. "Why

doesn't she like me?"

Michel often passed the phone to me when he called her in a futile attempt for us to bond, but she was unengaging. I asked her questions about the sewing job, the compensation per piece, and the production quota. She behaved as if she did not know what I was talking about.

"Her feelings are irrelevant. I caught the tap-tap to Genovous and wired her the one grand she needed to secure housing until her receipts post to her bank account."

I removed bread and a half of a piece of cake he saved from a hotel guest and the half of piece of fish he scavenged from the Etiennes. We had eaten scraps from his job for the past three years. We spent money only on necessities. We were doing better than most in our community. We were both employed. We had to be very careful, as it was not uncommon for peasants to learn of those with plans to leave and kidnap family members for a ransom.

"Are you sure we can't leave from Port-au-Prince? It will be much cheaper."

"No!" He rubbed his hand across my face and softened his tone. "We go from Cuba." He looked deep into my eyes and scanned my face. "Your surname is Gomez. Practice it. You can easily pass for Cuban. Soft skin, loosely curled hair, and your fake Cuban accent should be enough to get you in America if we are confronted by customs." He removed two official documents from his bag and passed one to me. "I paid for Cuban birth documents. If they should contact the registry office in Havana, our information will be verified. If a Cuban touches the American soil, clemency is automatically granted." He laughed as he touched his tightly coiled hair. "I may not be so lucky. I may not pass. They throw Haitians in the ocean for shark feed, so the sharks do not swim close to the beach and eat the Americans."

"Stop fibbing." I laughed. His expression was serious.

"You should start packing our things." I looked around our almost empty one room shanty and pick up a photo of my mother and siblings. "No photos. We must remember family in our minds. We are Cuban with no connection to Haiti."

"Then there is nothing to pack." We both laughed. He pulled me close and removed the used condom from the foil paper. We carefully washed our condoms after the first use and discarded it after the second. Michel was obsessed over saving and not having babies until we reached America.

God had other plans. My Jean-Jacques was not planned but he was not a mistake. He was the image of his father: the broad, curved shoulders and angular nose were exact replicas. His father never laid eyes on him, but he would have been very proud of Jean-Jacques.

I will clear Jean-Jacques' name. I owe it to Michel to clear his name. Our sojourn to American was the worst and best thing to happen in my life. Michel and I were not unique in our fight for a new life. Many people pooled their monies to support family members who desired to leave as an investment. Having someone on the outside to send money back for maintenance, school fees, or to set up a business was how we survived in a country with thirty percent unemployment. It was a luxury to have someone outside of the country to send money back. Many never had those connections and would sabotage those who did. It used to be people would put their gourdes together to pay for a brother, sister, or cousin to catch a ride on one of the boats. Sometimes, people were successful in crossing and the investment paid off, but many times, people were sent to America and were never heard from again. Some were taken by the ocean; others made it to America and were taken by greed and totally forgot those left behind in Haiti.

Michel planned to leave for years. The Etienne family was half cast and had permanent residency in America. They freely traveled back and forth between Haiti and the United States. They shared beautiful pictures of life in America. Sometimes, they passed Michel some of the American clothes they or their family members did not want. Every once in a while, Michel would take a dress for me when no one was watching.

Our desire to leave our beloved Haiti grew stronger with Michel each day he worked for the Etiennes. He became obsessed with the idea of America that we worked as if we were training for the Olympics. We mastered breathing underwater through reeds. We practiced holding our breath for long periods of time, our swim, and floating techniques daily. We ran miles a day to prepare our bodies for the trip.

I was walking with a friend in Jacmile Town Square to the Tap Tap when the Haitian National Police swarmed on the town square. A group of people stood shouting outside the US Embassy, "Laisser seul Aristide." Leave Aristide alone. The police stormed the area. The Tap Tap came along but did not stop. I stood at the stop for over an hour when Michel showed up. "Were you going to stand here forever?"

We walked five miles to our home. By the time we arrived, my feet were too swollen for my shoes. I was so tired. I went to sleep without dinner.

• • •

"Let's go!" He shook me so hard my shoulders popped.

"What time is it?" I looked through the makeshift window toward the sky. The sun had not risen. The only light came from the moon.

"Don't worry about the time." He gave no advance warning. I did not know the exact date we would depart. We splashed water on our faces and quickly changed our clothing. We dropped to our knees, said our prayers, and placed the best clothing we owned into our plastic tote. We divided the money to ensure we were both prepared should we become separated. Michel gave me thirty-five hundred dollars of the five thousand left after paying for transport. I wrapped the money in plastic, squatted low, and inserted them deep inside. I spent months practicing squeezing my vaginal muscles by holding small marbles inside to make them strong. Even if I had to cough like I had whooping cough, the money would not fall out.

We walked barefoot three miles on the gravel and then two miles in soft mud to save our second hand almost new shoes for our arrival in America. I remained at the dock while Michel spoke with the captain of the small boat. There were twenty other people traveling with us on the boat including two Mexicans, a Haitian teen with no accompanying family, and two Cuban males. Somberness covered all our faces. We were leaving our home countries for a better life and opportunities. I loved Haiti, the smell of the food and the happiness the people found in the most destitute situations. The zeal we Haitians have for freedom can be found in no other people I have ever encountered. We put our lives on the line for our freedom. Haiti was home. I might never see my country again, but Haiti will always be home.

The sun began to rise. We caught a truck from Port–au–Prince to Jean-Rabel. We waited for an hour for the boat then traveled by boat for almost six hours to Santiago de Cuba, then nine hours to Havana. We circumvented Guantanamo Bay, as many Americans inhabited that part of the island. I was afraid the smoke from the boat's engine would catch the attention of customs. We were behind schedule, as the small boat stopped three times totally shutting down the engine.

When the small boat docked at the Cuban port, people were already boarding the boat that would transport us the ninety-mile trip from Cuba to Florida. Michel paid another fee, and we took our place next to a young mother no older than twenty maybe twenty-one with a small girl child sitting on her lap. The baby had a gold bracelet with the name Jasmine Gomez engraved. I think to myself that Gomez must be a popular sir-name in Cuba. It was the same one Michel gave to me. She was a plump happy baby, appearing to be just over a year old neatly tucked in a yellow life jacket.

There were twenty of us on a boat meant to transport ten or fifteen at the most.

"Captain, should we wait?" One of the deckhands inhaled deeply; his nostrils expanded outward. "I smell a big storm."

"We leave now!" The captain dismissed his deckhand's concerns. "Our connection says customs will be miles from our port giving these people time to get off the boat, touch the American soil, and give us time to get far from the American waters." We traveled well over two hours in the sea for what should have been a ninety-minute trip when the water began to toss the boat. The waves pushed so much water in the boat that a small child could create a swimming hole.

"Hold on, everyone!" Fear and excitement collided in my gut as I could see the American shore above the horizon. "We are five minutes from our destination." The boat tossed and turned at one point and felt as if it was standing straight on its stern. People sitting in the bow slid all the way back, landing on top of those holding tight to the port and starboard.

A tall wave rose above the bow. The water felt like cement when it made contact with my head. Gravity pushed me backwards. Bodies in front of me hit hard against the water. It felt as if my head would explode when I unexpectedly went under. I panicked and began to fight the water sinking deep into the ocean. The many days of training with Michel were in vain. It seemed to take forever for me to relax my body, stop fighting the water, and come to the surface. Waves of blood mixed with the ocean water flowed away from a gash in Michel's head. I swam to him and flipped him on his back. He was in and out of consciousness. I grabbed his hand and tried to propel us forward to the shore. American boats left their ship and sailed fast toward us. He peeled my hand from his and thrusts me forward as he sank to the bottom of the ocean. I grab on to a yellow life jacket and flipped it over. A loud wail bellowed out of the baby's mouth as she kicked and screamed.

We floated in the ocean for several seconds

before I gathered my composure. The baby grabbed my sleeve and held on to me for dear life. She alternated crying and locking her eyes with mine. I grabbed hold to the baby and swam to the shore. I swam hard with one arm pulling the baby and the other fighting to reach the shore as the boats sailed toward us. I found myself propelling away from the shore and back into ocean. I went under and positioned myself on the other side of the baby and used my strong arm to swim towards the shore. The wet clothes and the baby almost weighed me down. The years training for this trip paid off. I rubbed the grainy sand between my toes, stood upright, and moved as fast as I could to the shore. I trip on the wet sand and fell to the ground. My eyes looked at the dull stars in the cloudy sky as I lay in the sand and waited.

"Hola," I greeted the custom officials as they ran to me and the baby with their guns drawn and pointed at us. "La hicimos a America! La hicimos a America!" The officers looked at one another as I screamed, "We made it to America! We made it to America!" Initially, they placed me in an infirmary. There were approximately thirty beds positioned side by side. I attempted to get up, but one of my hands was strapped in a metal cuff to the side of the bed.

"Nous avons soeur. Nous avons soeurnous sommes vivants," she told me with tears in her eyes. "We made it. Sister, we made it. We are alive!" I looked around and spotted the very frail Haitian teen. One of her arms were cuffed to the iron bed, and the other arm was wrapped in a white gauze and lay to her side. "Nous avons soeur." Her skin was dark like mine. She spoke French, but I could detect Haitian dialect in her voice.

"Habla Española!" I scolded.

"Si," she whispered back, still crying with joy. "Si."

A nurse accompanied by a female escort in what appeared to be military gear entered the infirmary.

"Your name?"

"Yo no hablo ingles." I do not speak English.

"Where is your home country?" Her broken Spanish made me comfortable. She most likely would not be able to detect my fake Cuban accent.

"Cuba." The female soldier stood guard as the nurse wrote on coffee-stained paper fastened to a clipboard. "Donde eta' mi bebe?" I asked.

"Your baby is getting medical care." She smiled and touched my hand. "She will be okay."

Anger boils in my belly as I reminisced on my journey to this country. I fought to survive in Haiti. I fought to get to this country for a better life for myself and those I left behind. Through it all with the help of my man, I raised a warrior. Now, I have to fight to find out what happened to my Jean-Jacques. I have called the police station, and no one will speak to me. I am unable to sleep. When I sleep, I wake up with Jean-Jacques standing over my bed.

"I did not do anything, Mama. I did nothing wrong."

I have had the same dream for the last five days. I will bury my son, and then I will fight for justice.

Chapter 11
Benazir

The savage softly knocks on my door. I do not answer. I sit on my bed and watch the doorknob slowly turn. He opens the door just enough to slide his head between the door and the frame. "Benazir, you are not eating again." His fake smile and soft tone cannot hide the evil in his spirit. His attempt at using the tools he learned in family therapy is inauthentic, well-rehearsed, and outdated. I am no longer the troubled high school girl. I am a young woman in love with a great guy. He is many years too late to have a civil relationship with me. The wounds are too deep. The trust is nonexistent. "We need you to work at the store today," he pleads. I look at him, turn my face to the wall, and cover my head with my pillow. I have refused to work at the store for the last week. My grief is heavy; I can barely leave my bed.

My parents believe I am depressed again. My mother wants to make an appointment with the expensive psychiatrist. My father behaves as if he is schizophrenic. He alternates between offering to purchase a new car for my depression and threats to send me to Pakistan for my rebellion. What they do not know, and I dare not share is I am grieving the death of a beautiful black man. Depression would be a nicer alternative. I wish I could communicate to these people I call parents, but we are miles apart in our thinking and experiences.

My Panther is dead. I want to shake myself awake and out of this nightmare. He was more than my friend. He was my rock. He helped me make sense of the world. He loved me. Unlike my mother, I am not stuck on Duty and Tradition. The Panther made it easy to love him. He helped me find my inner beauty, not based on a Caucasian, Eurocentric standard but my own Pakistani beauty. The loving way he touched my curved hips and cupped my rotund buttocks helped me celebrate the body I was taught to loathe. Panther was unlike other guys I dated. I did not have to dumb myself down to make him comfortable. I am a biology major. He helped me study for exams and would willingly act as a sounding board when I would explain different concepts like meiosis versus mitosis or the differences between deoxyribonucleic acid and ribonucleic acid.

"Dead." The murder was breaking news the first few days after Panther was killed. The news anchor pushed the words from his mouth void of emotion. His affect was flatter than a pancake. "Officer involved shooting." The words seemed unreal. It was out of the ordinary to report crime on Central Drive. Reporters would have to camp out twenty-four hours, seven days a week to report all the crime that occurs on Central Drive. People get robbed, mugged, and shot all the time, and it is never newsworthy.

This time is different; an honest police officer, loved and respected by the community was killed. This shooting was breaking news on all five local channels because Chandler was special. Chandler was the nicest, most honest cop in the county. The police allege he was killed by a young black male with possible gang affiliation. Nothing is farther from the truth. Panther was not a thug, nor was he in a gang. He was a gentle giant. He did not, could not, kill anyone.

His spirit was beautiful. His heart was pure. I wanted to spend every moment of the day with him. I would volunteer to make the daily bank deposits as an excuse to meet Panther. He became part of my daily life. Panther changed his workout schedule to spend those few precious moments with me. "Officer involved shooting," every time the news reporters speak these words, my heartrate increases, and my blood pressure rises. Panther did not own a gun, and if he did, there is no way he would point a gun at a police officer, especially Chandler.

Panther had no problems with anyone in the community until Officer Whitley began to harass him. Out of nowhere and without provocation, Officer Whitley began to single him out. Officer Whitley doesn't look like the typical police. There is something criminal about him. He often comes in our store for free refreshments. Most of the officers get a free coffee, but this one always grabs a handful of candy and a package of powdered donuts as he leaves the store, never offering to pay.

The first time Officer Whitley and Panther crossed paths was surreal. Panther was running. As usual, he calls me at the end of the run when he is walking to cool down. We were in the middle of a conversation when the sound of his voice became muffled. It sounded as if he stuffed the phone in his pocket without ending the call, but the conversation with the officer was clear.

"Stop, boy!"

"Is there a problem officer?" Panther was breathing hard.

"Why are you sweating so hard, boy?" His southern accent was inauthentic and became more pronounced when he said "boy."

"I have been training. I just ran five miles, Sir." His voice cracked. "I am unarmed, Sir. There is no reason to draw your weapon."

"You telling me how to do my job, boy?"

"No Sir, I just want you to know I am unarmed." His breathing should have been relaxed. Yet it sounded as if he was still fighting to catch his breath.

"You have any drugs on you? You look suspicious, my niggah." The officer's laughter was not jovial. Instead, it was mocking and condescending.

"No, Sir, I don't do drugs. I…"

"Place your hands on the car and spread 'em, boy."

"Ouch! That's my head. I don't sell or do drugs!" There were three loud thumps that sounded like a basketball hitting concrete; two minutes later, the call ended. I waited a couple of minutes and dialed Panther's number. The call went to voicemail. I volunteered to work late at the store hoping to see him. The next morning, I drove by his house and parked on the corner waiting for him to enter or leave his house. It was like he fell off the face of the earth. Three days later, he suddenly reappeared. He stood in front of the cash register with a bottle of water in one hand and a five-dollar bill in the other. A raised purple bump sat awkwardly on the side of his head. A fading purple circle surrounded one of his eyes. I smiled, and he returned my smile. We both contained our joy, as the Brute was in the back of the store and most likely eavesdropping.

"Jean-Jacques, what's up? Let me get that change, man." The new neighborhood junkie interrupted our clandestine reunion. He walked in the store. He looked as if he lost ten pounds since I saw him the day before. Panther passed the junkie two singles, and they walked out of the store together. I didn't like him associating with White Junkie Boy. White Junkie Boy did not fit the typical stereotype of the drug addict on Central Dive. He was articulate. When he was not high, he could hold an intelligent conversation. He was one of the many Caucasian junkies who now called Central Drive home.

He and Panther had nothing in common. I didn't like White Junkie Boy hanging out with Panther. I didn't like sharing Panther. Panther quickly became an integral part of my life. I would share with him the trials of growing up with a crazy father and submissive mother in a country where we all are supposed to be free. He would share his gratitude for his stepfather and his inquisitiveness about his biological father who died before he was born. Unlike me, he had an open and honest relationship with his family.

I miss him. He convinced me to stop dying my hair blond and straightening my natural curls. Though he would sometimes get his fingers caught in my natural curly hair, he found my hair beautiful. I started eating a healthy diet and jogged on the treadmill every morning because I enjoyed it, and it was good for me. My out of touch parents believed my new outlook is because I finally began to apply the coping tools introduced during the therapy sessions, but it was Panther.

The Panther was well respected in the community. His celebrity status in the boxing world was expanding beyond the southern states. Boxing promoters from all over were courting him. Many trainers were offering large amounts of money to lure him away from his stepdad. Businesses wanted to invest in him. He refused. The Panther named Jean-Jacques by his Haitian mother was adamant about keeping his independence and working with his stepdad. He was strong and lived a very principled life. He would have never shot Chandler. No one in this neighborhood would hurt Chandler.

I sit in the middle of my bed surrounded by piles of clothes I have thrown to the side in search of something appropriate to wear. I am beyond frustrated. My bra is now too small; my breasts are falling out the top and sides. My granny panties I reserve for my monthly flow used to fit loose; now they are tight around my waist. I am overwhelmed and suffocating with grief. I have lived a double life for a while now. In front of my parents, neighbors, and traditional Pakistani community, I am the ideal Pakistani girl making good marks in my college courses. In my other life, I am a vibrant young woman in love with a beautiful black man whose life ended violently and tragically. Panther was murdered, plain and simple. I do not care what the news reports say about the officer who shot Panther. I don't care that the District Attorney and the Chief of Police have pledged to stand by Officer Whitley. He is a murderer. My Panther was murdered.

I carry the heaviness of this grief alone. There are no girlfriends to lend a shoulder to cry on. I have crossed the taboo cultural, racial, class, and economic thresholds no decent Pakistani girl would ever cross. If my secret came to light, close allies would quickly align themselves with my parents and at best, ostracize me from my home and community. The worst-case scenario is too scary to think about. I have heard stories of young men and women drunken with romance, throwing Duty and Tradition out the window, and when the transgression comes to light, the penalties are horrendous. Some disappear and are never heard from again. I am terrified of this new trajectory. I had the power to adjust the sail and navigate in a different direction. I have procrastinated so long that it may be too late to make that decision.

My mid-section is quickly expanding. My clothes no longer fit comfortably. I am determined to show my respect for Panther. Tears burn the wells of my eyes as I fight to contain my grief. I can't believe he is dead. Some people deserve to die. Some, like Panther, deserve to live as long as desired. He was good. He had so much to offer the world.

I try to ignore the arguing outside of my door. He shouts at my mother with the threats of purchasing a one-way ticket to Pakistan with my name on it. His threats mean nothing. The power to intimidate me or manipulate me with fear disappeared a long time ago. She pleads and begs him not to send me away. I have come to believe this is some type of sick ritual for my parents. I do not understand why she is affected by idle threats. If he were to buy a one-way ticket to Pakistan, how would he get me on a plane? I am a legal adult. Who in America would enforce this ridiculous notion?

Today is the Brute's weekly civic meeting. No one seems to know which civic group he attends. It does not have a name, and as far as I can tell the membership is small and very exclusive. Our community is small. None of the other Pakistani parents whose children I befriend seem to belong to this exclusive group. The meeting requires his absence from work for an entire day. A greedy man like my father has no concept of civic duty. My mother is the only poor soul who believes his lies.

He has always been self-centered and self-serving. When I was younger, he would bring me to the store so he could bathe in the customers' comments on my beautiful skin or listen to the blacks marvel at the softness and thickness of my long, jet black, curly hair. I have often observed him flirting and tapping the buttocks of some of the flirtatious female customers when he thought no one was looking; many were barely legal and just old enough so he would not go to jail if his dirty deeds came to light. I would give subtle hints to my mother in my child-like language about those awful black girls visiting him in the back storeroom at thirty-minute intervals. She would respond as if I said he was purchasing soft drinks and start dinner after a long day of work. As a child, I knew the Brute was taking advantage. One day after becoming frustrated with her lack of reaction to my subtle hints about his infidelities, I shouted, "Daddy fucks the black girls in the back of the store!" I mistakenly thought I would feel a David vs. Goliath euphoria of exposing his deeds. I imagined the taste of revenge would be sweet like guava nectar. Instead, the defeated look on her face made me sad. I instantly regretted telling her what she must have known.

She is a college professor, highly esteemed among her peers, but married to a common shopkeeper who cheats. After a few arguments, one that escalated to an almost violent exchange where the police were called, the Brute modified his behavior. He now leaves the store around the same time every day, always leaving the parking lot the opposite direction of the places he conducts business and in the direction of what he calls the nigger jungle. He returns two hours later; his clothes wrinkled and shirt misbuttoned. He is so confident in his mischief that he often makes careless mistakes and returns with cheap lipstick stains that could never be mistaken as my mother's. This Duty and Tradition seem to work in favor of my father and men like him at the expense of women like my mother, too afraid to bathe in their own glory, running for shade to dim the light of their own shine. Honestly, both of my parents disgust me, but I stand in solidarity with my mother. We are both his victims.

"She is spoiled and too Americanized! If you would have allowed me to send her to Pakistan just for one week, I promise you..." He leaves from the other side of my bedroom door and walks down the hall. He intentionally speaks loudly so I can hear. "You have allowed her to get away with this level of disrespect! No decent Pakistani mother I know would raise a girl child to be this disrespectful!" He returns to my door. He attacks her mothering skills as if I am not the age of consent as if she can make me respond against my will. It has not dawned on him that he as well as my mother are powerless in my decisions. He yells, screams, and hits the walls hard. I stand my ground. I am going to pay my respect to Panther.

"We will lose money, Benazir. All the other stores are closed. We will be the only store open. This is a cash cow." I leave my room, walk past him in the hallway, and go downstairs to the laundry room. He follows behind me as I remove a pile of clothes from the washing machine and transfer them to the dryer.

"I am going to the funeral!"

"You will miss all of this money to attend some black gangbanger's funeral? Are you crazy?" He stands with his hands open, shoulders raised. A look of bewilderment covers his face. "Some nigger boy you barely know?"

"He is no gangbanger! He is my friend! He has more integrity in his pinky finger than you have in that entire bloated body!" He follows me to my room. I enter, turn around, and close the door as hard as I can in front of him. I remove my shirt and rummage through the pile of clothes again.

"Benazir, Benazir." Her voice is especially annoying today. "Benazir."

"What happened to knocking and waiting to be invited in?"

"Do you have to go to the…?" She stands still in the threshold, her hands on her hips dressed in her favorite black Kuti with the heavy Rashan. Suddenly, her high energy and elevated voice falls flat. Her chest rises abnormally high as she inhales. I quickly pull a T-shirt from a pile of clothes on the bed and cover my mid-section. She closes the door and moves her head from side to side not in the Indi-Pakistani way but in a this cannot be true kind of way. I toss my T-shirt to the side, and I pull the covers to my chin. "No, Benazir, no," she whispers. She covers her mouth to muffle her scream.

I look deeply into her intense eyes. Her expression is more fear than anger. I turn away and whisper, "I am sorry." I quickly stand, go to the closet, and find my robe. Her hand is so close to her mouth that it looks as if it is suctioned to her lips. "I am afraid. I am terrified. I do not know what to do," I whisper. She walks to me and wraps her arms around me. I allow my body to relax in her arms, believing and praying that motherhood will overrule Duty and Tradition. She shifts her body to adjust to my weight.

"Mina!" We both jump at the sound of the Brute's voice. "Where are the keys to the truck?"

"On top of the freezer in the garage." She removes her arms from around me, wipes the tears away from her eyes, and smooths her thick henna colored hair with both hands. We stare intensely at one another. We hold our breath as we hear him move closer to the door. We jump when he knocks.

"What are you guys doing in there?" His cologne is so thick I can smell it on this side of the door.

"Girl talk." A fake giggle leaves her mouth. Her sullen face does not match the happiness in her voice.

"I am leaving. Please have dinner prepared when I return. Please don't be too heavy with the curry this time." We exhale, simultaneously relieved when we hear him walk away from the door.

"Who is the father?" she whispers. "Is it someone we know?" A beam of hope at the thought that she may be able to fix this problem lights up in her eyes. "Is he Pakistani or at least an Indian boy? We can speak with his parents and make proper arrangements to protect your honor."

"He is not Pakistani." I lower my head and whisper, "He is not Indian."

She stands, holds her stomach with one hand and massages her heart with the other. "Is it a white boy?" Her lips spread into a slightly hopeful smile.

"One of your classmates?" I do not respond. "Please, Benazir, he cannot be a black! Please tell me the father is not a black!"

My lack of response confirms her worst fear. She steps away, turns her back to me, and places her head in a corner. She makes no sound, but her shoulders slowly rise and fall. Her body shakes as if she has epilepsy. Her hand is suctioned to her mouth again. She wipes her tears away, looks at me with no expression, opens the door, and leaves.

I lie down on my bed. I close my eyes tight; I see Panther. If he were not taken away, this would be easier. He would have the answers. He would reassure me I am not bound to Duty and Tradition. He would pass his confidence to me. He would protect me.

I love him. I begin to cry, not loud, but the worst kind of cry. The one where you must hold emotions tight inside. The kind that reaffirms my loneliness. I wish he was here.

Panther impacted my life from the onset. I was almost his stalker. I stared out the window at 9:47 every morning rain or shine to see him run past the store toward Memorial Drive. Forty-five minutes later, I would look up and find him on Central Drive sparing with the air or talking to White Junkie Boy. Power is the first word that comes to mind when I think of him. He was big and tall like a tree trunk. His muscular body radiated power. After his run, he usually walked to the Korean store and came out with a pint of milk.

Panther called me his angel. He credited me with saving his life. There was an incident that resulted in a squadron of marked and unmarked police vehicles converging into the parking lot of the Korean store. Ten black males sat with their hands cuffed behind their backs waiting to be taken to jail. He came into our store, clothes soaked with perspiration, purchased a pint of milk, and drank it straight out of the carton.

"Thirsty aye?"

He waved his hand and finished half of the carton before placing it on the counter and passing a five-dollar bill. "I need the calcium."

"You can get it from broccoli, you know?" His smile was so bright I turned away. "Milk is for baby cows. It is not for human consumption." As I passed his change to him, two officers, one in uniform and Officer Whitley in plain clothes swarmed in the store with guns drawn and pointed at Panther.

"Raise your hands! Get on the ground!" Panther immediately fell to the floor and lay on his stomach. His legs and arms were spread wide apart. "Why were you running, boy?"

"I am in training, Sir! I am a boxer!"

"It is you again." Officer Whitley manipulated Panther's face with the tip of his shoe. "Pass me your ID, boy!" Panther did not move. The officer stood over Panther, lowered his weapon, and pointed it at Panther's head.

"Sir, please look in my left sock. I do not feel safe moving my hands, Sir!"

"I said pass your ID, boy!"

I ran from behind the counter, reached into his sock, removed his ID, and passed it to the officer, who snatched it from my hand.

"Jean Jackass." His southern accent is inauthentic.

"It is Jean-Jacques, Sir." He proudly pronounced his name with Haitian dialect and French accent. The Panther lay so still he did not look like a live human.

"What the fuck ever." The officer scanned the ID with his red-rimmed eyes then threw it on the floor next to the Panther. Panther still didn't move. "You can get up, boy! Everything checks out." Panther laid still on the floor until the officers left. He rolled over, covered his face with his hands, and sat totally still on the floor for two minutes. One long tear flowed down his cheek. He wiped it away and picked up his ID from the floor. I stood next to him, unable to move. He finally stood, and we embraced one another for what felt like an eternity. His body felt like concrete. My shirt became damp with his perspiration.

"Thank you." He kissed my forehead, looked into my eyes for several seconds before leaving.

I did not plan to love him but loving him came easy. No Pakistani girl with my family status would view Panther as a viable suitor. He would not fit with my responsibility to Duty and Tradition. It is expected that I will marry a Pakistani boy from a family of doctors, lawyers or possibly an engineer with at least a PhD matriculating from an Ivy League university or at the very least a highly ranked state university. I could get away with marrying a white boy from a prosperous family but never a black no matter the wealth or family status.

I never challenged the social dynamics of my family. I never gave them much thought. If our paths never crossed, I would have never bucked the status quo. It was impossible not to love Panther.

Panther became my everything. I was willing to give up everything for him. I honestly wanted to maintain my chastity. I wanted to bathe in the pride of my future husband checking the sheets for the blood stain on my honeymoon night. Making love to Panther was not planned. We were both virgins. It simply happened.

If anyone is to blame it is me. Prior to the day our baby was conceived, our intimate interaction consisted of exploring our bodies with our hands, heavy petting, and kissing. I remember the day I lost my virginity as if it happened yesterday. I had not seen Panther in a couple of days; I went to his house. I could not remember the address. All the doors of the townhomes connected to his were the same color. I parked my car next to the fire hydrant and walked along the sidewalks until I saw a heavy boxing glove lying on grass next to the walkway. I knocked, waited several minutes, and was about to leave when he opened the door. He was exercising as usual. Perspiration dripped down his bare chest and settled in the middle of his pectorals.

"I was in the back working out. I have to finish." He invited me inside. I followed him to the back of the townhome to a patio filled with exercise equipment. I looked like a dwarf standing next to him. His chest was massive, and his arms unnaturally extended from the sides of his body.

He lay on the weight bench. His tight upper body fit perfectly on the platform. His shoulders extended outward like angel wings. His appeal was magnetic. I stepped closer to the bench. I stood next to him and took in the hard, bulging muscles in his arms as he lifted the weights high above his head. After completing eight repetitions with two hundred-pound weights, he placed the weights back in the holster. Our eyes locked, and he pulled me down on top of him.

"I am in training." I felt him hardening against my thigh. "I have a fight in two weeks." We continued to explore each other's mouths with our tongues. He put his hands under my shirt and lifted the cups of my bra above my breast and softly kneaded them with his fingers. It felt as if a million butterflies had taken flight between my thighs. We rolled off the bench onto the floor, our mouths still locked together.

He fumbled with the string that held his jogging pant on his waist. I moved his hand and untied the knot without removing my lips from his. I took his hand and guided it to the moist opening between my legs. I arched my back and cried out when he inserted one finger then two inside of me. He gently massaged my insides until they were stretched and lubricated enough to receive him.

"How do you know how to do this?"

I ignored him and guided his hardened member inside me. My sexual IQ came from reading magazines and watching pornographic movies when no one was around. I thrust against him waiting for that feeling that have women in the movies screaming, body shaking, and eyes rolled back as if they are having convulsions. However, there was nothing about this experience that garnered loud screaming and uncontrollable moaning of pleasure depicted in the movies. He instinctively grinded his pelvis against mine. My insides felt wet and mushy. After three or four minutes, a burst of liquid erupted inside me and flowed onto my thighs. He collapsed on top of me. His weight was uncomfortable. I lightly pushed him, and he rolled off me. We lay still next to one another looking straight into the ceiling, both too shy to look at each other.

"This was your first time?"

"Yes." I did not look at him. I stared at the ceiling thinking of the importance my mother placed on chastity, and in a few seconds all those things she stressed were important flew out the window.

"It was my first time, too. I will keep this moment special in my heart."

"Thank you." We lay next to one another in silence until we heard movement in the front of the house. We quickly and quietly dressed. When his sister passed the patio, we were fully clothed pretending to spar. They greeted one another; she looked at me suspiciously as she slowly walked away.

We left the patio and went to the kitchen. He opened the refrigerator, removed two eggs, cracked them open with one hand, and allowed the inside to drop in a cup.

"I don't know how you do that."

"It makes me strong. You want to try it?" His thick brows raised, and his smile widened. I walked in front of him and wrapped my arms around his tight waist. "I have a match in two weeks." He stepped away from me, scanning my body from head to toe. "I should not have done that." He smiled. "You will make me weak."

"Let's go to your room."

"My sister is in the other room." He smiled. "But if she wasn't..." We both laughed.

My tears sting my eyes as I think of him. I remove a brown dress from the hanger; it's one I wore when I was twenty pounds heavier. It is a straight dress, without buttons or a zipper but still uncomfortably tight. I turn the lights off, set the intrusion alarm, and leave through the garage. I cry the entire twenty-minute ride, as memories of Panther flash through my mind.

Traffic came to an almost complete stop five

miles from Central Drive. Several Cars were parked on the sidewalk along Harrison Road. The line to drive into the church parking lot is a mile long extending into the street at all entrances.

I knew the funeral would be well attended. The neighborhood is angry. No one believes the police account of the shooting, but I did not imagine so many people would attend his funeral. Panther is accused of killing a police officer, and not just any police officer, but Chandler Davis. Allegedly after several commands to lay the weapon down, Panther raised the gun, pointed it at Chandler, and pulled the trigger. Office Whitley alleged he had no other choice but to use deadly force. The officers who arrived on the scene after the murder corroborated Officer Whitley's statement. No one in the community believes the officers' accounts. The people have very little faith in the police. Chandler was different; he was loved by everyone in this community. No one would cause him harm. I gave up on finding a parking space in the church lot. I maneuvered my car between two others on the hill along the side of the parking lot.

Jermaine is the first familiar face I see as I enter the crowded church. His appearance is mind boggling. He stands in line waiting to view the body. There is no evidence of his thuggish past. He looks like a clean-cut choir boy.

I stand in the long line of people waiting to view his body. It seems as if the entire neighborhood has attempted to squeeze inside of the church to pay their last respect to Panther. My heart beats fast and hard against my chest. I begin to perspire profusely with each step I take toward the casket. My body becomes overheated. My head feels light. I stand still in front of the casket to get one last view of my Panther. I am oblivious to the long line of people behind me waiting to view the body. His chiseled face even in death is one fit for a god. His skin color is gray, absent of his natural glow. It seems as if the mortician used the wrong color makeup. What I would not do to see Panther's smile just one more time. I close my eyes and reflect on the smile three months ago when I told him I miss my menses again for the second time.

"What are you saying?"

"I am pregnant." My eyes were glued to the floor. I did not want to see his reaction. Neither of us needed this in our lives. I was still matriculating, and he recently signed contracts with sponsors to support his boxing career.

"Wow, this is unexpected. What do you want to do? I support you no matter the decision."

"I have two more years of college. If I keep the child, I will have to find a place to live. Living at home is not an option. I would most likely have to go into hiding, so the Brute cannot find me." He laughed. "You are laughing, but trust I am very serious."

"My mother will most likely go crazy. She has invested a lot of money and time in me, but she will not allow us to do this alone. I have signed contracts with sponsors. I have enough money to provide for you and the child." His smile, initially reluctant, gradually spread wide and bright.

I feel a slight nudge almost a push but not quite as hard from a middle-aged woman with long dreadlocks. Her face is covered with tears as she stands in front of the casket holding tight to a young boy no older than seven. I recognize the boy as one of the kids from the neighborhood Panther mentored and taught boxing techniques. I pass the casket, walk down the red carpeted aisle, and see Jermaine who has taken his seat. We lock eyes; he stands and embraces me as I pass. He is well-dressed and does not reek of stale beer. I turn away from Jermaine and stare straight into Panther's mother's eyes. She has turned away from the casket and looks toward the back of the church. I turn and walk toward the usher directing me to the next available seat on a half-filled pew. My legs feel as if they weigh a ton. The room begins to spin. The bright lights make me dizzy. A quick penetrating ache travels from the back of my head to my shoulders. Everything goes black as if someone turned off the lights.

Chapter 12
Marie

He has spent every second with me since Jean-Jacques' murder. The media labels my son Cop Killer, but I know better. My son was murdered. I have handled many things in my life. I have endured many disappointments and beat many odds. The fact that I am Haitian living in America is indicative of my resilience. I manage to pass the Sertifico examinations and made it to Tertiary, something almost unheard of in Haiti for a peasant, as education was not always available.

I thought I would die when I lost my first love to the ocean. Somehow, I managed to make it to the American shore. I have endured much, but nothing can prepare me to bury my son. Perhaps if he died of natural causes, if he was a reckless young man or perished in a car accident, it would be easier. My Jean-Jacques was murdered, and to cover their misdeeds, they tainted his name. Emotions bounce inside me like ping pong balls. I don't have to tell Jikki; he already knows I cannot handle this. He knows my needs before I know them myself. He canceled all practices, spars, and fitness classes to attend to me and keep me safe from myself.

The gym has been closed for two weeks. Half of the gym is outsourced on the weekend for tumbling classes. Those coaches also canceled classes in memory of Jean-Jacques. Jean- Jacques' soft personality did not match his powerful six-feet, two-hundred-and-forty-pound muscular physique. His spirit was calm. He was gentle. He is incapable of doing the thing he is accused of.

No words exist that can describe this pain. Nothing can fill this hole inside me. There are no letters that create a word to describe this feeling. They murdered my child. The pictures of him in the news are dark and obviously altered. They use clips from footage taken after boxing matches. They do not show schoolboy photos or pictures of him in his Sunday school suit. The slander is nefarious, deliberate, and calculating. On the contrary, lightly enhanced still pictures of Chandler Davis in his police uniform with his beautiful family are placed next to pictures of Jean-Jacques wearing his good luck hoodie. The media and the police seek to destroy Jean-Jacques' image.

The tranquilizers the doctor prescribed finally begin to work. I have not slept in two days. Lack of sleep is causing a mental imbalance. My sanity is under attack. I struggle to filter the real from the unreal. Jikki is worried about me and so am I. I caused an unimaginable stir when I left the house yesterday. I thought I heard Jean-Jacques call my name. There was panic in his voice. I remember leaving my bed. I do not remember how I reached Central Drive. My thighs and hips felt chilly. I rubbed my hands up and down my arms for warmth. People were staring and pointing, as I passed the bus stop in front of the Pakistani store. Jean-Jacques' voice became louder, and it sounded as if his breathing was labored. His speech was uncommonly fast. I followed the voice to the side of the Pakistani store and then to the fence that separated an apartment complex from the store.

"Jean-Jacques! Jean-Jacques! Jesuis prise de vous accueil!" I called out to him and said, "Come to me. I am going to take you home."

"Ma'am." The nice boy who used to be a bum removed his jacket and threw it around me. "Let's get you home."

"I am waiting for Jean-Jacques. I need to take him home." I pointed behind the store. "He is just there. Venez Jean-Jacques, maman est prise de vous accueil." Come, Jean-Jacques, I said. Mommy is taking you home. "Jean-Jacques, obtenez jusqu'à partir du sol." I tell him to get up from the ground.

"I know, Ma'am, but let's get you home. He will come later."

I reached down and picked up a deflated pink balloon from the ground. I pushed it up in the air. It slowly fell back to the ground. The young man extended his hand, and I took it. I used my free hand and wiped the long tear from the boy's face and wondered why he was crying.

"His name is Jean-Jacques. He is named after the powerful and fearless Haitian warrior Jean-Jacques Dessalines."

"Yes, Ma'am, but let's get you home. Your family is probably worried about you." The nice boy who used to be a bum knocked on the door. It was slightly ajar and opened wider after the boy knocked. "Is anyone here?"

Jikki came to the door in his pajamas. "What happened?" His mouth was open wide. His voice cracked, rose, and fell in pitch. "Where are her clothes?"

"I found her like this. She was on the side of the Pakistani store calling for her son. Just like this." Jikki escorted me to the back of the house to our bedroom where I sat on the bed. He removed the young man's jacket, spread the coverlet over me, and left our room.

"Thank you." He left our bedroom door open.

"I understand, Sir. The entire neighborhood is having a time with this. No one deserves to be gunned down by police, but your son of all people did not deserve this. Everyone in the neighborhood respected him. No one believes the police account of what happened on the side of that store. "

"Thank you." I heard the door close and then the deadbolt lock engages.

"What were you thinking?" He was frustrated but not angry.

"I went to get my son from the Pakistani store." I felt water flow from my eyes. He sat next to me and wiped the tears away. "Jikki, I heard his call to me. Jean-Jacques yelled, 'Maman! Maman!' He was afraid. He needed me."

"Look in the mirror." He pulled me to my feet and walked me to the mirror. I was wearing nothing except for my panties, but I was in too much pain to feel shame. "This is how you left the house. We will get through this. I promise."

He left our bedroom and closed the door behind him. I heard cabinets opening and closing in the kitchen. I wished he would stop cooking; the food is wasted.

My lids were heavy. I wanted to close my eyes, but I didn't want to relive the scene that was on repeat in my mind. I was returning home from retrieving a package from the post office. Fine cloth I was expecting from Italy arrived. I was excited. I passed the mail clerk the beige notification the carrier left in my mailbox. She took the notification and walked through large gray double doors to the back of the post office. I stood in line like a giddy schoolgirl waiting for her to return. I began tearing the box open as soon as the mail clerk gave me the package.

I was excited imagining the finished product as I ran my fingers across the delicately woven raw silk cloth, I ordered to fill a custom drapery order. The contract with the local celebrity was such that it was going to open doors for other high-profile local clients. My excitement was contagious; Jikki always bathes in my accomplishments with me. We were deep in conversation about the particulars of my new client. Traffic immediately slowed to a crawl as we turned on Harrison Road. White Junkie Boy, a drug addict new to the neighborhood, waved the car down as we turned the corner on Central Drive in front of the Pakistani store. I ignored him and believed he was on a binge begging for money. I was not alarmed by the crime scene tape surrounding the Pakistani store or the sea of blue lights in the parking lot. The neighborhood was fast declining, and it seemed the police were constantly responding to criminal activity. Jikki, as loved and respected in the community as Jean-Jacques, rolled down the window. I looked in the console for change so I could throw it to the White Junkie Boy so we could be on our way.

"Jean-Jacques," I heard my son's name, yet was still unalarmed. Jean-Jacques is known and loved by everyone. I am accustomed to his name thrown around the neighborhood. "Killed, Cops, Dead." The words were scrambled but should not be used in the same sentence as Jean-Jacques'. I quickly threw the expensive fabric on the back seat, opened the door, and ran to the crowd standing in front of the yellow caution tape. The Pakistani storeowner's daughter who runs the store stood on the outside of her car, dropped her purse, and ran behind me.

I maneuvered my way through the crowd. My heartbeat increased as I got closer to the scene. White chalk that surrounded his body made his massive build appear larger. His body lay flat and awkward on the ground. One of his heavy legs was tucked under as if it was broken off and no longer part of his body. A gun lay next to his right hand. Blood formed a stream in the cracks of the red Georgia clay. It took several seconds to take it all in and process the scene of my son's lifeless body on the ground. I choked on the scream lodged in the back of my throat. I ran toward the crime scene tape with the quickness of an Olympic runner. A slim, unshaven Caucasian man with oily hair grabbed me before I could reach the body. His breath reeked of alcohol; a stale odor seeped through his skin. I did not know he was a cop until I saw his badge.

"Jean-Jacques." Jikki came to the tape, removed the officer's hands away from me, and took me in his arms. He maneuvered himself between me and the officer. The officer placed his hand on his gun then slowly move it, but Jikki remained stoic. He did not flinch at the officer's subtle threat. The officer turned away and joined his comrades on the other side of the crime scene tape. The Pakistani store owner's daughter stood next to me. Somehow, I felt a sense of solidarity with her. Instinctively, we embraced each other. Jikki unwrapped the girl's arms from around me carried me from the scene as I wildly fought to get away from him to get back to my son.

It was an out of body experience. It was surreal. I saw my boy alive and thriving this morning going about his business and now he is dead. I felt life leaving my own body.

I can't eat on my own volition. My body does not crave nourishment. I want to die. Jikki does not trust me alone. All sharp objects have been removed from the bathroom and our bedroom.

I trust Jikki. We have been each other's rock for the last nineteen years. It began as an awkward friendship that blossomed into a love, I thought I would never know again after Michel. We both were beginning new lives, learning to live with loss and pain. He was my rescuer and caretaker. My voyage to America was traumatic. After I made it to the American shore, I stayed in the detention unit for one hundred and sixty days before I was granted asylum as a Cuban refugee. They gave me the papers and the child who they believe was my niece. It's odd how a woman and child can form a bond even when there are no blood ties. I know she has a family somewhere waiting for her. We immigrants leave our homes and come to a country where people expect our arrival. Our voyage is thought out and well-planned years in advance. I spread the word around the Cuban and Haitian community about a lost Cuban child. No one claimed the child. I became her parent.

Our arrival in America was hard from day one. Michel's cousin, Genevieve, was supposed to meet us upon our release from the detention center and transport us to the apartment Michel helped financed. She came to the interview and provided check stubs to prove she had the means to accommodate me and the child. I suspect her documents were fraudulent. I walked out of the detention center with one small bag of our belongings in one hand and the child holding tight to the other. Michel's cousin was nowhere to be found. I went to the bathroom in the lobby.

"Stand here." I told the baby to stand in front of the stall so I could see her feet. I closed the door, squatted, and pushed out the money wrapped in the foul-smelling plastic. I walked across the street and purchased food for the baby. When I returned, there was still no sign of Genevieve. I was nervous and too anxious to eat. I took the baby's hand and stood in the long line of people calling loved ones announcing their release from the detention center. After several hours, I went back to the restroom and placed the money back inside me.

"Bonjour." I called again. Michel's cousin finally answered the phone. It felt odd speaking French again. Michel demanded we converse in Spanish or English. His cousin sounded as if she did not recognize my voice.

"Genevieve, c'est l'épouse de Michel d'Marie." I told her it was me, Marie, Michel's wife. I called her every other week to inform her of my progress and my expected date to be released from the detention center, I've sat across from her during an immigration interview, but that day, she behaved as if she did not recognize my voice. My stomach turned. I had come too far to have nowhere to lay my head. She inquired about finances, and I would remind her of Michel's payments to her before we left Haiti.

I told her I had been released and was on my way to her.

"Qui venir." She paused. "Oui venir mais nous n'nt pasd nourriture. Je n'ai pas petro pour la voiture. Vous devrez prendre un taxi." I listened as she told me to come but quickly noted she had no food or gas, so I would need to take a taxi.

I told her I had money, and she quickly provided the address to her house. I hailed a taxi from the line of taxis waiting outside of the detention center to transport lucky detainees who had been released. When I arrived, I was beyond afraid. I got out of the taxi in front of a concrete house. The yard was littered with paper, empty cans, and bottles. A car with no hood sat in the yard on concrete blocks, and old flat tires were thrown about. Cardboard paper was put in place of a broken window in front of the house. I picked up the baby and held her close. She wanted to walk and tried to wiggle out of my arms, but I held tight to her.

This was not the America pictured in the magazines Michel brought home from the hotel. It was nothing like the America the Etiennes bragged about to Michel while he cleaned their yard. People walked around aimlessly engaged in full conversations with invisible people. I was anxious. The sun was beginning to set; darkness would soon come.

Genevieve opened the door, her hair in disarray. It was late in the evening, yet she looked as if she just left her bed. She had lived in America for eight years, having left Haiti when she was 18. She was not yet thirty but looked much older. Gone were the perfect white teeth and blinding bright smile. Genevieve looked nothing like the picture Michel kept in his wallet. The perfect, smooth dark skin was now dry and covered with black spots.

Genevieve was Michel's favorite cousin. He was always proud of her zeal and looked up to her for leaving Haiti and making it in America. Michel would be shocked to find her in this condition. The smell of urine mixed with marijuana hovered in the air. Before we left Haiti, Michel wired her 1,000 US dollars to get a nice place. She led us to believe she owned a small sewing factory and was waiting on payments from a large order her company filled. I had never lived in America, but even I knew that this place did not cost a thousand dollars. "Evangeline!"

"No, I am Marie." The background of her apartment was absent of light except for one candle that had almost burned down to the wick and the amber from the cigarette hanging out of the mouth of a tall skinny male standing close behind her.

She removed my bag from my shoulder, opened it, and removed the twenty-dollar bill and several lose bills I received when I purchased food for the baby and myself. "This is all you have?" Desperation mixed with anger permeated her voice. She rubbed trembling, dry hands across my chest, feeling for more funds. "Where is the rest?" She grabbed my shoulder with an aggressive force. I looked deep into her eyes. She detected the uneasiness in my spirit and attempted to ease my discomfort with an ingenuine smile. I wrapped my hand around her bony wrist and pushed her away hard enough for her to know my displeasure with her touch but gentle enough not to incite violence.

"They will send my declared funds in the mail. I gave them your address." I lied.

"It will be time to pay the rent again soon. When will they send the funds?"

"Dix jours ouvrables." I told her ten business days. In the detention center, everything was tied to what they call business days. It appears everything in this country happens around business days. Her actions made me anxious and almost fearful. Her face was a mixture of anger that I didn't have immediate funds but relief at the thought of monies arriving in her mailbox.

"Okay." She touches my protruding stomach and pats the head of the child that stood next to me. "Michel said nothing about a child."

"She got anything?" The tall, slim, black man with a British Jamaican accent stood close behind her scratching his head so hard I was expecting blood to squirt out of his scalp at any moment. She stepped out of the apartment and closed the door.

"This child is now my niece who was on the boat when it capsized." I searched her eyes. "Were you able to contact family to see if Michel made it back to Haiti?"

"Yes." Her voice contained no emotion. She has grown tired of my inquiry. "I call Maman, no one has seen Michel." I lost hope he would resurface. I grieved Michel's death while in detention. I cried every night praying to God he somehow would resurface. I finally had no choice but to accept Michel's fate.

"You have to come back later. Go down the street to that bench over there." She scratched her arm incessantly and pointed to a strip mall with overgrown grass growing through the cracks in the asphalt parking lot. "I need to get money to add to this so I can get us proper food." She held up the bills she removed from my bag. "Are you sure you don't have more?" I didn't answer. I took the child's hand and walked the half block to the strip mall and sat on the graffiti covered bench in front of a beat-up garbage can overflowing with trash.

The child slid close to me and placed her head on my lap, as I sat on the bench. I heard people moving about and the command from a strong voice yelling, "Hit harder," from the building behind us. A tall male walked outside; I tried not to notice the bulging muscles that protruded from his tight, form fitting shirt. He looked at me and the small child. His massive size was intimidating, but his eyes were warm.

"This is an old stop. There is no bus coming here."

"Oui." I turned away and rubbed the small child's shoulder, and he went back inside. My eyes were locked on Michel's cousin's apartment. An hour passed; Genevieve did not leave her apartment. My body shook with emotion. The big man from the gym returned, placing a carton of milk to his mouth and taking very long swallows.

"The bus stop is two blocks over lady; no bus is coming here." He appeared frustrated that I was sitting on the bench.

"Oui, merci, Monsieur." I thanked him; he slowly turned around and reluctantly walked back inside the building. I sat on the bench for over two hours watching the apartment. Various people entered, but no one left. Michel's cousin had not come for us, and it was well into the night. I picked up the child and lay her down on the beach. I lay next to her with her safely tucked between me and the back of the bench.

I was awakened by loud voices leaving the building behind me. I sat up; the baby that I had come to know very well began to cry. I could read her emotions as if she was my own child. She was uncomfortable in this new environment.

"You still here?" A group of young men stood next to him. "Go on, guys. I will see you tomorrow." The men shook hands, said their goodbyes, and continued to their vehicles.

"Oui."

"Do you speak English?" He spoke louder as if I was hard of hearing.

"Yes."

"This is a very dangerous place. You cannot stay on this bench."

"My cousin lives there." I pointed to the apartment down the street that was no better than a Haitian Shanty. "She says she will come for us when she acquires food."

"Acquire food?" He laughed. "Your cousin lives there? He pointed to the dilapidated building down the street. "You are still waiting for your cousin to get food?" He laughed and walked toward a black truck parked under the streetlamp in the parking lot. He got in the truck, turned the lights on, and backed out the parking space. He drives back into the parking space, gets out of the truck, walks to the bench, and stares straight at me. "Follow me."

I picked up the baby, and she started to cry again, wrapping her arms and legs tightly around my body. I gently rubbed her back until she went back to sleep. "You stay here." I followed him into a small office. Pictures of men in boxing gear were taped to the walls. He removed a blanket from a locker and spread it on a blue mesh cot that sat low to the floor. "When your cousin comes," he laughed, "lock the door when you leave." He stood in the threshold and laughed louder than before. "I am sure I will see you tomorrow morning." He laughed again, this time holding his stomach as if he was trying to contain himself.

Thus began our journey. Most of our years have been good. We have had an argument here or a disagreement there, but we have weathered every storm with our relationship intact. He rescued me from a bus stop bench, but he cannot rescue me from this.

I slept through the night. I took a double dose of sleeping pills. I was afraid to leave the bedroom. I don't trust myself. It is noon. The sun should be at its highest peak, but the abundance of overcast dims the light. It is the beginning of spring, but the temperature is abnormally cool. I leave the bed and begin to get dressed. I don't have the energy, so I lay back down. Faint but powerful footsteps become louder as they near our bedroom. The silver knob slowly turns. The squeaking from the door hinges sounds unusually morbid. I do not move. I know it is time, but I lay on the bed in my slip. One strap barely hangs on my shoulder while the other hangs to the side. I did not have the energy to put my arms through the strap. My nylons are pulled up past my knees. I attempted to get ready, but an overwhelming fatigue immobilizes me. I hear movement in my daughter's room, but I lay still on my bed.

He stands in the threshold of the open door. The lights are off, and the curtains are drawn close. The silhouette of his body looks more like machine than man. He slowly walks closer, stands motionless next to the bed, before sitting next to me. I lie still and look at him. I am too weak to utter words. I am not going to make it.

He says, "We will get through this." He touches my shoulder; I pull my knees to my chest. I cannot speak. Tears flow like a river from my eyes and down my cheeks. I have no energy to cry out. I can only moan. I wrap my arms tight around my knees to hold myself together. I want to scream.

He spoke: "You can let go. You can scream if you like. You can scream as loud as you want." I think, I will not make it.

He said, "We will get through this together. We will make it through this." I close my eyes so the light cannot penetrate the darkness I feel inside. He unweaves my fingers, spreads my arms, wraps them around his neck, and pulls me close. He leans back and lies down on the bed; he wraps his legs around me. Tears roll down my face, but my voice is stuck in the back of my throat. He rubs my back then softly pats it like a mother burping her baby.

"Jean-Jacques! Jean-Jacques!" I choke on the scream as it escapes my mouth. "Je vous aime son fils. Mama va vous manquer." I scream to my son that I love him, that I will miss him. Jikki pulls me closer. "Qu'est-ce que je vais faire san votre fils?" What will I do without you, son? Jikki continues to hold me close. I hear movement on the outside of our bedroom door. I lower my volume.

"We have to get ready." He places a series of soft kisses on my face and gently wipes away the tears. "We will bury our boy today, and then we will fight for justice if it takes the rest of our lives." He removes my arms from around his neck and stands in front of me. He extends his hands, and I place my hands in his. He pulls me to my feet. I stand, I cover my face, and I cry.

"It's okay. Cry as much and as long as you want. I am here for you. I am strong for you. I will cry later." He pulls the nylons over my hips to the top of my waist and secured the slip straps on my shoulders. He removes the dress from the chair next to the bed. I raise my arms as he slides the dress over my head. He leaves, goes to the bathroom, and returns with a hand towel. The warmth of the damp hand towel against my face is soothing. He stands behind me, pulls all my hair together, and holds it in place with a black rubber band. "It is time."

My mind says, okay, but no words leave my mouth. I will lay my son in his final resting place in the church graveyard across the street. He should be laid to rest next to my mother and grandmother. I have given up a lot to live this fantasy called America. When I received word Maman passed, I was in the middle of getting permanent residency and could not risk attending her burial in Haiti. Too many family members depend on the money I send for their sustenance to take a chance, leave, and not be able to return. Jean-Jacques should be buried next to the grandmother he saw in pictures and whose voice he heard on the phone. I pray my mother will see my Jean-Jacques in the heavens, and pray he remembers her face and the sound of her voice.

I bump into my daughter as we walk out of our room. She falls into my arms. I hold her so close we are almost one. "It should have been me. You loved Jean-Jacques so much. It would have been easier if it were me." I cradle my daughter, entertaining the thought, would it in fact be easier if it were her. The truth is it would not. She is my daughter given to me by the ocean. No matter how she became my daughter, I love her as if I had given birth to her. The pain would be just as intense.

"It is time." Jikki continues to guide me. In one movement, he raps his arms around me and my daughter. He holds us close then separates us by maneuvering himself between us. We walk arms linked together to the door. The limousine is parked in front of my townhome. My legs become weak and unable to hold my small frame. My mouth is wide open, but the scream is stuck in the back of my throat. He grabs me as I fall to the ground. He picks me up and carries me to the limousine. Neighbors stand in front of the homes watching the long line of cars on route to the church. He places me on the ground, and I crawl in the limousine and maneuver myself in the corner to get one last cry before the funeral.

Cars move to the side as our limousine approaches the church. The church is a five-minute walk from our house. The line of cars moves so slow that onlookers have time to walk to the cars and embrace the occupants, some engaging in lengthy conversations as they walk next to cars waiting in the line to get into the church parking lot. We would have gotten there sooner on foot as opposed to maneuvering through the cars and onlookers.

The pastor of the mega-church donated the limousine to our family. Honestly, I do not believe the Pastor knew anything about Jean-Jacques, but he speaks to the media as if they were the best of friends. The news reporters lined up on the street are insignificant to me. I am amazed at the crowd of people from the neighborhood. The parking lot is filled, but cars are still lined up along Central Drive searching for parking spaces. Cars maneuver to the side of the road giving honor to my dead son as attendees pass. Flowers cover the sidewalk that leads to the church. A young woman in a long dress is surrounded by three black males dressed in black suits with neat bowties; they stand at the end of the church parking lot, she with a handwritten sign held high over her head that reads, *"We Demand Justice."*

The driver parks the limousine in front of the church. I sit still as the door opens. We exit the limousine and walk with Jikki in the middle; his strong arms are tightly wrapped around me and my daughter.

The church is filled to capacity. Ushers line

the aisles between the pews with metal folding chairs to accommodate the overflow. Others had to stand along the walls. I am overwhelmed at how many people cared for Jean-Jacques. The two stores on the corner closed for the funeral. People from the neighborhood created a makeshift memorial on the side of the store where he was murdered. The Pakistani store owner's daughter stands at the back of the church waiting among members of the community for our small family to be seated. I am not surprised to see her, but her emotions are over the top. I recall Jean-Jacques mentioning her, but I did not get the impression they were close friends.

White Junkie Boy, with an athletic build almost like Jean-Jacques, stands uncomfortable in the back of the church. He looks out of place as the only white face in a sea of black and brown faces. I almost did not recognize White Junkie Boy as he is called by people in the neighborhood. I often warned Jean-Jacques to stay away from him. I noticed him hanging out at the corner stores about a year ago. Some days, he is clean shaven while other days his clothes are dirty, his hair greasy, and he appears as if he has not bathed in days. He seems to make a living doing odd jobs for the seafood restaurant owned by a Russian immigrant and Korean store. "White people have every advantage in this America." I would tell Jean-Jacques. "This boy has to be a bum of no character and a total loser to be white in America and live the way he lives." My warnings fell on deaf ears. Jean-Jacques was unassuming and always gave people a chance.

The community raised over twenty thousand dollars through the church and gave it to me. For some reason, people assumed I did not have insurance for burial expenses. I live this simple life by choice. My finances are above average. I came to Georgia after living in Florida for several years and purchased my townhome with cash.

Before relocating to Georgia, we often traveled with Jikki to Atlanta with the intent of visiting his daughter. We would park outside of a brownstone style townhome and watch a young woman, a young man about the same age, and a lovely young woman who appeared to be in her late teens or early twenties. I found it strange that we would watch these people and never make contact. If we did not park and watch the young woman, we traveled to the opposite side of town and park in front of a brick house. Again, we made no contact as we watched a young man and two elderly women. Over the years, I simply accepted this as a way of life.

In Florida, Jikki worked in a gym training boxers. The owners decided to sell the gym, so we use the change as an opportunity to move to Atlanta and opened a gym of our own.

On a to visit Stone Mountain, a national monument, we stumbled upon Central Drive. We had no family here, but this was close enough to the family he visited but never contacted. The townhome was large enough to accommodate our family and reasonably priced. I purchased it with savings from seamstress jobs. Many women find sewing demeaning, but I saved every dime and used what was left after purchasing the townhome to help Jikki purchase the gym. I sell clothing in boutiques as far as New York. Jean-Jacques created a website for me to sell online. My clothing generates enough income to sustain me, but my main income is from custom drapery. It provides enough income to supplement my daughter's college scholarships without student loans. Clients fly me to New York, California, and I have even been flown to Madrid to measure and design custom drapery. One job can easily gross $10,000. I am by no means struggling. Michel taught me to live frugally, even more frugally than the poorest Haitian. I occasionally buy nice things for myself, but I never overindulge.

Michel taught me many things. He did not get to see our beautiful son on this earth. I pray they will meet in the heavens. It takes everything out of me to hold myself together as I walk down the aisle to my son's body. It appears as if Jean-Jacques is asleep in the extra-long mahogany coffin. His skin looks gray. Fashion models would die for his chiseled features. His hair is cut to precision. The barber did an excellent job. I lean over and kiss his lips; they are hard as a rock and rough against mine. I rub my fingers through his tightly coiled hair. His hair feels the same. Jikki wraps his arm around me and attempts to nudge me along. I snatch my arm away from his with such force he stumbles backwards. Tears burn my eyes; I wipe them away. I turn around to the sea of faces, many are covered by handkerchiefs to mask tears of their own before I take my seat.

The church choir sings beautiful spirit filled hymns. People stand and speak of Jean-Jacques's intelligence. Many speak of his kindness. I never knew so many people adored Jean-Jacques. The White Junkie Boy and several others speak of Jean-Jacques' protective nature. A couple of women from the neighborhood share the confidence their children developed by working with Jean-Jacques. Every testimony to his greatness fills my heart with pride.

Chapter 13
Myrtle

I separate the blinds in my bedroom with my fingers. There are a plethora of cars and people lined up to attend the funeral; our neighborhood has never seen this much movement at one time. It almost feels as if we are under siege yet again. News reporters are everywhere. The church across the street is hosting the funeral for the thug who killed Chandler. I don't understand Blacks. I have lived among them for years. I can say some I call friend, but many seem to not take accountability.

I was standing in the back yard a few weeks ago when I saw the thug run past at lightning speed. I have seen him on the corner several times talking to a white boy who is obviously on drugs. The thug always wears a hooded sweatshirt as if he is trying to disguise himself. Whit was visiting with me. Our relationship was slowly developing into a nice friendship where we often converse and enjoy a glass of iced tea. Whit and I lock eyes as he ran by.

"If we could get all of these drug dealers out of the neighborhood, we could get back on track."

"I am working on it, Myrtle."

"See that one." I pointed in the direction the thug running. "He is always at the corner talking to that white boy who cleans up around the Korean store. I bet he is his personal drug dealer."

"Are you sure?"

"Well, what could they have in common other than drugs?

"You have a point." He looked away as if he was in deep thought. "If we can get rid of the dealers, the drug addicts will stop coming." I looked at Whit and found that I liked him more each moment we spent together. Chills traveled all over my body when Whit gently took my hand in his. He gently squeezed it, brought it to his face, and planted soft kisses on the back. "This place is getting dangerous by the second. I will stop and check on you from time to time if you don't mind." It felt good having someone looking out for me, and it was a plus that he carried a gun and was easy on the eyes.

I walk to the front of the house and look through the kitchen window blinds. Several neighbors have congregated on the corner; some sit comfortable in lawn chairs as if this is a parade as opposed to a funeral procession. I leave the house and join the neighbors when I see Jermaine walking toward the church. The neighbors are all gossiping about his new look. I could not believe my eyes when I saw him. I had to look twice to make sure my eyes were not fooling me. His notorious tall can of beer wrapped in a brown paper sack is nowhere to be found. A clean black suit has replaced the dingy oversized T-shirt and jeans that hang below his hips. His hair is cut neat and short. His new look reminds me of when he was a young schoolboy before he started hanging with the neighborhood thugs.

"Jermaine!" I yell to him. He waves with one hand and continues to walk to the church to join the others attending the funeral. I am embarrassed by the attention this shooting has bought to our community. We have good police officers who have a hard job to do. The troublemakers alleged the shooting was racially motivated. Detective Chandler was a great man. He was black. His killer was also black. I do not see a racist connection.

We used to have a nice community. We have always had Blacks in our community, but a different type of black people moved in, and all hell broke loose.

We predicted this deterioration and did everything we could to stop it. Our fight began when the apartments started going up. Our local politicians ignored our complaints accusing the neighborhood association of racism and prejudice ignoring the diverse racial makeup of the association. Yes, the association had more white members, but there were a couple of blacks heavily involved. One served as secretary. We were not racist or prejudice. We were simple people who wanted to maintain our property values and lifestyles. We could adjust to any group of people as long as they could adhere to our community standard.

Gentrification in Atlanta could have almost been tolerated. Eventually, with police involvement, we could have persuaded our new residents from Atlanta to adapt to our community standard, but Katrina was another story. I am not saying all Hurricane Katrina victims are the same. I know they are not, but the Katrina victims that settled on Central Drive appeared to have suffered from undiagnosed and untreated Post Traumatic Stress Disorder as they brought with them unfamiliar mannerisms and behaviors that were more foreign than the actual foreigners that migrated from across the ocean and settled here. It was a domino effect. Test scores in our once high performing neighborhood schools became abysmal, school ranking became unsatisfactory, and property crimes increased sixty-three percent within one year. Having no faith in our council members, the remaining few homeowners who called Central Drive home for decades and generations slowly packed up and moved.

All of this happened while generational poverty in public housing became number one on the agendas of Town Hall forums and City Council meetings in Atlanta. The poor were used as pawns in an unprecedented land grab hidden by a made-up agenda to decrease concentrated poverty and push those suffering from it into mainstream communities. In the spirit of helping the poor, housing projects all over the city were systematically bulldozed to the ground. The former residents were given housing vouchers and relocated to the suburbs. Of course, there was no public discussion of the beneficiaries of the billion dollars land deals, nor was there transparency in the transfer of land deeds.

This sideshow is pathetic. Blacks and so-called civil rights leaders have come out of the woodworks to put on a show. They are attempting to make this thug a martyr. This thug is a murderer. People should be angry at this boy instead of the police. Chandler was good for this community, and he helped a lot of the Blacks.

The burial of the kid that murdered Chandler is more of an event than a funeral; I have never seen anything like this. White people and black people have a different protocol in burying their dead. I am white; the only true white woman left in the neighborhood, the other one is married to a black man, a very nice black man I may add. I have been here a very long time and over the years I have become close like family with some of the black neighbors; I have attended a few black funerals over the years. I have witnessed the passing out on the floor, loud outbursts, and emotional hymns where even if you were not attached to the deceased or believed in a God, the beautiful hymns stirred the spirit.

I have witnessed the painful cries from people not ready to depart with their loved ones and no matter how low down the deceased, family members are convinced they will see their loved ones again in heaven. I have witnessed emotions so high; family members engage in full out brawls brandishing knives and guns in the church.

This funeral is over the top even for a black funeral. It is like a red-carpet affair as attendees stop to give commentary to news reporters standing outside of the church. Neighborhood rival gangs stand in unity in front of cameras, making crazy gestures with their hands while making subtle threats against law enforcement. News crews from several affiliates were camped out before the services began. People get shot, killed, and maimed on Central Drive all the time; none of the killing garner news coverage.

"I have never seen such a ting in all me life." I step close to Ernestine, the Jamaican who stands at the corner with a half empty coffee cup in her hand. "Look at the long line of cars trying to get into the church yard."

"Did you see Jermaine?" I place my hand over my heart and breathe deep to catch my breath. "He looks like an entirely different person."

"Me saw him walk past with him sign under him arm last week. He is spreading some conspiracy nonsense." She takes a long sip from her coffee. "I can't be bothered with the nonsense. If you pull a gun on a cop, what you think going to happen?" She places her free hands on her chest. "Who would hurt Chandler? Bless his heart. He was the best."

"He was carrying a gun." I am happy Ernestine and I share the same point of view. "Why do people make excuses for those with bad behavior? You don't pull guns on cops!"

"Jermaine is a one-man protest." I try to mask my contempt. Jermaine is just like all the other black boys, Muslims, and foreign gypsies who have come and torn our neighborhood apart. "No one is paying him any attention. Don't worry Ms. Myrtle; in a few days, this will all go away."

"I hope you are right." I formed a bond with Ernestine after our encounter with Jermaine before he disappeared and came back with an almost a complete makeover. Jermaine and a couple of neighbors were standing in front of my yard discussing the shooting and possibly starting a charity fund for Chandler's children.

"We should also raise money for Boxing Boy's family."

"Are you kidding me?" I said. "The thug shot a cop. He killed Chandler, one of the best things to happen to this community."

"You don't know what you are talking about, old lady. Rage, I had never seen before ignited in Jermaine's eyes. I have known him since he was a little boy. I treated him as if he was my own child. The entire community, black and white, looked out for him. I have even bought Christmas gifts for him and his sister after his father left the family. I have

never witnessed Jermaine display this type of anger.
He placed the can to his lips and swallowed hard.
"You think every black person in this fucking
neighborhood sells drugs!" His face was contorted.
His eyes begin to fill with tears. He wipes them
away before they began to flow. "Folks tolerate your
crazy racist ass cause you old. You don't know shit."
I stood, shocked, fearful, and unable to move. "You
just as racist as the rest of these low-down ass
crackers!"

"Jermaine, I have known you all of your life."
I found myself almost pleading with him. "You
know I do not have a racist bone in my body!" I was
beyond insulted. I have lived on Central Drive with
the blacks long after my friends either left or died.
My sister calls me crazy. She and my niece often
threaten to put me away in an institution; they
accuse me of senility because I stay around so many
blacks.

"You need to mind your business. You either
on the team or not! Everybody knows this shit ain't
had anything to do with Boxing Boy. This is just a
distraction." The neighborhood consensus was
Jermaine was crazy. He constantly talked of
conspiracy theories.

"Shut your disrespectful mouth, boy!"
Ernestine shouted. "Ms. Myrtle has always been on
our side. She does not have a racist bone in her
body." I was grateful for Ernestine coming to my
defense.

"Kiss. My. Ass. You. Nappy. Head. Boat.
Monkey. Plantation. Overseer. Bitch!" Jermaine
jerked his head side to side to the beat of each
syllable in his tirade. Ernestine and I grabbed our
chests with one hand and on to each other with the
other. The verbal assault was unexpected and

caused us to lose our balance. "If you believe that boy, who never did anything to anybody killed Chandler, you are an idiot. That boy stayed out of trouble. Everybody in this hood respected his game. If you believe he shot a cop, you old bitches are crazy. Even these so-called gangsters in this crappy ass hood had a hands-off clause on Boxing Boy." The Jamaican and I looked at one another in disbelief as Jermaine took a long sip from the can in the brown paper bag. He no longer bothered to wipe the tears away. "Chandler was shot by one of his own and framed that kid for it. Shot the kid, too."

"Boy, take your crazy lazy ass to your momma! Everybody says they have it on film. They were chasing that boy, them cornered him, and he shot Chandler dead, leaving him to die on the ground to get eaten up by the maggots." Ernestine had one hand on her narrow hip and the other hand with one finger extended and pointed in his direction.

"You crazy bitches believe anything the cracker cops say." He stood in the middle of the street. "Y'all punk asses the reason this country so fucked up." He poured a few drops of beer on the ground, placed the can to his mouth, and threw the empty can on the ground. "Boxing Boy and Chandler were good friends. Mr. Chandler recruited him to teach boxing to some of the neighborhood kids y'all call thugs." I stood still, shocked and speechless at the way he behaved. Now, he looks like a totally different person, but he still makes me uncomfortable.

The sounds of screams and moans redirect my attention back to the funeral. Cars are still lined up to get into the parking lot. Detective Whitley turns on his police siren and blue lights and drives around the slow-moving cars. He turns the corner into the subdivision so fast his tires scrub against the curb. He quickly exits the car, steps to me, and places a soft kiss on my cheek.

I turn from the Jamaican and give my undivided attention to Officer Whitley.

"How are you doing? What brings you back?" I smile and slightly turn right so my one dimple is visible. Fire ignites in places I long thought dead as he rubs his suntanned hand up and down my arm.

"Making my rounds. Be careful out here. With all that is going on, things can get crazy. Have you heard anything?" Officer Whitley stops by almost daily and talks about ways to improve the neighborhood. I was immediately impressed when he was transferred to our community. He and Chandler were very interested in getting rid of the neighborhood riffraff and cleaning up the neighborhood. Last year, Chandler started a neighborhood cleanup the first Saturday of the month where we all met on the corner of Central Drive and picked up debris from one end of the street to the other. He called code enforcement to write tickets to residents who did not take heed to cutting their grass and removing old junk cars and appliances from their yards.

"People are upset about the thug getting shot. I don't know what makes this any different than any of the other shooting. People around here get shot all the time. What do people think will happen if you pull a gun on the police?"

"You are one of a kind, Ms. Myrtle." His smile is bright. Too bad neighbors like you are few and far between."

I smile and think to myself, If I was twenty years younger, I would give him a run for his money.

"I don't know what is wrong with people. The gangs and drugs have taken over this community." I smile. He smiles back, this time his eyes travel from my baby blues and land on my breast enhanced by my favorite push up bra.

"I don't know either. I am getting hungry. I guess I will get a bite to eat." He reaches in his back pocket as he leans to get in his car. He steps back outside of the car and quickly runs his hands on the outside of his pockets. "Damn." He leans in the car and moves things around.

"What's wrong?"

"I must have forgotten my wallet. I have to drive thirty miles to my house and get it." He shakes his head. "Oh well, crime fighting will have to wait."

"You don't have to do that. I have a few dollars." I gladly reach into my bosom and remove tightly folded bills. I unravel a twenty from a one-hundred-dollar bill.

"Ah, Ms. Myrtle, you don't have to do that." He rubs the side of my face.

"It is no problems for all you do in this community. Someone should buy lunch for you every day."

"Well, thank you. Do you know which townhome that thug lives in that harassed you the other day? I could arrest him for disorderly conduct."

"Jermaine? He is harmless. He is the neighborhood crazy. He believes there is some type of conspiracy."

"Conspiracy?" He steps back and away from

his car.

"Thinks the boy was set up to take a fall for something else."

"Set up?" His smile does not appear genuine.

"He is crazy, Whit." I smile. "No one pays him any mind." Officer Whitley leaves, promising to stop by tomorrow.

I go back inside my house and start dinner. I open the fridge and realize I don't have tomatoes. I get into my car and exit the neighborhood from the back entrance on to Harrison Road to avoid the mourners and fame seekers on Central Drive. The grocery store parking lot is unusually empty. I walk around the store with ease, grabbing an item from every other aisle before making my way to the cashier. I miss our old cashiers. This one is covered from head to toe. She is pleasant. She attempts to have conversation in broken English. I do not want to be rude, but I do not understand one word she says. It would be helpful if I could at least see her face. I simply smile and nod. "Twenty-five dollar, two cents." She announces my total. I remove the money from my bra and realize I mistakenly gave Whit the one-hundred-dollar bill as opposed to the twenty-dollar bill.

Chapter 14
Benazir

My head rests comfortably against the usher's soft bosom. I have no idea how long I was out. The breeze from her hand fan feels good against my face. We are in the back of the church sitting on the last pew by the exit sign reserved for grief-stricken mourners. She hums the hymn the choir sings and rocks me back and forth.

"Were you a relative of the deceased?" She smiles; her false teeth appear too big for her mouth.

I shake my head side to side. I sit up and use my hands to brush my hair back in place.

"You feeling better, baby?" She does not wait for a response. She adjusts her wig, lightly touches my shoulder, leaves the pew, walks to the back of the church, and stands with the other ushers. The funeral director leaves his seat and walks to the rhythm of the music to the front of the casket. He thanks Panther's family for trusting his funeral home with their loved one and directs the six pall bearers to take their place, three on each side of the casket. The ushers open the large double doors at the back of the church. Everyone rises from their seats in honor of Panther and his family as they walk down the center aisle behind the casket. I found it odd no other relatives attended. He never mentioned cousins, aunts, uncles, or grandparents. I assumed he had other relatives and they lived far away. His mother, sister, and stepfather leave the church walking behind tall muscular pall bearers, some past boxing opponents, holding the casket high above their shoulders. They exit through the double doors to a waiting hearse.

I step in the long line behind a sea of mourners. I do not go to the gravesite. I am too overwhelmed. I cry the entire trip home for Panther as well as for myself and this dilemma in which I have found myself. It's not too late to change course, but this life I carry inside me is all that is left of Panther.

Even if I choose to end the pregnancy, the logistics would be cumbersome. My mother knows, but I doubt she would accompany me to a clinic. Our community is small; many work in the medical field. We could possibly run into someone we know. We dare not allow this secret to come to light.

I drive around Interstate 285 two times before going home. The sun is beginning to set. Night will soon come. I stop in front of the gate at the subdivision entrance and enter the gate code. As I wait for the gate to open, I use the hem of my dress to wipe my face while I finger comb my hair in place. An eerie feeling comes from nowhere when I reach my house. I proceed with caution; I remove my feet from the accelerator and allow the car to coast in the driveway. I sit in the parked car in the dark driveway to gather my composure; I am overwhelmed with emotions. It feels as if a dam has been released, and the flood gates have been opened. I try with all my might to stop crying, but grief and anxiety overwhelms me. I wrap my arms around my body, close my eyes, and try to imagine the last time I was in the safety of the Panther's arms.

When I stop crying and can finally open my eyes, I press the garage door opener. The custom-made mahogany doors slowly rise. The Brute's car is inside. The truck is gone. My mother's car is in place. She would never sit in darkness alone in the house. She is uncomfortable with the size of the house and often worried someone will follow us from the store and rob us. I walk on the tip of my toes like a thief until I am inside of the foyer. I flip the light on. I call her name, but my mother does not answer. I run upstairs, open my bedroom door, and find my mattress is turned upside down. Fist size holes are sporadically placed through my bedroom wall. *Duty and Tradition*. I grab a bag from the closet and quickly throw clothing inside. My heart pounds heavily against my chest. I grab all my important documents including my birth certificate, social security card, and passport and throw them inside the bag. *Duty and Tradition* always wins with my mother and takes precedence over the mother-child bond. I remove the covers from pictures and remove all the money I saved. Four thousand dollars is not enough money.

My motherly instincts are in full throttle. I panic as I imagine all the things the Brute could do to me and my baby that would make death seem like a walk in the park. I grab my favorite picture of my mother. I look into my mother's lifeless eyes and see the result of being at the mercy of an evil spirit that beats you over and over with your own shame. I throw the picture to the floor, grab my things, and run downstairs to the garage.

I quickly get into the car and drive to the store. I drive around the store several times to make sure he is not inside. I park across the street and run to the store. I unlock the door, turn off the alarm, and lock the door behind me. I move throughout the store so fast I create a current that moves items from the shelf as I pass.

I sprint to his office, open the safe, and remove several stacks of money he keeps in the safe to hide from my mother. I grab a stack full of lottery tickets. As I turn off the light, I see stacks of DVDs in jewel cases labeled by dates. I take the DVDs and place them in my bag. I lock the store and walk to the bus stop. The car is in the Brute's name. If I take it, it will be easy to find me. I remove the SIM card from my phone and drop it in the trashcan as I wait for the bus, constantly looking around prepared to fight or flee if the Brute or my *Duty and Tradition* incubator show up.

The half-filled bus finally arrives. I quickly board, pay my fare, and take a seat in the front of the bus. I am on edge, constantly looking over my shoulder until we are on Memorial Drive. I lean deep in my seat and turn my face toward the window. I close my eyes and see him. God, I wish he was here. I don't know if he told his mother about our baby, but I am sure he would not have felt the need to flee. His fear would be centered on his ability to provide for our child. I doubt he would fear for his life.

"Ma'am, are you okay?" I use both hands to wipe the tears from my eyes. "We have arrived at the station. If you stay on the bus, you will have to pay another fare."

"I am fine." I stand, grab my things and look out the graffiti covered window. Kensington Station is almost empty. "Sir, how do I get to the Greyhound Bus Station?"

"Take the West Bound Train to Five Points,

then get on the Southbound Train to Garnett Station." The driver does not make eye contact. His eyes are glued to his cell phone. I exit the bus and enter the train station through the turnstile. It is late, and the train is not as crowded as I would have imagined. It feels like a ghost train. A woman in torn clothing with matted hair walks from car-to-car begging for spare change. I take a seat next to a mother sharing a seat with two small children. The mother leans back in the hard seat and closes her eyes. The two children lean against her as she sleeps. I lean against the window and close my eyes. Just as I was getting comfortable, the automated operator announces my stop. I exit the train at Garnett Station. A strong stench of urine assaults my nostrils, as I walk through the parking lot to the bus station entrance.

This does not look like the city I live in. Men and women lie around on cardboard. This looks like a third world country reminiscent of photographs my father has of himself standing barefoot in front of old buildings near puddles of water.

I walk inside the bus station. The waiting area is crowded. A group of children chase after each other as if they are playing in the park. Young military soldiers barely out of adolescents carry human sized duffle bags on their shoulders. Everyone looks tired and filled with worry. Perhaps we are all on the run. I step over luggage, dodge running children, and walk to the map that lists various destinations. I spot Columbus, Georgia. I move my finger east and find West Point, Georgia; it sounds like a military fort. I move my finger south and next to West Point is a small town called Lanett, Alabama. My parents never left Atlanta. I doubt if they have ever heard of Lanett, Alabama. I purchase a one-way bus ticket with cash and wait among the crowd to board the bus.

The line to board the bus is long. Most of the travelers are women with small children. I scan the tired faces and find I am the only Pakistani among the passengers.

My parents should have never had children. My mother is too weak to protect an offspring. The Brute totally missed the love gene. I used to loathe being an only child. Now, I am thankful they spared potential siblings the pain of having parents ill equipped to raise a child. I will be different. I am going to love and protect my child with all my being.

I stare out the bus window. After leaving Atlanta, the bus travels on back roads I never knew existed. The seats on the bus are close together. There is very little leg room. After an hour, my shoes began to tighten as my feet began to swell. What should have been an hour and a half ride at the most has taken almost three hours. It seems as if we stopped in every little town on the route to West Point. We arrive at one o'clock in the morning. The bus parks into a parking lot on the side of a hotel in dire need of a major renovation. I look around waiting for something that indicates this is a legitimate bus station like the one in Atlanta.

Most of the passengers are greeted by people waiting in the parking lot for their arrival. I had not worked out this part of my trip. There is no one waiting for me. Helplessness, loneliness, and fear creep in. I exit the bus and walk across the broken asphalt parking lot with faded parking lines to the hotel with the cracked half lit sign sitting high above the office that reads, "Patel Inn." A young woman who appears to be in her early twenties greets me at the desk. It is difficult to tell at first glance if she is Pakistani or Indian, as peasants usually have the same mannerisms.

"Hello." Her dialect is Indian. Her eyes are locked on the 24kt jewelry on my finger and the ruby encrusted bracelet on my wrist.

"Hello, I will need a single room for the night."

"How old are you?"

"Excuse me, what does it matter?" I move my bag from one shoulder to the other. "Do you need ID?" I do not wait for a response. I remove it from my wallet and drop it on the counter.

"You look very young." She scans my body and again focuses on my jewelry. "You do not look like our usual guests." She smiles and never looks at my identification. "Just for you, I will get the best room in the house, Ma'am." She removes an application from the clipboard and passes it to me. I sign a fictitious name and pass the sixty-five-dollar fee for the nightly rate. "Follow me."

I hold tight to the handrail and follow her up the unstable metal stairs that are in desperate need of a paint job to the third floor.

"Do you know anything about Lanett, Alabama?"

"No, not very much. I work most days. The owner's son attends school at a nearby university, and we pass through Lanett to visit him." She has gold earrings and a very small gold bangle. Her parents probably scraped together the funds to pay for the jewelry. "Will your husband join you?" She looks at my slightly protruding belly.

"Actually, he is away in college. We will be moving to the area after he completes his studies. I thought I would surprise him by looking for a house." I am sure my story sounds bizarre. In my culture, the elders, even second and third generation Pakistani, no matter the social status, would never allow an expectant mother to travel alone. I am positive she found my story suspect. However, she can look at my bracelet and the craftsmanship of the matching ruby encrusted earrings and know I am from a well to do family. She would dare not question me. "Does Uber come here regularly?"

"Uber?"

"A taxi service."

"I never heard of Uber."

"No worries; I will call a taxi."

"Taxi? That will be expensive. Tomorrow is my day off. For a small fee, I can drive you around."

"That would be great." I place fifty cent in the rusty newspaper stand outside of my door, purchase a newspaper, go to my room, and engage all three locks on the door.

My parents would die if they learned of me fraternizing with a peasant. My mother is from a very established, well-connected and very educated family. The Brute is an imposter who has used my mother's status to improve his own. He and his two brothers came to this country on student visas. Both of my uncles were shipped back to Pakistan after the first World Trade Center bombing in 1993. The Brute managed to go underground and worked in convenient stores or washed dishes in Indian and Pakistani restaurants where he was paid cash. He lived in a rooming house sharing one room with three other men until he met my mother who is second generation Pakistani American. He thought she would be the answer to his prayers. She thought the nightmare she married would restore her status after she was ousted from her family for betraying *Duty and Tradition*.

My parents do not socialize with people lower than their social status. My mother is less assuming, but she is influenced by the Brute. The Brute is pretentious and rides on my mother's position. He was nothing until he met my mother.

Chapter 15
Josh

There are people in this neighborhood who deserve to be gunned down and left in the street for fly, maggot, and buzzard feed. Most people in this neighborhood are law abiding citizens doing the best they can, but a small few raise more hell than the devil. I have met some wicked people on Central Drive. I have witnessed behavior I never knew existed until my addiction landed me on this five-square mile of hell. I have met murderers, rapists, and an army of thieves who make a living taking from people just as marginal. I have used drugs with people who are nothing shy of sociopaths. I also live among true victims who carry scars so deep they will never heal, and using drugs is the only reason they have not blown their brains out. To be honest, society should be thankful for Central Drive and the drugs that keep the psychos here so not to spread the negative behavior to other communities.

There are a lot of shitheads roaming around the earth, and an abundance of them live on Central Drive; many are due for a killing, but not Jean-Jacques. He did not fit in the shithead category. He was a great kid. I have never witnessed him engage in any of the illicit activities rampant on Central Drive. He was always kind, even to junkies like me.

I am not far reaching when I call him friend. I am obviously not the only person who feels this way. His funeral was the most attended I have ever seen. People get shot, stabbed, or just plain beat the hell up for no apparent reason all the time on Central Drive, and no one seems to give a fuck.

Though I have never attended a funeral in these parts, I bear witness the church parking lot has never been as full as it was for Jean-Jacques' funeral. The ambience was beyond sad; an overflow of empathy was expressed toward the family. The incident, though tragic, was a catalyst for a camaraderie I have never witnessed. People who would never speak, somehow, are embracing one another. So many people attended the funeral that streets were blocked. The two-lane roads turned into one on each side of the median as people parked their cars on the side of the road because the church's massive parking lot was full.

Jean-Jacques was good. He was the nicest unassuming person I have ever met. I am a junkie; people in the neighborhood look at me sideways, and some treat me like scum. I deserve the second looks and the occasional shove. Jean-Jacques was different. He could see past my addiction and could always share an encouraging word despite my situation. I still wrestle with the fact that he is gone. Like others in the community, I too, believe he was murdered.

The day of his murder was unreal. Nothing seemed to line up for me that day. I worked all morning, picking up trash left on the side of the Korean store where day laborers wait for construction trucks. I cleaned the bathrooms and mopped the floors for Vladimir, trying to get enough money to score a sack. Once I had the fifteen bucks, I went from one dealer to the other; they were all waiting to replenish their supply. There was so much media and police activity on the corner since the shooting that the distributors were uncomfortable moving their product.

The consensus on the street is the cop who killed Jean-Jacques is dirty. He is mocked by many. Some call him by his true name, Officer Whitley. Some mock him and call him Officer Whitey. I lay low and mind my business, but I have seen him leaving the back of the Korean store in the wee hours of the morning after they close the gambling parties. I have witnessed him shaking down drug dealers, leaving them with their drugs but removing wads of cash from their pockets and quickly stuffing it in his.

Whitley is a cop, but if he were not wearing the badge, one would think he is an honorary member of the Central Drive crime syndicate. People in the neighborhood are used to low down cops and accept the behaviors as part of the game, but something happened after Jean-Jacques' murder.

I was leaving the store in search of medicine. Suddenly pedestrians began to scatter as Whitley drove onto the sidewalk and quickly jumped out of his vehicle. He grabbed a young schoolboy and threw him against the car. He immediately handcuffed the boy and used his heavy combat type boots to kick his legs apart. Young kids almost on cue began filming with their cell phones. I have never seen anything like this. There were groups staked out on every corner with their cell phones held high in the air recording Whitley brutalizing the young boy.

"Whitey!" A young kid yelled then ran to the

side of the Pakistani store through the path toward the apartments. Whitley looked up and scanned his surroundings while holding the kid by the back of the neck with one hand. He placed his hand on his weapon with the other.

He released the gun from the holster when another kid stood on the corner across the streets with his phone extended and yelled, "Whitey!" A pretentious smile was plastered on Whitley's face. Realizing he is on camera and there was no way to catch all the kids, he released the boy from his grip, removed the handcuffs, slammed the kid's head against his car, then let him go.

I wish someone would have recorded the incident between Officer Whitley and Jean-Jacques a few weeks prior to his death. When I saw Whitley follow Jean-Jacques into the Pakistani store, I was concerned but not worried until I glanced through the store window and saw his gun pointed at Jean-Jacques' head, but Jean-Jacques was cool to form and handled it like the gentle person he is.

I miss him. I miss the light conversation. He was a big guy with a boy-like smile. Somehow, his parents saved his innocence among the crazy around him.

I am a certified junkie. My addiction has taken over. I am the epitome of selfish and self-centered. Most days are spent finding ways to feed my habit, but I was determined to pay my last respect to Jean-Jacques. I cleaned myself up as best as I could. I spent the early part of the morning the day before the funeral casing the laundromat down the street at the corner of Memorial and Harrison Road looking for my body double. I thought of going home and getting clothes, but the thought of seeing Rebecca was too much. I cannot deal with the guilt right now. After a couple of hours, my body double exited an old-style Cadillac with two large duffle bags of dirty clothes. I sat in the corner and watched him place his clothes in the washer. I spotted a nice pair of khakis and a white polo shirt. When he left the washer to get change, we made eye contact. I quickly looked away. He stood in front of the washer and inserted coins. He glanced in my direction then went to his car. I waited for his clothes to complete the wash cycle before walking outside to make sure he was not in the immediate vicinity. He was nowhere in sight, so I went back inside and quickly opened the washer, removed the wet slacks, peeled the white polo from deep inside the washer, and placed them in my bag. I quickly walked up the hill past Central Drive to another laundry mat and dried them.

Staying clean or even trying to get clean for a day on Central Drive is almost an impossible endeavor. As I sat in the laundromat, the smell of cannabis floated past my nostrils. The desire to walk to the group of teen boys sitting on the dryer smoking weed and ask for a toke was overwhelming. I have been using long enough to be aware of my patterns. If I start using any mind-altering substance, I will end up searching for a sack. I won't stop until I get one, and then that one will start a vicious cycle of trying to get another one. I was determined to pay my respect to Jean-Jacques. I wanted to use, but I knew the routine: one sack and attending the funeral would be a passing thought. I purposely stayed away from the apartment and Simone. I used my last sack the day before. I did not want to sit in the church nodding. I drank a couple of beers and purchased several shot bottles to help me get thought the day yesterday. I did not go to the apartment to sleep. I slept behind the dumpster in China Town. I have yet to understand why the dump is called China Town since no Chinese live there.

I was dozing off but was jolted awake by a sharp pain that traveled through my back and down my legs like a lightning bolt. Perspiration seeped through every pore and dripped off my skin like a faucet. Before Monster, I never stole, but earlier that day, I stole a roll of tissue from the corner store to wipe the constant flowing mucous from my nose. The few hours without the drugs were taking a toll.

Homicidal and suicidal thoughts occupied my brain as I began to withdraw. Images of my past began to haunt me; guilt for being an absentee father and a neglectful husband began to seep in. I felt like a zero, but I was determined to pay my last respect.

I pulled my knees to my chest and wrapped my arms tight around my legs to hold myself together. This should not be my life. I am a fifth-generation college graduate. I grew up in a mansion with one brother and two sisters. My mother is a society woman, and my father, like his father and his father's father, is a successful surgeon.

I should not live like this. Everything in my life was well-planned before I was born. My father purposely married a woman like my mother. She is arm candy who produced the prettiest blonde-haired blue-eyed babies in the state of Georgia. My father owns real estate in every state south of the Mason Dixie line. We can trace our roots as far back as the late 1700s. My mother is a woman of quiet Southern grace on the exterior, but she can outthink and outsmart my father in her sleep. She plays the demur, Southern belle who must be protected and saved from the world. If she was on stage, her performance would garner an Oscar. There is nothing demur about her. She is calculating and stronger than anyone I have ever known, including my father.

In my mother's world, appearance is everything. All my siblings are Yale or Harvard graduates. I did not have it. The best tutors, hours upon hours of studying, nor family connections could prepare me for Ivy League, so I matriculated at the state university. It took mother many therapy sessions, a variety of anti-depressants, and one-on-one prayer with her church minister before she could finally accept, she had an average child. She loved and protected me despite me being her greatest disappointment. I love my mother because no matter my shortcomings, Mother made sure that even in my dimmest light, I shined brighter than those around me.

What I did not have in academics, I had in athleticism. I was top in my private school of White Anglo-Saxon Protestant descendants who knew very little of hard work. My private school was in the same sports conference as some of the public schools located in upper middle-class neighborhoods. My elite school offered scholarships to mostly black athletes under the guise of diversity, but truthfully it was because of their outstanding athleticism. In football, I competed against those who played with the hope of making football a career. Though I could hold my own, many on the team were far better, but Mother paid the coaches to ensure I was the star quarterback. She began paying news reporters to interview me. I was more hype than talent. I was blessed to have a publicist in the form of my mother working on my behalf. I inherited many of my manipulative ways from my mother.

I blame Mother's persistence in me playing college football for my current situation. I decided I was going to be the hero in the last quarter with less than two minutes on the clock in a championship game. Instead of throwing the ball to the tight end who was open, I ran the ball in the end-zone myself. I heard my fibula crack when the three-hundred-pound linebacker tackled me to the ground and landed on my leg. The injury was career ending. To be honest, I was happy for the curtain to close on this act. The pain of my fibula cracking was a relief. I hated football, but it was the only thing that separated me from being a regular guy.

Initially, I took the pills as prescribed for pain. Then slowly, I took them to sleep. Instead of taking one as needed for pain, I began taking two. The euphoria from the pills was something I never felt. It felt as if I was walking on a cloud. After a couple of years, I began to ingest the pills whether I was in pain or not. I found so much comfort in them that I could not do without them. I was sitting at home taking care of Avril while watching the evening news. Breaking news was a Drug Enforcement sting that resulted in multiple arrests. I leaned closer to the television when I recognized the Buckhead office park. I panicked when I saw Drug Enforcement officers lead Dr. Feins from his office with his hands cuffed behind his back to a waiting police car. Agents entered and exited the office carrying boxes to a white cargo van.

Dr. Feins would write my prescriptions and call them into the pharmacist. After the third office visit, I never saw him again. My co-pay along with a monthly convenience fee of $500 was debited from my bank account the first business day of the month. As usual, when I was down to the last three pills, I called the pharmacist to get a time to retrieve my new prescription.

"Sir, your prescription has not been called in."

"What?" I had been tripling the dosage. I shook the bottle as if the pills would magically appear. I called Dr. Feins and left several messages on his answering machine but did not receive a return call. The first day of withdrawals was the worst.

After the second day, I panicked, left the house, and drove to Dr. Fein's office. There was a line of patients waiting in front of the locked entrance. Some so anxious they paced back and forth like zombies. Others were on the brink of violence.

"Hey, do you know if someone will open the office today?" A middle-aged white male who reminded me of myself and looked like what I believed I would look like, minus the beer belly and receding hair line, in the next ten or fifteen years. "He can't still be in jail. Can he?"

"I hoped one of his partners would see his patients." I massaged my fibula to ease the pain. I shifted my weight to my other leg to take some of the weight off.

"Fuck it. I'll go elsewhere." The desperate looking middle-aged male walked to a top-of-the-line Audi.

"Hey, buddy, where are you going? Do you mind if I tag along?"

"Suit yourself." I walked to the passenger side of his car, opened the door, and slid in.

"Where are we going?"

"I know where to get something close to the meds until I find another doctor to get a prescription." We left Buckhead and drove to GA 400 at top speed. We exited Interstate 285 East to Highway 78 East and drove ten miles before exiting at Mountain Industrial. We drove three miles and turned left onto Central Drive. The fall of the year had settled in, but people were still out and about. We drove past a small shop and passed a group of rundown apartments to a community of duplexes. "You got 20 bucks?" He opened his hand. "I just have enough cash for me." He removed a folded bill from the visor and stuffed it in his pockets.

"Sure, dude." I open my wallet and pass him the money. He walked next to a group of small children playing outside of a rundown duplex with the front door wide open. Dogs and cats with matted fur entered and exited the duplex apartment at will.

Walking back to the car, he nervously scanned the environment of trash, household debris and abandoned cars parked in front of the rundown duplexes that appeared one electrical wire from being uninhabitable. An older Mexican woman stood next to an over-filled dumpster talking to a younger African woman with a small child tied to her back with bright orange and green cloth. He removed the key from the ignition and grabbed a small, black key with a plastic cover and placed it in a secret compartment under the console. He removed a plastic bag that contained a spoon and needle. I was speechless. His hands began to shake uncontrollably as he scooped the beige powder onto a spoon and added a couple of drops of water. Perspiration dripped from his face as he melted the lumps of heroin on the spoon. He somehow managed to tie a tourniquet around his arm. He injected himself and slowly leaned back into his seat.

"Man, what the fuck are you doing?"

"I am doing the next best thing. It is cool as long as you use clean needles."

Initially, I sat still and watched the guy sitting next to me transform from manic to calm. A sharp pain wrapped around my entire fibula and traveled to my hip. I reached for the needle.

"Pass it to me."

"Hell no, brother!" He removed a clean needle from the console. He pulled the liquid through the syringe. My stomach turned. "Tie this around your arm tight and never share needles." He stopped looking at me eyeball to eyeball. "Always use a clean needle!"

I tie the tourniquet tight the first try. I grab a clean needle. I do not search for a vein; I stick the needle in the first raised green line I see. The warmth of the liquid relaxed my entire body. The excruciating pain slowly subsided. I lean back in the seat; it feels as if I am floating on a cloud.

"This is some good shit."

"Here is your sack. You used some of mine. I will replace it from yours." He removed half of the lumpy powder from my sack and placed it in his.

"I have to go back to my side of town. The wife is waiting." He cranked his car and quickly backed out the parking lot.

He stopped in front of Dr. Fein's office. My car was the only vehicle in the parking lot. I looked at the clock: 9:45 p.m. I glanced at my phone and saw Rebecca had been calling nonstop. I placed the phone in the console and drove home.

I coasted into the gated community of mini

mansions I called home. All the lights in the house were off. A dimmer of light from the baby's night light provided just enough illumination to lighten the hallway to my bedroom.

I slowly opened the door and saw her blonde hair pulled to the top of her head in a messy bun. The covers were pulled to her chin. She did not move nor speak, but I could feel her energy. She yelled at me without speaking. She raised her head from the pillow, and our eyes met before she turned over and pulled the covers over her head. After taking a shower, I climbed into bed, lay close to her, and wrapped my arm around her. She didn't respond to my touch.

I woke up the next morning before sunrise and drove to Central Drive to search of the magical medicine.

I have been stuck here ever since. Unlike Jean-Jacques, someone like me deserves to die. I am a horrible husband and the worst father. The cops should have shot me. Jean-Jacques was good. He made the right moves. He was an angel among demons in this Godforsaken place.

I am determined to make this funeral. At sunrise, I wake up and walk to the Pakistani store. The Koreans announced their closing to attend the funeral days earlier. My plan was to wake up early and use the bathroom at the Pakistani store to freshen up. The parking lots of both stores are filled with cars parked in no particular order. I pull the door handle on the Pakistani store. The lights inside are dim. I jerk the handle a few times. I'm in total disbelief; the store is closed. The Pakistani is greedy; I doubt if he would close the store for his own mother's funeral. I walk to the back of the store, use the water spicket to clean up, and quickly change clothes.

I am nervous. This is the longest I have been in a long time without my medicine. I am uncomfortable partly due to feigning and partly because I am nervous about stepping inside a black church. I cross the divided highway on Harrison Road. The line to get inside is wrapped around the church twice and extends down the sidewalk that runs parallel to Central Drive. I try unsuccessfully to blend in with the other attendees. I am sure I stick out like a sore thumb among the well-dressed attendees. Women in dark suits with decorative hats and men in clean suits, some I have only seen in jeans that hang below their bottoms, fill the church. A few Hispanics showed up with their wives and children in colorful, festive dress. The Pakistani girl was the first familiar face. My eyes landed on her slightly protruding abdomen. Her eyes are bloodshot red. Her body trembles as she walks toward the casket. Her skin is dark and blends with the other attendees. I could not possibly understand what she must be feeling. The father of her unborn child is dead. From the size of her stomach, she looks too far along to abort. But if she was anything like Jean-Jacques, she is nervous and full of fear about becoming a parent.

"I am having a baby." Jean-Jacques' eyes were watery, but he was slightly smiling. I was sitting behind the Pakistani store when he approached me after his morning run. He was drenched with perspiration.

"What the fuck, man?" I did not know if I should be happy or sad. "That is a big responsibility."

"How would you know?"

"You are looking at the number one failure at

daddying. You ever heard of a condom?"

"It just happened."

"What the fuck you mean?" I felt kind of fatherly, like this was what I would say to my son if this were to happen, and I was actually parenting him. "I guess you were running, tripped over your big feet, and fell in some pussy." I laughed at my own joke before noticing the long tear traveling down the side of his face. "Can she get it taken care of, you know have an abortion?"

"I am a gentleman. I would never suggest such a thing. I will support whatever she decides." He slid down the wall and sat next to me.

"Don't ever do this shit." I removed a blunt from my bag and lit it. I looked at him eye to eye. "This is the devil, and don't ever take pills either. I don't care how much pain you are in. Don't ever let them give you pills. Just deal with the pain." I puffed on the joint, choking as I was trying to give fatherly advice and inhale at the same time.

"I have royally fucked up." Before I could stop him, he snatched the blunt from my hand, placed it to his lips, and inhaled. He quickly jumped up and beat his chest, coughing so hard I was waiting for his lungs to fly out of his mouth. "How do y'all smoke this shit?"

"Stay away from dope. You are looking at your personal Say No to Drugs billboard."

Tears burn my eyes as I reminisce on our last encounter. I continue to walk down the aisle. My feet feel like concrete as I approach the long mahogany casket. My body shakes so hard it feels like I am having a seizure. When I see the Pakistani girl hit the floor, I want to rush to her and assist, but there are too many people blocking my passage. I turn my attention back to Jean-Jacques after the ushers manage to get the girl to one of the pews in the back of the church. Jean-Jacques looks as if he is asleep. His body is stiff. Most dead people look peaceful. Jean-Jacques looks restless.

Chapter 16
Ayanna

I lay in bed thinking about him after I hung up the phone with Che'. She called to remind me the non-stop flight from London Heathrow will land in Atlanta on April 24. Osei' is once again allowing her to take charge. He is the parent; he should have the maturity to speak with me directly to finalize the children's travel arrangements. If I am honest, I am not looking forward to their visit. I am dreading it. Talking to this girl child who has always believed she is my equal on the phone is one thing. Dealing with her face to face is totally different. I have not been in a mommy routine for a few years. My ex-husband has always been the primary caretaker of the children. When they were small, a trip to the library, zoo, or park was enough to entertain them. I have no idea how to entertain them now, and honestly do not have the desire to learn.

OJ will be easier. He is non-combative and goes along to get along, but his sister is another story. Che' has always been oppositional where I am concerned. Her father has always given her reign. I can only imagine how Nana, his new wife, must feel living in the shadow of a thirteen-year-old girl. Che' sends family pictures of Osei', OJ and herself always posing with her arms wrapped around Nana. The smirk on her face in the picture stands out. She believes I will somehow feel envy of Osei' and Nana. What Che' does not know is Nana has been around. Nana was Mrs. Badu-Bonsu's choice for a daughter-in-law. I am happy Osei' rekindled his relationship with Nana. It removes some guilt for the role I played in the failure of our marriage. He and I were going in totally separate directions. He wanted children; I never really wanted them. I felt obligated to have children with Osei', as I cannot deny, he introduced me to a lavish life I would not have experienced as quickly on my own. I would have made money, but Osei' was a product of generational wealth. His family was firmly planted in high society. We lived a good life, but I always wanted more. Playing wife and mother was too much pressure, so I explored relationships outside of the marriage. For a brief time, I found what I needed in Trevor, but he became too emotional and somehow believed he could dangle his money and power and snatch it away at will. No one controls Ayanna Williams. I needed his connections for a quicker route to the State Bench; he has purposely not come through.

Now, I have found another route with better connections and a hell of a lot more money.

Katsa knows I have children. I have shared photo albums with him, but I do not see him as the stepparent type. I need him in my corner; he has long, global purse strings and is connected with people with long global purse strings. Getting to the State Bench was my goal. With Katsa, I can go further; the United Nations or an Ambassadorship is within reach.

I would rather spend time with Katsa than chauffeuring two children around for the summer. I am too busy with work to host the children for the entire summer. I pick up the phone and dial Osei'. I don't feel like talking to him. I end the call before he picks up and decide to text him instead. "Osei, I hope all is well. I am working on a tedious case. It is not a good time for the children to visit." I press "send" and immediately feel the pressure subside.

Katsa is a hard nut to crack. I have given him every opportunity to seduce me. Low cut blouses and push-up bras that expose firm, perky breasts that costed a fortune do nothing for him. Tight fitting dresses that accent curves from spending hours in the gym do not cause a stir. If it were not for the bulge I feel when I sometimes casually brush against him, I would question if he was attracted to women. I take matters in my own hands. I have been doing this relationship with no title with Katsa for over a year. I hired Katsa's company to assist in prosecuting a criminal case three years ago. Our relationship has slowly evolved from professional colleagues to hang out buddies to romantic involvement, but he is slow as hell. He does not seem to notice subtle hints and reacts slowly to conspicuous ones. I roll over and look at the clock. It is seven a.m. I pick up the phone. He answers after the first ring.

"Do you have plans for the weekend?"

"Nothing in particular."

"Let's spend the weekend together."

His response is slow and unenthusiastic. If I were to suggest the weekend with Trevor, he would be packed and at my door in ten minutes.

"I have an appointment with a client." He pauses. "I guess I can reschedule it."

"Let's go to the German town in Helen, Georgia, come back, and enjoy a hotdog at the county fair. Get ready. I will pick you up at 10." I look at the clock. "That is less than two hours." I emphasize the time. Unlike me, Katsa is not a stickler to time.

I make a mental note to purchase a few cases of wine while in Helen. The town with German inspired buildings is also known for its vineyards that produce quality wines comparable to those in Napa Valley. My cell phone rings as I leave the house to get my nails and hair done. I look at the Caller ID and see Trevor's name. I throw the phone on the sofa and leave. I can't take his back-to-back phone calls and constant texting when I do not respond. He is becoming more problematic than a crazed stalker.

I arrive at my hair appointment twenty minutes early. There are two ladies under the dryer. Kelly, the receptionist, escorts me to the back where the shampoo girl is waiting. I sit in the chair and relax as she messages my scalp with her fingers. The shampoo feels good on my scalp as she folds it into my hair. I was so relaxed that it took a few seconds for me to realize her fingers stopped working the shampoo into my hair.

"Is my husband paying for this?" I open my eyes, and Trevor's wife stands in front of me. I look up; the shampoo girl's eyes are wide open. Her mouth is so wide open her chin almost touches her chest.

"It's you, yet again." I do not move and do everything to appear unfazed. I am fully aware that I am at a disadvantage as Mrs. Bordeaux stands over me. "I will ask you one time to move away from me. Please remember I am an officer of the court."

"Is that right?" She smirks. "You are a lowlife homewrecking Jezebel." She takes a sip of the coffee in her hand that is so hot steam escapes through the small hole in the top. "Don't worry, you can relax."

She smiles. Her eyes are bloodshot, and her skin has darkened. "You are nervous as most sidepieces are when confronted by their lover's wife. What did he tell you? I am boring. Probably complained I was needy?" She takes a sip of the steaming coffee and smiles. "You can have Trevor. You will soon find he is not worth the aggravation. I wish the two of you the best. We have been married for over twenty years. When I am done, there will be nothing left."

She transfers her Hermes bag from the left shoulder to her right shoulder, turns, and scans the women's faces in the shampoo area. "Just like the rest of them you will soon find I am the brains behind Trevor." She smiles. "His brain is in his pants." I inhale and exhale deeply as she steps over my feet and walks to the front of the salon.

The shampoos girl stands still, her mouth wide open. "You can finish. I have an appointment." I ease back into the chair. No one reacts to the scene. We all go on as if nothing happened. I am nervous, but I have always had a good poker face. I tip the shampoo girl, take my seat under the dryer, and wait my turn with the stylist. Before leaving the salon, I take a quick peek between the blinds to ensure Mrs. Bordeaux is nowhere in sight. My car is parked across the street. I open the door and stand in the threshold to check my surroundings before advancing to my car. I sit in my car; relieved Mrs. Bordeaux went about her business. I remove my phone and dial Katsa.

"I am jumping in the shower. I will leave your name with the Concierge. Park your car on the first floor and enter through the lobby. I will leave the door open." To say his lack of punctuality is annoying is an understatement.

I arrive at his apartment in less than thirty

minutes. I walk to the concierge desk. A handsome, young, black male with a Caribbean accent greets me. His fresh tailored suit fits his toned body perfectly.

"Greetings, Ma'am."

"Hello, my name is Ayanna Williams. I am here to see Katsa."

"Yes, Madam." He does not allow time to reveal the last name. I am sure there is probably only one Katsa in the building. "He informed me of your arrival. I will press you in. The Concierge was going through piles of mail as he spoke.

"Do you have mail for Katsa? I can take it to him."

"Yes, actually I do." He places the mail in a plastic tote bag and passes it to me. I try to resist looking through the stack of magazines and mail, but I can't help myself. I step on the elevator, and when the door closes, I scan through one of the tech magazines and find myself basking in admiration of Katsa's intellect. I place the magazine back in the bag. I reach his door and notice an odd shaped, envelope with *Correctional Institution Mail* typed in bold capital letters standing out against gray recycled paper. He opens the door as I attempt to get a quick look at the name of the correctional institute and inmate number, but I quickly drop the envelope in the bag and pass the bag of mail to him.

"The concierge gave this to me to give to you." His expression was not one of anger, but it was obvious he was not happy about this slight breach in security. He takes the mail and steps aside as I enter the apartment.

"Let me get my shoes, and I will be ready." I want to ask about the prison letter and then realize I had no business looking through his mail.

He slipped on tennis shoes with no shoestrings. The T-shirt looked too tight for comfort, but after rubbing my fingers across the sleeve, I realize it's cashmere. His hair is gathered in a rubber band at the nape of his neck. He takes my hand in his, and we walk to the elevator.

"Have you ever been to Helen?" I ask.

"I can't say that I have."

"I think you will like it."

We talk about children and marriage on route to our destination. I am surprised that he wants children. To be honest, it is somewhat of a turn off because I have no intention of having more children. He shares that he has a sister who lives in New Zealand and a cousin who lives in this country that cannot seem to stay out of trouble. I assume this cousin is the sender of the prison letters.

My ears pop due to the change in elevation, as we pass the Welcome to Helen sign. I knew Katsa would like the German inspired buildings. He is so excited he exits the car before it fully stops. We walk around the small mountainous town, peering into the many German shops. The aroma of confections pulls us into a small bakery. He becomes excited like a little boy when he sees fresh Marzipan. I am impressed as I listen to him speak German with the many business owners we visit. We visited a variety of restaurants and shops. We end the day with a hike in the mountains. We are so tired after visiting Helen, we immediately head to his house as opposed to going to the county fair. He goes to his bedroom and returns with a robe.

"This is for you." I take the robe and go to the shower. When I return, the mail that was on the table is gone. He leaves me on the sofa and goes to shower while I sample a glass from one of the bottles of wine we purchased in Helen.

He returns from the shower with loose fitting gym shorts that hang low off his waist. His abdominal muscles are so defined they look like a washboard. Water drips from his dark curly hair. He makes his way to the kitchen and returns with a bowl of fresh fruit and cheese. He places the bowl on the coffee table, and we quickly begin to engage in a heavy petting session. I remove my shirt; he fumbles with the hooks on my bra. I untie the string that holds his shorts below his waist and begin to give him the best head I hope he has ever had. Our movements are in sync. I think he is ready to explode when he suddenly stops. I look up. His eyes are glued to the television; the remote is in his hand.

"You have got to be kidding me." He does not respond. It is as if I do not exist. "Katsa, Katsa!"

"I am sorry." He looks at the television. "The news has been covering the story for a couple of weeks." He points to the screen with coverage of a group of people demonstrating. A young black male dressed in a suit holds up a written sign that reads, "We Demand Justice!" I grab my bra and throw it in my bag.

"You are something else." My self-esteem hit the floor. "You would rather watch these hoodlums protest against a justified police shooting than…" I shake my head after I step into my jeans.

"Babe, it is not that." He turns the television volume down, leaves the sofa, stands close behind me, and plants soft kisses on my neck. I push him away, grab my purse, and leave. "Hey, I am sorry." He follows me to the door, pleading for me to return, as I wait for the elevator.

I can't figure him out. He acts as if he is interested, and then he does some off the wall, cornball shit. I ignore the pleading as I walk away and think I have to change my priorities. Instead of pursuing Katsa, I will throw myself into my work.

My anger is short lived. After a day without talking, he begins to ring my phone with the frequency of a stalker. I refuse to answer the phone for three days. On the fourth day, I walk into my office and find it filled with Calla Lilies. I open one of the cards and find a forgive me note along with an invitation to a four-day trip to the Caymans.

The phone rings as I fold the note and place it back in the envelope.

"Hello," I answer on the first ring, thinking it is Katsa.

"You have to be the worst excuse for a parent known to man."

"Osei'?"

His voice is low as if he is attempting to conceal his anger. "You are a sorry excuse for a mother. Make that a fucking human. You are a sorry excuse for a fucking human."

"What are you talking about?"

"Our children were in the airport for half a day waiting for you to gather them. Are you fucking insane?"

"What? I left a message."

"I called you. The airline stewardess who escorted them called you. Luckily, I found your mother's phone number so she could gather the children before the airline notified the authorities."

"I texted you to inform you that I had a change in my plans. Look at your phone."

"Text? Are you fucking serious? You have to be kidding me!" He quickly stops speaking. After about ten seconds of total silence, he continues, "Your children are traveling across the ocean, and you text at the last minute that your plans have changed."

"I will get the children from my mother."

"Don't bother. I chartered a private jet to get them to London." He exhales. "What in the hell did I ever see in you?"

Chapter 17
Marie

The sweet and spicy aroma of curry hovers in the air. He made my favorite dish exactly the way I like it. The extra dash of hot pepper sauce is so potent it opens my sinuses. I have not eaten a full meal in days. I have eaten nibbles of food, but barely enough to sustain life. I have isolated myself from the world as well as from the only two people I have left in it. There is no light in my life. It was taken away when my son was murdered.

My bedroom is dark. A thin line of light from the bottom of the bedroom door illuminates the outline of the furnishings. I wince as tiny hairs are torn from my skin as I peel the covers away. Days of dried tears, mucous, and perspiration have turned into an adhesive. I have been in the bed five days to the hour I buried my son. I only leave the bed to relieve myself, which is not often because I have ingested very little food and drink.

He opens the bedroom door as I was returning to my bed from the bathroom. I use my hand to cover my eyes from the sudden burst of bright light.

"Hi, Sleepyhead." He stands in the threshold with a small bowl in one hand and a glass of tea in the other. I turn my back to him and face the wall.

"You have to eat something."

"I can't. I do not have an appetite." He steps closer, sits on the bed, and places the food on the side table. "You have not eaten a meal in days. You have to eat."

"Later. My throat muscles are too weak. I cannot swallow."

"Don't be ridiculous. You must eat something just a few bites. I insist." He places bite size portions of curry goat on the fork, and places it under my nose. "Smells good? I made it just the way you like it." I part my lips and reluctantly open my mouth. He gently glides the fork with small amounts of food on the end inside my mouth. As usual, the food is delicious, but I have no desire for food.

"It was a beautiful funeral." A tear rolls down my face.

"Yes, it was." He pats my hand, brings it to his face, and softly kisses it. "Let us hold onto the beautiful memory of our boy right now. It is time to start healing."

"So many people. Have you ever seen so many people in one place at one time?" Dried tears feel like small pebbles as I rub my fingers across my lids.

"Our boy was special." He takes the towel and softly dabs the tears away from my face.

"Did you find it strange the Pakistani girl from the corner store attended?" I shake my head to stir the memory. "I hope she is okay. She hit the floor hard. She was very emotional."

"It appears as if the entire neighborhood came. Everyone was emotional." He places another bite size portion of food to my mouth. I turn away from the food. "Open, our boy was special. A gentle giant, who would not love him?"

"The murderous cop did not love him! What is today's date?" I reach for the bottle of pills the doctor prescribed to help me sleep.

"It is Wednesday." He removes the bottle of pills from my hand and places it on the table. "It is time to stop taking the pills." I do not protest. I agree. I have become dependent on them; I need to learn to sleep again without them.

"I have a 3:00 appointment with the district attorney today. I need to be calm." He brings another spoon filled with curry goat to my mouth. I turn away from it. I throw my legs off the bed and plant my feet on the floor.

"Wait a minute." He grabs my arm and holds me still. "Her receptionist did not confirm an appointment; she said she may have an opening. Did she call you to confirm?"

"Yes." I remove my arm from his grip. He knows I am untruthful but does not stop me.

"I will go with you."

"No, I want to go alone." I open the closet to find suitable clothing. I grab a black A-line form fitting dress, go to the shower, and close the door behind me. I undress and stare at my body in the mirror. I have two children but gave birth to one. I use my finger to follow the raised lines on my stomach. I was always proud of my stretch marks. I have lost the desire for food. My body is thinner than normal. The outlines of my ribs are visible through my skin, and my abdominal muscles are more pronounced. He opens the door and looks around the bathroom suspiciously. He removes his clothes dropping them on the floor as he walks into the bathroom. His fifty-year-old body looks like the body of a well-toned twenty-year-old. He walks behind me and cups my bare breast. I feel him harden. My insides normally drip wet when he touches me. I am dry as the desert sand. "Apologies."

"It's okay." He removes his hand from between my thighs and plants soft, quick kisses on the back of my neck. "There is no hurry." He steps away and turns on the water. I take hold of his outstretched hand for balance as I step into the shower. The water feels good on my skin. He squeezes a generous amount of bath wash on the sponge and lathers my entire body. The lavender body wash removes days of funk off my skin. I stand under the shower where my tears blend with the water. It feels as if my grieving ticket is about to expire. I rinse the suds away, step out of the shower, and grab the towel. He turns the water off. He wraps his towel tight around his sculptured waist, sits on the commode, and watches me as I use the towel to pat myself dry.

"You are beautiful."

"I feel sick and ugly. I am of no use. I could not protect my own child."

"Maybe we should get away for a while."

"I will carry myself with me." I leave the bathroom; he follows me to our bedroom and sits on the bed. I step into my underwear. They are loose. I make a small knot on the side to keep them on my waist. My bra is so loose, my left breast falls beneath the cup. I adjust my breast into my bra. I never knew one could lose weight in their breasts. I step into my dress. It used to fit snug, but now it is very loose.

"Are you sure you do not want me to go with you?" He slides his jeans over beautiful muscular legs so thick they remind me of tree trunks. He pulls the pants over his bottom to his waist. I think to myself I hope his pubic hair does not get caught into the zipper.

"Positive" I remove my phone from the drawer and turn it on. It's fully charged. I have not touched my phone since Jean-Jacques was murdered. Several messages pop up. I type the District Attorney's office address in the GPS and grab my purse. I pass my daughter's room on route to the front door. I look inside; she is not there. I find her in the dining room sitting at the table next to the clean-cut boy that used to look like a bum. He stands as I enter.

"Hello, Ma'am." I tilt my head to acknowledge him. I do not have the energy to verbally respond. I assume he is helping my daughter study, as a pile of papers are spread all over the table. I am happy my daughter has a friend.

"Are you sure you do not want me to come. You do not have to handle this alone."

"No, I can do this." He places a kiss on my forehead and follows me to the front door. I get in the car, buckle the seatbelt, shift the transmission to reverse, and back off the parking pad. I notice graffiti on the stop sign that reads, *"Not This Time"* as I turn right onto Central Drive. People have gone about their business. The makeshift memorial is still present, but stuffed animals and boxing gloves are thrown about. Tire prints stand out on a large white Teddy Bear propped against the electric pole on the corner. Two young men walk up and down the street with a sign that reads, *"We Demand Justice."* The White Junkie Boy in front of the Korean store is doing what junkies do. I was surprised to see him at the funeral. The Korean and Pakistani stores are now open, flowing with business. Beer bottles, empty candy paper, and soft drink cans are mixed in with dirty stuffed animals and dead flowers at the makeshift memorial for Jean-Jacques. My daughter returns to school tomorrow, and Jikki will reopen the gym. Everyone is moving on, and my son is still dead.

I think of what I will say to the District Attorney. There is something repulsive about her spirit. She is cold. She uses words like neglect and accountability as if I am somehow to blame for my son's murder. I practice my words to keep occupied. I have no expectations of this meeting with the D.A. I have made several attempts to meet with her regarding prosecuting the criminals who murdered my son. Each time, her assistant promises a call back that never comes. Days of watching the news media paint my Jean-Jacques as a thug, drug dealer, and menace has taken its toll. I need to set the record straight. I was so desperate to speak with the D.A. that I once staked out her office and followed her to Stoney's Bar and Grille. The bar is a hole in the wall, but it is an established meet up for the well to do and politically connected.

She sat at the table with a middle-aged white male. She appeared enamored with him as her eyes did not leave his face. Perhaps it is the lighting, but when she is on television, she appears heartless. However, she was soft and attractive as she enjoyed the company of her friend. I was disheveled, hair uncombed for two days, clothing wrinkled, and probably musky, but I needed to speak with her. I needed to tell her who Jean-Jacques was. She needed to know the countless number of young neighborhood boys he mentored at the gym. She needed to know Jean-Jacques worked closely with Detective Chandler trying to keep young boys away from gangs. Jean-Jacques would never cause harm to Chandler.

I stood at the bar and observed them for several minutes, ordered a drink, and gulped it down in one swallow then stumbled to her table. I stood next to her for several seconds before she noticed me. Her eyes almost popped out of her head when she finally recognized me. She immediately yelled for security. I removed my cell phone to show her beautiful pictures of my Jean-Jacques. Her security team quickly surrounded me with high powered rifles and threw me on the floor. Patrons ran over each other trying to leave the scene. She raised her hand to stop security from doing whatever it is her security does.

"Ms. Gomez." She stood and motioned for the security to lift me off the floor. Her acquaintance looked familiar, but I paid him no mind as he observed the fracas.

"The police murdered my son. The police are feeding the news media many untruths." I looked into her eyes, searching for her spirit. Her eyes were void of empathy. She had no spirit; she had no soul. "My Jean-Jacques was no thug!"

"Ms. Gomez," she slightly raised her voice, "this is not the place or time." She briefly paused, and in the most unsympathetic tone a heartless person could muster, said, "Due to possible litigation, I cannot discuss the case with you." She assumed I had a lawyer and advised that she would speak to me through my lawyer.

"I do not have a lawyer." Many lawyers have contacted me to offer free representation. The lawyers want to file lawsuits to get money and notoriety. Money means nothing. I want to remove the tarnish from my son's name. The media alters pictures of him. They darken his skin and photoshop facial hair that makes him appear much older than his eighteen years. I have current pictures of him smiling in Sunday suits. I have school pictures of a little boy with a toothy smile. I have offered these pictures through the Pastor. None make it to the public.

"I will ask that you allow the judicial system to run its course." Her smile was disingenuous. "I will have my security escort you to your vehicle." A tall, white male wrapped his fingers around my arm so tight my arm became numb. He dragged me to the exit, lightly pushed me out the bar, stood in front of the door, and blocked the entrance.

To many, Central Drive is the eyesore of the county. The recent shootings between the Mexican and Black gangs have bought unwanted, negative attention. Most of the residents in our community are hardworking and live responsible lives. We work and pay taxes like everyone else. The troublemakers are a small number but wreak so much havoc that their negative behavior outshines the many positive things that also happen in the community. Chandler was our hero. He worked diligently for the betterment of our community. He held many forums, though he never said it, he always implied what many know: much of the criminal activity is connected to the corner stores.

Chandler was a great community organizer who just happened to wear the badge. The community loved him. Pictures of his children and his beautiful wife pull on the heartstrings of everyone, including me and my family. The community has created a college fund for Chandler's kids while the media constantly shows altered pictures of my son in dark hoodies. I empathize with his widow, but my son did not murder her husband. Chandler was popular with everyone. He was the buffer between the police and the community. No one on Central Drive, and especially my son, would harm a hair on his head.

I circle the office building three times before I enter the parking deck. I immediately feel burdened and weighed down when I step out of my car. Her office is on the tenth floor. I park the car and take the stairs to clear my head but lose the energy by the time I reach the fourth floor. I exit the stairwell, enter the atrium, and find my way to the elevator. I press the button for tenth floor. My stomach feels as if it dropped to the floor. The elevator is super-fast. In no time the bell rings, and the elevator opens to a spacious reception area. Her office is modern and appears to have been professionally decorated. It looks more corporate than the office of a government official. A young black female in her mid-twenties sits at the receptionist desk. She does not respond when the bell rings as the elevator door opens. Her facial expression is uninviting. I stand in front of her desk for at least two minutes while she peruses social media sites and surfs the internet. She does not acknowledge me until I clear my throat. Without her asking, I provide my name and ask to speak with the District Attorney.

"Do you have an appointment?"

"She is expecting me."

"Wait here." She pushes her chair away from her desk and turns her monitor off. She throws Indian hair woven into hers over her shoulders and walks in front of her desk. I walk two steps behind her. She quickly turns and goes back to her desk, almost pushing me to the floor as she reaches for her cell phone. She never takes her eyes off the screen as she navigates the twists and turns from the reception area to the D.A.'s office. She opens the door to the D.A.'s office. I immediately regret not bringing a sweater. Her office is colder than the morgue that kept my son's body.

The D.A. immediately stands when I enter. She is average height but petite. Her arms are well toned, stomach flat as a pancake. If she has children, there is no evidence. A small half-consumed smoothie sits next to a bowl of colorful fruit in the middle of her desk. Her hair is cut to precision in a short pixie much different from the picture that sits on the wall next to her predecessor.

"Apologies." The assistant slowly walks away. "Ma'am, I asked your guest to wait in the lobby!"

"No worries, Tiffany." She consoles her meek assistant without taking her eyes off mine. It is as if we are in a duel to see who will blink first. I do not wait for her to offer a seat. I sit in the chair at the end of the conference table close to her desk. My eyes are glued to hers.

"Apologies for barging in." I do not blink; neither does she. My face is bland, no affect. "My son was murdered. My son was murdered in cold blood. I do not understand why anyone would want to take his life. Jean-Jacques was a good boy. I was promised transparency, yet I have not received one update on the investigation."

"Ms. Gomez, again, I would much prefer our meetings take place in the presence of your lawyer."

"I do not have a lawyer. I don't need a lawyer. I need justice." I fight back tears. Her demeanor is cold. I hold my composure.

"Mrs. Gomez." She leaves her desk, takes a seat in a soft, dark brown leather chair in front of a stack of folders. "I was actually going over your son's file before you barged into my office. Sometimes, our children can disappoint us. I am sure your son was a great young man." She opens a file that contains school records as far back as fifth grade. "He appears to have violent tendencies that may have played out on that horrific day." She smiles. I do not blink. "It seems his penchant for violence started very early." She removes a school report documenting a suspension for beating three boys in the bathroom. Behind the report is a prison photo of Jikki, my man. She slides the picture across the table close to me.

"We really have to be careful of the type of people we introduce to our children," she glances at Jikki's photo then at me, "particularly during the impressive years."

"Jikki." I sit in the empty chair in front of her, as I take the picture from the table. I knew he spent time in prison, but I had not seen the mugshot. "He was such a handsome man even back then. He did his time; he has been a wonderful influence on my children and many in our community." I smile, look into her eyes. Pride replaces grief. I am ready to battle. "My daughter graduated valedictorian and has earned a scholarship to college. She is making straight A's as a pre-med major. Jean-Jacques was a great boxer." I hold my head high and extend my chest outward. "You speak of the incident in the fifth grade where he disfigured three schoolboys." I smile. "You should have seen their faces. The punks' eyes were swollen shut. Their parents tried to sue, but the courts found that Jean-Jacques was defending himself against three bullies attempting to violate him." I turn my nose upward. "It seems that kind of thing is rampant in this culture." I smile. "Keep looking further you will find in the ninth grade, the last year he was in public school, two eleventh grade boys tried to force him in a gang. He broke their noses and cracked their ribs."

"Yes, and I believe charges were filed against your son." She rambles through papers.

"Yes, keep looking and you will see they were dropped. The school's cameras showed he acted in self-defense." I raise my head higher and extend my chest further. "I imagine those bullies will never forget the powerful blows of Jean-Jacques." I smile. Her face remains flat with no emotion. "The bullying was constant. After begging the schools to intervene, meeting with principals, filing police reports, I removed him from the savagery you people call school to keep the bullies safe."

"Yes, I was getting to that."

"Jean Jacques is..." I pause to gather my composure. "Jean-Jacques was an amateur boxer getting ready to turn professional. We signed a contract for sponsorship one week before he was murdered. God gave Jean-Jacques powerful hands and quick movements." I shake my head, stand, and walk toward the door. "My Jean-Jacques was a gentle giant. Everyone loved him. He has never owned a gun, never touched one." I point to the folder on her desk. "The evidence in that folder suggests he never needed a gun." I take another step toward the door and turn back to face her. "You have gone through a lot of trouble to research the life of a dead boy. I hope you spend the same energy investigating the rogue cop who murdered my son."

"Ms. Gomez, the procedure..."

"Procedure?"

"Yes, procedure." She attempts to engage me in the stare down game again. "Jean-Jacques is…was a citizen. What is your status?"

"Jean-Jacques was a citizen born in this country. I am a naturalized citizen."

"From Cuba?"

"Yes, from Cuba." This is the first time anyone questioned my nation of birth since I left the detention center.

"You don't look Cuban." She removes copies of Money Transfer receipts showing monies I regularly send to Haiti.

"You seem to have strong ties to Haiti." Her voice carries an accusatory tone.

"Is that a crime? Many people live a global existence. I have relatives in Haiti, Cuba, England, and Australia."

"How much money do you send those relatives?"

"They don't need money. Haiti is poor, kept poor by sore losers who lost a true war of independence."

She smiles. "You do not look Cuban."

"How does a Cuban look?" I smile and visually peruse her cold office. "You should travel more. Please tell me what my nationality has to do with the murder of my son? He was not murdered by a Cuban or Haitian. He was murdered by a white American cop." My tone subconsciously elevates. I remind myself to stay calm.

"Ms. Gomez, I am truly sorry for your loss." She fails miserably at her attempt to express empathy. She flips through papers. "All of the evidence suggests your son was the aggressor. Gun residue was found on his hands. The officer had just cause to use deadly force after your son killed

Chandler. Perhaps it was the marijuana found in his system that caused your son to act out violently."

"Marijuana? No, my Jean-Jacques did not do drugs. He was an athlete, a celebrated athlete." The smirk on her face as she removes the toxicology report feels like daggers imploding every artery in my heart. I walk back to her desk and remove the toxicology report from her hand without taking my eyes off the she-devil in front of me. I scan the report; cannabis was highlighted and underlined twice.

"I am glad you stopped by. An appointment would have been appreciated." It takes all that I have not to wipe the smirk from her face.

"Rubbish! My son did not do drugs!" I don't know how many insults a person can take and keep their sanity intact. She expressed her disingenuous condolences again. "The police killed my son." We engage in the duel of the eyes. This time, she concedes and looks away.

"Your son had a weapon and killed Chandler Davis while under the influence of drugs. We are still investigating, but all evidence suggests..."

"What investigation?" I step closer to her. My voice elevates; I immediately lower my volume. "Testimony from the cop that pulled the trigger? Testimony from crooked cops who support his lies? My son did not have a weapon! He never carried a weapon! The only thing he carried besides his wallet was his phone." I walk toward the door and stand in the threshold.

"Ma'am." She walks to the door. She passes a picture to me. "This is your son. Please take a look." She points to the dead body with a gun lying to the right of his dead body.

"No!" My tone is flat, void of all emotion.

"My son is lefthanded." The gun is lying next to his right hand. She does not respond. "The gun was planted."

"All of the officers on the scene have the same reports. I know this is hard. I am a mother, and the best raised children can sometimes make bad decisions."

"My Jean-Jacques had a promising future. He is...was a boxer. He was going places. He was going to make a lot of money."

"Jean-Jacques?" She flips through her folder. "That is not a Cuban name."

"You should travel more." I proudly extend my chest. "Many people of color all over the diaspora give their children heroic names." My face remains blank as she smiles to soften the conversation. "My son is dead at the hands of a murderous cop. I will not quietly allow his murderer to go free. If it takes the last breath in my body, I will have my justice. My son will have his justice." I look around her office. "You say you are a mother? I see no pictures of children. Odd."

Chapter 18
Josh

"No more butter! No more butter!" The protestors are so loud the restaurant's thick glass doors and loud conversations between customers do not drown the chanting. Jermaine successfully turned his one-man advocacy into a neighborhood movement. I peer out the window to see if Donovan is lurking in his usual spot on the corner. The word on the corner is I owe him money, and he is looking for me. Simone has been telling anyone who will listen that my family is wealthy believing she will gain leverage for credit. I asked her to stop with the rich white boy rumors reminding her that I am grinding along with her trying to get another one.

I owe no one. I learned the hard way early on not to ask for credit. I am not in the mood for confrontation with Donovan. Avoidance is the best option. I look left and right before leaving the store to make sure everything is cool. Onlookers gather around several men dressed in tailored suits adorned with bright bowties and holding handwritten signs high in the air that read, "We can't go back. Justice Now or..." Initially, people would pass the protestors, annoyed at the attention they brought to the corner where a lot of illegal transactions takes place, but eventually the love and admiration of a fallen, neighborhood hero changed from annoyance to admiration.

"Hey, brother." I look to the left and right, not sure if he is talking to me, and if he is, wondering why. Jermaine is no longer part of the scene. He no longer hangs on the corner waiting for something to jump off. If you are not associated with the drug life or part of the hustling network, I really can't be bothered. "White Boy!"

"Talking to me?" I lean back, raise my shoulders and slightly tilt my head to the side. It is amazing; my dialect has changed. My mannerisms are almost unrecognizable.

"Yeah you." Jermaine motions for me to come closer. "Weren't you and Boxing Boy friends?"

"Who?"

"Boxing Boy, I used to see you running with him in the mornings."

"You mean Jean-Jacques?"

"Yeah, you know he was murdered." He lowers his tone; his eyes become glassy. "You know he did not shoot Chandler."

"Jermaine, of course, Jean-Jacques would never to hurt anyone. He was the nicest kid I have ever met." We instinctively bump fists in agreement.

"Nuri, my name is Nuri." He smiles. "I have been transformed brother. I am a new man. Jermaine is dead."

"Cool." I smile. I am happy for Jermaine and hope one day I can leave this lifestyle and go back to my old life, but for now, I am on a mission.

"See this, ladies and gentlemen." He raises his voice and points in my direction. He is oblivious to my discomfort. Attention from law abiding citizens is not something I need, and I am trying to avoid a fool who believes I owe him money. "Even the Caucasian knows they are lying." More people began to gather around. "We can't go back to business as usual." He looks around. "Who is going to be next?" He directs his attention to a small crowd of Mexicans. They could actually be Guatemalans or El Salvadorians but to the residents of Central Drive anyone who speaks Spanish is Mexican. He yells in their direction. "Is it going to be one of you border brothers? They already blaming you for crime and taking away jobs no Americans want. Hell, some of the politicians believe the lot of you to be rapists." He captures the attention of a young Mexican with tattoos all over his face as he leaves the Korean store. Instead of standing under the tree with the other day laborers, he walks closer to the small group of protestors and listens to Jermaine who now calls himself Nuri. "We have to have our justice. Justice for Jean-Jacques is justice for all of us."

Nuri returns to the corner sidewalk holding the sign high in the air. His fellow protesters stand on the sidewalk talking to people as they pass.

I walk across the street to the Pakistani store to take advantage of a two for two-dollar beer special. I look around the store for his daughter. I was surprised she was not working. She usually works in the store six days a week. I wanted to check on her and make sure she is okay.

"Two-dollars and fifteen cents." I look past the register, thinking she might be in the corner reading a book as usual. I pass him one wrinkled dollar bill, four quarters, one dime, and a nickel; I take my beers and leave. I make my way to the tree and wait with the others for work. It seems as if the crowd has now doubled in size. The beer does not taste as good as I expected. It is flat, no fizzle. I look at the date and find it expired two years ago. I have been trying to wean myself off the medicine by drinking beer and cheap liquor. It is not working. The high I wanted does not seem to come. I toss a half-full can of beer in the trash.

"I ain't seen you in a minute." Miguel joins the day laborers under the tree. He looks out of place counting his money.

"Yeah. Just laying low."

"Why are you out here under the tree? This is for working people."

"Trying to find some work."

"Why don't you call your family?" A slick smile covers his face. "Simone says you're a rich white boy." He laughs. "But seriously she is using your name to get credit. Donovan, the crazy black dude is looking for you to pay up." He stuffs a wad of cash in his pocket. "You should stop dealing with the Negros. The pork is driving them crazy." I don't respond. I doubt if anyone is truly giving Simone credit. She is probably getting a pebble as opposed to a rock. Some dealers are more deranged than dope fiends. The dealers will make themselves believe they are owed hundreds of dollars for twenty dollars of credit. Donovan is more deranged than most. He goes through extraordinary lengths to intimidate. In actuality, he is a scared piss ass. He is never alone. He surrounds himself with young kids from fucked up families. He walks around with three oversized pit bulls on thick chains. He will probably come up with some outrageous amount I owe on Simone's behalf believing my rich parents will bail me out.

This game is wicked and becomes more insidious by the day. I want out. I don't know how to stop using. I started hanging out with the day laborers to distract me from the needle. The contractors usually pick up workers they believe to be Mexicans because of their reputation for working hard for low wages; for now, I will be a Mexican. I never kick it with the Mexicans but found they are hard workers. The first day I stood under the tree, none of the contractors took me seriously.

"What's your skill?" The first time I was asked, I stood still with a blank stare. I watched the Mexicans and listened to their answers and found I had a skill set. I am a good painter. I heard one laborer scream demolition. I began to yell painting and demolition when asked about my skill. It took three days to get work.

The Mexicans come prepared to work with lunch boxes so not to spend money. I am also holding tight to my cash but for different reasons. The contractor works us hard allowing only two fifteen-minute breaks. The Mexicans do not complain and neither do I. The paint job lasted all day.

After work, the contractor drops us off in the Korean store parking lot. The protestors are still protesting, it appears as if the crowd has tripled in size. Nuri has a blow horn talking to the crowd. "There is footage somewhere. We live in a world where everyone is taking pictures. There is a scene behind every selfie. Look at the pictures in your cell phones. Look at all the pictures you have taken in the neighborhood. Bring them to us so we can look together. Talk to your children. Tell them to ask their friends to do the same. There is footage. It may not be the day it happened, but there is footage of the rogue cop doing rogue cop policing." He has the crowd's full attention. They are speaking to themselves, some removing their cell phones from their pockets to scroll through pictures and videos.

"This store here," he points to the Pakistani store, "has the best angle. Boxing Boy was murdered on the side of his store. Look at where his cameras are pointing." He points to the small devices extending from each corner. The crowd almost in unison turns their heads to observe the cameras. "The owner says he does not have footage. Are we to believe a man with no respect for us? Are we to believe a man who watches every move we make when we enter his store? A man who looks at your daughters, wives, and sisters with a lustful eye." He scans the crowd. "Brothers and sisters, are we stupid? Do we believe the Pakistani?"

"Hell no!" the crowd screams.

"Ladies and gentlemen, brothers and sisters, I ask you, why are we spending our hard-earned money with the patsy Pakistani who has aligned himself with the rogue cops? Let us show him who butters his bread. Let us tell him until he aligns himself with the people who line his pockets with their hard-earned money there is NO MORE BUTTER!" The smile on his face says it all. He has captured his audience. The crowd stands on the sidewalk as cars turn into the parking lot. They chant, "No more butter! No more butter!" Nuri stands on the sidewalk and tells patrons as the exit their cars, "Please don't support this store. He does not support you or people who look like you." Some enter the store; however, just as many walk away, go back to their cars, and drive across the street to the Koreans.

The Pakistani owner stands in the threshold of his half empty store shouting obscenities to the crowd. "Ladies and gentlemen, brothers and sisters, give it a day or two, and he will be calling us Nigger." He turns his attention back to the store and chants with the crowd, "No Butter! No Butter!"

Chapter 19
Marie

My saliva is thick and pasty. I push my tongue through my lips to pry them apart. I force myself to suck ice cubes, but the cubes no longer quench my thirst. I leave the safety of my bed, walk into the kitchen to get water, and find my daughter sitting at the table in front of a stack of books. I am proud of her spirit. She loved her brother. She looked after him like a mother hen. Losing Jean-Jacques is painful to all of us, but she continues with her studies and remains focused. I smell food but have no interest in eating.

"Mommy." I continue to walk back to my room. "Mommy!"

"Yes." I turn around, and our eyes meet. We lock eyes for what feel like an eternity. Guilt is overwhelming. I turn away. I have yet to ask of her well-being.

"Ms. Bailey called and asked about her drapery order."

"Is she kidding me? My son is dead, murdered in cold blood, and she worries about drapery!" I rush back to the kitchen and snatch the phone from its cradle so hard the screws that hold the cradle to the wall loosen.

"Mommy!" She quickly stands. "Mommy, who are you dialing?"

"I am going to let this bitch know where she can put her fucking drapery. She can shove them…" My daughter pries the handset from my hand.

"No, Mommy, go lay down." Her beautiful eyes are filled with tears. "I will bring your dinner to your room. Mrs. Bailey is a good client."

I reluctantly follow her instruction, go to my room, and lie down, but sleep will not come. I open the drawer next to me and remove the bottle of pills I promised I would stop taking.

"You promised to stop taking the pills." He opens the door slowly and walks softly on the carpet. I smell sweat on his skin. He must have worked out hard. He steps into the walk-in closet. I hear drawers open and close. He leaves the closet and goes to the shower. I try to drown out the sound of the shower, but the shower mixed with his singing interferes with my sleep. I pull the pillow over my head but can smell the fresh scent of African Black Soap when he opens the bathroom door. He tosses the towel on the bedroom floor. The covers slide from my shoulders to my waist as he eases in the bed. His touch is light.

"Wake up, baby," he whispers as he places soft kisses on my face. His strong hand softly kneads my breast. I lie limp, purposely not returning the affection, hoping he will get the hint and leave me alone. He lightly pushes me on my back, rolls on top of me, and spreads my legs with his knees. My underwear cut into my skin as he pulls them over my hips.

"Are you kidding me? Get off me!" I push him away with so much force his six feet, two-inch frame tumbles off the bed and onto the floor. "It's your fault! She looked at me like trash. She says I am a bad mother because I keep house with a murderer!" My breathing is labored. I can't catch my breath. "Je suis une mauvaise mère." I am a bad mother, I scream. "You gave my son drugs!"

"What?" He behaves as if he does not know what I am talking about. "Drugs?" He stands.

"I saw the toxicology report!"

"Toxicology report?" The dumbfounded look on his face enrages me. I grab a glass from the nightstand.

Water splashes all over me and onto the floor as I hit the glass against the nightstand and leap toward him. I feel blood dripping from my hand as I hold the sharp edge of the broken glass, but I feel no pain. He grabs my hand as the glass makes contact with his face. He stands naked in front of me. Life has left his eyes. He does not speak. He uses one hand to pry the broken glass from my hand and the other to wipe the thin line of blood away from his cheek. Our eyes are locked for several seconds.

He steps away, opens the closet, goes inside and closes the door behind him. I hear hangers sliding against the metal rod that holds our clothes. My adrenaline slowly returns to normal. The sound of zippers brings me back to the present. The pain in my hand is excruciating. I go into the bathroom, run water over my wound and wrap a tight bandage around my hand to stop the bleeding. I hear my daughter outside of the bedroom door. I ignore her. I grab a cold towel and blot the red blood stains out of the carpet. I climb back into bed. I reach for the bottle on the nightstand, twist the cap off, and pour two pills in the palm of my hand.

"Daddy, Daddy." The intrusion alarm beeps as the door opens. She calls out to him, but he does not answer. Jikki is the only daddy she knows. The sound of the front door closing is unusually loud. She comes to my bedroom, opens the door without knocking, and steps inside. "What happened?" Her face is filled with anger, but she is respectful; she does not say what is probably on her mind.

"Nothing." I lie. "Go back to your studies." I roll over and face the wall. I still feel her presence. I turn over and yell, "Get out of my room! Go back to your studies!" She stares at me two seconds too long. We lock eyes. She steps away and closes the door with a force so hard the pictures on my nightstand vibrate.

I wake up in the middle of the night and reach for him. His side of the bed is empty. I feel my way around in the dark and look around the living room for his silhouette. I rub my hand across the empty seat cushion. I am surprised he did not return. We are both shaken. In all the years we have been together, we have rarely had disagreements. He set the course of how we relate early in the relationship. I am from a family of loud voices. In the beginning, when we had disagreements, his response was no response. His only comment was "Respect, everything we do and say is done with respect." I want to cry and feel great remorse because we have never spent a night apart since we began living together. I dial his cell; his voicemail answers the call. I grab my pills take a double dosage, and immediately fall asleep.

I awaken to a sun so bright the light penetrates my eyelids. I look at the clock. It is noon. I was going to swallow another pill when my daughter knocks on the door. "We have guests." I leave the bed and walk toward the door. She takes my hand and guides me back inside of my room. "Mommy, let's get cleaned up first." She removes a face towel and washes my face. She places the hairbrush under water and uses it to detangle my hair. I look in the mirror and do not recognize myself. My cheek bones protrude. Dark circles surround eyes. My face is sunken. I am thin and appear frail. My daughter removes my gown and slips a frock over my outstretched arms.

I did not expect to see the minister. I was grateful he organized the funeral and insisted Jean-Jacques' home going was held at his church. I cannot think of a building in close proximity that could accommodate the number of people who attended the funeral. I am not a member of his church. I am not surprised by his interest; it seems that many people were affected by Jean-Jacques' murder. I understand the reason so many admired him. Jean-Jacques was focused. He stayed out of trouble. He played by the rules; he circumvented all stereotypical indices that trap young black males in this country.

The district attorney has it wrong. Jean-Jacques was not a drug user. He was focused on becoming a world champion boxer. Of all the black males living near Central Drive, Jean-Jacques was the least likely to have a run-in with the law. After Jean-Jacques' murder, the minister and his wife befriended me and helped me navigate the burial process. Initially, I wanted to bury him in Haiti, but decided it best to make his final resting place in America.

I walk into our living room. The front door is wide open. The Reverend and his wife stand outside. The mesh from the screen door creates a shadowy image of the heavenly couple.

"Jasmine, invite them in." She looks as at me then at the door then me again before finally inviting them inside. I stand close behind my daughter. The Mrs. Pastor scans my home; her eyes finally lock on my hair then slowly on my face. She clutches her beaded necklace and attempts to mask her disapproving look with a fake smile. She quickly removes an envelope from her purse and passes it to the Reverend who quickly passes the envelope to me.

"Sister," He lightly pushes my daughter to the side and takes my hand in his. The First Lady stands beside him with one hand covering her heart and the other lightly brushing against my arm. "We hope this is not bad timing. We know the wounds are still fresh." Mrs. Pastor mumbles, "Thank you Jesus" followed by a series of "Amens" as she removes a fan from her purse with a mortuary advertisement on the back. The beads of perspiration on her forehead slowly evaporate with the quick back and forth motions of the fan. She fans herself with one hand and continues to softly rub my arm with the other. "We are so sorry." The Reverend looks at his feet then back at me. "We must rest knowing Jean-Jacques is in a better place. He will have no more worries."

"Amen, yes, Jesus." The Mrs. Pastor throws her hand in the air and stares into the ceiling." I smile as I hold back my tears.

"How are you, sister?" The Mrs. rubs my arm in the same spot for so long it becomes irritated. I slowly step away from her and fold my arms across my chest. "I know it is hard, but God knows best, but dear, you have to eat!" She turns her nose upward; the wrinkles she attempts to hide with layers of makeup are pronounced. "You are about to disappear," she whispers.

"I am doing the best that can be expected. I

am still in disbelief." I walk to the sofa. They follow. "I am trying to press them to investigate."

"Sister, it appears to be an open and shut case." He looks at the Mrs. Pastor then casts his eyes on me. "Sometimes, our children are involved with things we know nothing about." I am surprised and insulted by the unexpected change in his position. The minister was the first person calling on social activists to mobilize. He stood on the church steps with a microphone at his mouth in front of news reporters demanding transparency. He opened his church to the neighborhood and the police with the hope of building a strong coalition. He led the call for an investigation. I don't know what has changed, but he sounds like the She Devil D.A.

"Boxing was Jean-Jacques's world. He did not own a gun. He had no use for a gun. He could take out a threat with one quick punch."

"Yes, that is what we want to talk to you about." He looks at the Mrs. Pastor. She bows her head as if she is giving the Reverend permission to speak. "The best way to bring attention to this is political mobilization." He looks at Mrs. Pastor; she is off cue. Their eyes meet; she quickly responds, "Thank you, Jesus. Amen."

"I am going to run for County Commissioner." He turns away from me and looks directly into the eyes of Mrs. Pastor. She smiles. They seem unnatural. It is almost as if they are rehearsing a part in a play, and the stage is my living room. "The best path to change is to work from the inside." He smiles. "The mayor appreciates all of the work done in our community." He looks toward Mrs. Pastor. "The best way to honor your son and the fallen officer is to honor them with a crime free community where we can all live."

"Amen, yes, Jesus, Thank you, Lord." They smile approvingly at one another.

"The relationship with the police has improved." The Reverend straightens his necktie and sticks his chest outward.

"Yes, Chandler was building bridges. He reached out to my son for help. He wanted Jean-Jacques to train some of the troubled young boys at the gym. Jean-Jacques would never hurt Chandler. No one in this community would hurt Chandler. Everyone loved him."

"There is a young man causing a lot of commotion at the corner." He interrupts and redirects the conversation. "Do you know anything about him?"

"No, I don't know anything about the corner." I stand. "My Jean-Jacques..."

"I do." My daughter quickly intervenes. "No one believes my brother killed Chandler. He is rallying the community to clear my brother's name. My brother would never..."

"Yes," he clears his throat, "We know he was a good kid."

I quickly become irritated with the Reverend and his puppet wife.

The silence becomes uncomfortable as the Reverend and Mrs. Pastor stare at me eyeball to eyeball waiting for a response. Words are running through my head but will not come to my mouth. My ability to make words seem to have suddenly ceased.

"My mother does not feel well." My daughter steps in front of me and escorts them to the door.

"I see." Mrs. Pastor scans me over again. She folds the hand fan and places it in her purse. She is a step behind her husband.

"There is surveillance of Gene Jack..." The Reverend stops at the threshold.

"Jean-Jacques," I correct him.

"Yes, excuse me, sisters. There is surveillance footage of the police finding drugs on your son. I have actually seen it with my own eyes."

"Liars! All of you are liars!" I shove the thick envelope filled with money in his chest. "Take your money! We don't need it!" My daughter quickly thanks them for their visit and closes the door. She stands still with her back against the door. Tears flow from her eyes like a river. She uses both hands to wipe them away. She walks to me with her arms open wide; she wraps them around me and pulls me close.

"Mama, come back to me," she whispers. "You are all I have." I want to open my mouth, but the words will not come. She leaves the living room and walks down the hall to the bathroom. A whiff of lavender hovers in the air. The water is turned on full blast. It sounds like a fierce rainstorm as it hits the bottom of the bathtub. She returns to the living room, takes my hand, and guides me to the bath. She helps me remove my clothes. I use her hand for balance as I step in the tub. She stares at me. Tears flow from her eyes. She wipes them away. "Come back to me. My natural family lost me. I don't have anyone. You are all I have."

Chapter 20
Josh

Strange vibes hover in the atmosphere. A camaraderie has formed among the *"I have to get me"* hustle crews. Neighborhood enemies have formed unusual alliances. Nuri, as Jermaine now calls himself, is no longer a lone ranger in his search for justice. His single man protest has morphed into a daily congregation of well-dressed men and women holding signs as they walk up and down the sidewalk demanding justice. Jean-Jacques was buried four months ago today. Except for a sporadic soundbite, the news media has forgotten the story. Law enforcement's promise of transparency was all in vain.

I am on my way to speak with Nuri about a twenty-dollar loan when a black limousine with dark tinted windows slowly passes the protestors. The driver exits the car and scans the surroundings before opening the rear passenger door. An olive skinned male with dark curly hair steps out the limousine and cautiously walks to one of the protestors who points in Nuri's direction. The man with dark hair approaches Nuri. They shake hands, exchange words, and Nuri gets into the limousine. The limo turns left on Harrison Road and leaves in the direction of Memorial Drive.

Jean-Jacques is not the first questionable

killing by a police officer. In the past, the community would accept the police account and eventually move on because most likely the deceased was a member of one of the many criminal enterprises that call Central Drive home. This time is different. Very few people are buying the police's narrative. Jean-Jacques did not fit the stereotype that led to his tragic end. The protests escalate each day and are parallel with the legal and illegal activity still flourishing on Central Drive. The only change is the community no longer patronizes the Pakistani convenience store. The Pakistani store parking lot is no longer filled with cars. Most cars that turn in the Pakistani parking lot have tags from out of state or addicts from the suburbs that come to score drugs. His neighborhood customers have abandoned him. In protests, they wait their turn in long line to buy gas at the Korean store.

I almost feel sorry for the Pakistani. He has somehow become the scapegoat for the neighborhood wrath. Jean-Jacques was killed behind the store, but the Pakistani did not pull the trigger. He is not taking his new position in the neighborhood very well. The wear and tear is all over his face. His hair is overgrown. The expansion of his abdomen to a beer belly seemingly happened over night. It is so pronounced that he walks like a baby just learning to take its first step. The protestors are relentless. They have no mercy.

"Please." His speech is slurred. "Leave from in front of my store." He places her hands together. "Please get away from my property."

"Give up them tapes!" The protestors scream from the sidewalk.

"Please." It is abnormal watching him exhibit manners and respect. "Please leave." He walks back inside his store. His distaste for black people is known throughout the neighborhood. Hell, I'm a junkie, and he speaks to me in a more respectful tone than he does the black law-abiding citizens who patronize his store. In the beginning, he cursed the protestors while hosting the police and providing free snacks and coffee. He allowed his store to be used as a place of respite for the police. He even assisted the police by pressing charges against the protestors for allegedly trespassing on his property. The protestors have proven to be a strategic group. After the first group of protestors were arrested, Nuri organized groups of men, women, and children who alternate standing in strategic places on the corner with their cell phones extended, filming all activity to fight bogus charges.

I sit under the tree with the day laborers. I reach into my bag for my beer when I see the black limousine approach Central Drive and Harrison Road. The limousine stopped in the middle of Harrison Road and then turned in the Korean store parking lot taking up three parking spaces. Nuri steps out. He walks to a fellow protestor. He leans close and speaks in his ear. They shake hands, embrace, and continue protesting.

"Mister," The Pakistani runs out of the store like a mad man when he sees Nuri. He stands bare feet with no shirt next to the gas station pump and yells across the street to Nuri. "Please, you are ruining my business. I have a family! Please stop this!"

"Give us the footage," Nuri mockingly yells back.

"Sir, I do not have videos." He places his hands together as if he is praying. "The videos are gone. I will pay you to leave. Please." His begging does nothing. His pleas fall on deaf ears. The protestors appear to yell louder, "No more Butter! No more Butter!" The defeated Pakistani storeowner walks back inside his empty store. I leave the almost comical exchange and hit up the Russian for work.

"Vladimir."

"I ain't seen you in a while." He scans me with his eyes from head to toe. "You are putting on a little weight."

"Yeah, I am doing better. I need some work. Need to send the kids some money." He looks at me a with hard stare. We both know I am lying.

"Send money to the kids?" He laughs. "You? Okay, today is your lucky day. Huey Newton and the gang reserved the banquet room in the back." I veer out the front store window. The crowd steadily increases in numbers. Cars pass honking their horns in solidarity. "Normally, I could care less about the hoodlums killing each other, but that boy." He shakes his head. "Damn that kid was a beast in the ring. If his crazy mother would have cooperated, we could all be filthy rich." He grinds his teeth and balls his fist.

"He was a great kid."

"Yeah, I have to agree. He kept his nose clean. Prepare the room. I will give you fifty bucks to your suicide fund." He laughs.

I grab a pan, fill it with water and bleach, and clean the tables. I place extra napkins and paper menus on the tables in the small private room in the back of the restaurant Vladimir calls the banquet room. The space is rarely used. Most people order their food and carry out. It is a fish joint, just a step above a fast-food burger joint, and a smart front for his illegal businesses. Vladimir does not deal drugs. He is a gambling promoter. He places bets on any and everything worthy of waging a bet. If you bet on high school, college, or professional sports, Vladimir is the man for you. He is an expert at fixing games for big payouts. The Russian agreed to allow Nuri space for a meeting in the back of the restaurant. Nuri's resilience and patience are paying off. He has replaced beer cans wrapped in brown paper bags with newspapers and posters protesting the police.

He is almost unrecognizable. The thin unshaven man with braids all over his head is now clean shaven, tie wearing, and rather handsome. He used to hustle on the corner but is now an entrepreneur. When he is not protesting, in addition to selling papers, every Friday and Saturday he operates a mobile auto detail business in front of the barber shop on the corner of Harrison Road and Memorial Drive. Nuri steps in Vladimir's office and stays about ten minutes then goes back outside. Truthfully, the Russian could care less about neighborhood politics; I was surprised he allowed space in his restaurant for the meeting until I noticed the line of protestors wrapped around the corner waiting to enter the restaurant. I did not expect a big turnout, but the space is standing room only.

"Josh, every attendant has to order ten dollars' worth of food and a drink before going in the back. Make sure you check the receipts."

I help everyone purchase their food and quickly guide them to the rear of the restaurant to the overcrowded banquet room. There were so many people the Russian agreed to give me five percent of the sales in addition to the fifty dollars. Nuri stood at the door and greeted each patron with a kiss on each cheek.

The crowd is diverse. Professionals, day laborers, and a few teachers from the neighborhood elementary and high school stand in solidarity with the protesters. A few of the neighborhood hustlers have also shown up. The scene looks like a black '60s or '70s civils rights gathering I have seen on television.

"Hello brothers and sisters" Nuri canvasses the room. "Brothers and sisters, I am going to get right to the point. Our brother we lovingly knew as Boxing Boy never carried a gun. He was never in trouble. Many of you have had the privilege of engaging him, and I am willing to bet my last dollar those encounters were nothing shy of pleasant and respectful. Sisters, many of you have given birth to gods just like our brother, but like me, they became distracted and unfocused. We are enamored by the flash, quick money, and made wrong choices that changed the trajectory our divine paths. We struggle in communities like this to take our rightful places." He looks straight into the eyes of the attendees. "Many of you knew Boxing Boy. Ask yourself, 'Have you ever seen him behave violently with anyone other than in the boxing ring or in self-defense?'" He canvasses the faces.

"Hell no!" One of the male attendees shouts. "He ain't fuck with nobody!"

"Brothers, our women are present." He raises both hands. "I know we are angry, but today we are going to show respect and love." He smiles. "Is that all right?" The crowd mumbles and nods in agreement.

"Every last one of these stores has cameras. Why haven't we seen footage? What are they hiding? I asked the Pakistani storeowner to pass the footage to a lawyer if he did not trust us. He called the police, banned me from his property, and tried to have me arrested for trespassing." He canvasses the room and appears pleased with the many heads nodding, affirming his position. "We all loved Detective Chandler. Not one of us would have hurt him. He has taken me to jail four maybe five times when I was drinking that poison or smoking that weaponized marijuana, but each time, it was for my own good. He loved this community." Tears slowly run down his face. "Each time, I would beg Detective Chandler for another chance. My tears and pleading did nothing to move him." He laughs behind tears. "He took me to jail anyway and would say, 'Give yourself a chance. Boy, stop being selfish. Think of your community and these youngins coming up. They are looking at you out here acting a fool. Don't your mama deserve more than this?' He would sometimes reach in his pocket and pass me a few bills for my commissary before taking me to jail." He shakes his head and looks into the sky. "Detective Chandler, I am going to give myself a chance."

"That's right!" Someone yells from the crowd.

"We can't let them get away with this. Not this time, brothers and sisters, not this time." He uses the back of his sleeve to wipe away tears. "We loved our Boxing Boy. He was our hope. He was what some of us wished we could have been." He wipes away another tear. "It has been four months." He holds up four fingers and scans the faces in the crowd. "Four months. What are the results of the investigation? Why don't we know any more today than we did the day Boxing Boy was murdered?" He looks around. "They are not investigating. Many of you have sent videos from your phones of the

Rogue cop who pulled the trigger. Some of the videos are very disturbing. Some of the shit our kids are subjected to with this rogue is unbelievable, but we need more when we take this to the media. We want heads to roll! We are not powerless!" He wipes tears from his eyes. "How much money did we spend in that Pakistani store?" He smiles. "That Pakistani would probably be willing to pay you to patronize his store. We have all but run him out of business. How much do you spend with the Koreans?" He looks around the room.

"We want justice! We want justice!" someone yells from the crowd.

"The storeowners do not care about you or your families." I want to stop him and remind him he is hosting a meeting in one of the storeowner's establishments. "We are using this facility because we are bringing business. The Russian don't give a damn about us." He smiles. "Some of you are good cooks." He points to an empty space next to the Shell gas station across the street. "I bet we could pool our money and cook for ourselves." Heads nod in agreement.

The meeting lasted two hours. This looks nothing like the community known for drugs and violence. The impact Nuri has made is unbelievable. The Russian probably made more legitimate money today than he made all week. As they leave, he invites the group back and promises to provide one free soft drink with each meal.

The impact may appear subtle but impactful none the less. It appears to be business as usual, but nothing could be farther from the truth. Miguel was back on the corner mixing in with the day laborers making sales only now he was not walking his kids to school; he was driving them. His customers are mostly white and getting younger by the day. The gun fights between the Mexicans and blacks continue, but there are intermittent moments of peace.

"Hermano qu podria maternos siquiente." Brother, they could kill us next, Miguel explains to a small gathering under the tree. "I will pay ten dollars for every photo or video I can use. If you have any pictures of this police officer." He removes a picture from his pocket, unfolds it, and raises it in the air so all can see. "If you have pictures of this cop harassing people, show it to me." Some of the crowd shake his hand in agreement while removing cell phones to scan through pictures. Others walk away whispering, "Inmigracion." Somehow, Nuri manages to make his fight a multicultural one, something no law enforcement officer, pastor, or activist could ever do in the community.

The community came together in solidarity to challenge the powers that be to clear a fallen hero's name, and after the meeting the protesters left a mess behind. Empty cups are thrown on the floor next to half-filled garbage bins. Ketchup is left splattered on several tables while napkins dispensaries are full and in plain sight. After the meeting, several attendees return to their protesting position on the corner while others congregate on the side of the building where the stench of marijuana stubbornly hovers in the air.

I go outside to pick up debris by the gas station pump and to see if Miguel is under the tree so I can let him know I would have cash later to do business when I notice someone has spray painted the outline of a dead body with the letters "R.I.P." on the side of the building. Graffiti has always been an issue but has gotten worse since Jean-Jacques' murder. Vladimir and the Korean agreed to pay fifty bucks each to paint over it.

It is late, almost one in the morning when I finish. As I put the cleaning supplies away and discard the paint, the cop with the new Rogue alias and two extremely muscular white males walk close behind a thin bald middle-aged white male with a graying goatee and tall medium complexioned black male with long locks. They walk down the narrow hall of the restaurant to the large room in the back. I assume the muscular men were bodyguards. I have never seen the four men before and become concerned when I notice all have dark metal semi-automatic pistols strapped underneath their shoulders.

The scene is odd, kind of like a board meeting; shot glasses surround top-shelf liquor bottles in the middle of the table. If this were downtown or Buckhead, it could be legit, but there is nothing legit that goes on in the back office behind the store late at night. Officer Whitley appears hung over. His clothes are usually wrinkled, hair a mess, and always in need of a shave, but he looks even messier and unkempt today.

I do not know whether to run or hide when I hear Vladimir speaking in his native language with the bald man with the gray goatee. One of the guards without warning casually steps to Officer Whitley and punches him in the throat. Whitley grabs his throat with both hands and rolls back and forth on the floor; strange sounds appear to be stuck in his throat. I make my way to the hall next to the kitchen and continue to sweep as the rogue cop fights hard to catch his breath. The two muscular men grab each of Officer Whitley's arms and pulls him off the floor. The thin one with the graying goatee inflicts powerful blows to his abdomen with a closed fist. Whitley screams, begs, pleads, and tries to negotiate with his torturers. The walls are thick; no one can hear him. The bald man removes a cigar from his mouth and presses it against the rogue cop's face until the embers turn to ash.

"You are such a fuck up! Stupid piece of shit!" He waves his hands and sits on the sofa. The two enforcers loosen Whitley's arms. He falls to the ground. "You have made a big mess!" One of the bodyguard's suspiciously stares at me and begins to walk in my direction until Vladimir calls his name.

"I was following your orders. It was you, Nicholai, who said any black boy in this neighborhood would do."

"You dumb shit!" The tall medium-complexion black male with the locks walks close to the beaten cop. His accent is thick and definitely East African. His shoulder and arm rise as if he is going to hit him. "You killed the best thing to these monkeys in this godforsaken neighborhood."

"How was I supposed to know? The old lady on the corner said he was a drug dealer." He reaches in his pocket, removes a small plastic bag, pours a small line of white powder on the back of his hand, and sniffs.

"You were supposed to get rid of the attention. You were supposed to get rid of these low-life thugs constantly attacking our heroin market. You were paid to get rid of the goody cop. The bitch cop was working with the community and making an unprecedented number of arrests, fucking up our business. Instead, you brought more attention."

Chapter 21
Benazir

It is 8:00, and I am still in bed. I have pressed the snooze button five times. It takes all the energy I can muster to leave my bed. My ankles are swollen, and my legs feel as if they weigh a ton. The baby has gotten so big I can no longer sleep in my favorite position. When I lay on my back, it feels as if the baby is pressing the air out of my lungs. My doctor says the baby already weighs seven pounds, and I have four more weeks until my due date. Gravity has maneuvered the baby to one side of my stomach. Navigating to a sitting position creates a lot of pressure in my back as the baby moves to the center. The load feels unusually heavy today.

I missed prenatal care the first trimester and half of the second, but the doctor assures me the baby is healthy. So much has happened, and I have not had the time to process it all. I am lonely, sad, and heartbroken. When I decided to have the baby, getting prenatal care was the farthest thing from my mind. I had not thought that far ahead. I assumed I would simply show up at the hospital and have a baby.

That is until I was questioned about my pregnancy by my coworker and friend Mina.

"How many months?" she asked one day while we were working.

"About three."

"Ooh?" She leaned back and propped her weight on one leg. "You too big for three." She pressed the large power button on the outdated vacuum and moved it up and down the carpet. "You should have the doctor check your dates again." I quickly looked away and gave my undivided attention to the bed I had been trying to make for the last ten minutes.

"You have gone to the doctor? Right?" She turned the vacuum off.

"My husband is in school." It took a few minutes to form a response. "All of our money is used for school fees."

"Ah, this is America." She smiled. "You don't have to pay."

"No?" I was used to the Brute complaining about the cost of health care, food, water, gas, and air.

"The government says you have a baby, you see the doctor for free, and you get free milk for the baby." She smiled.

"Really?" I was excited but reluctant. I was an adult running away from home. "We want to keep our news away from our parents for a while. They will be disappointed that we have children before he finishes the degree."

"Who will tell them?" She laughed. "This is America. You are a big woman? For a small fee, I will take you to the county office to apply for medical care. Do you have your documents?"

"Documents?"

"Birth certificate, social security number."

"Yes. I have documents."

"That is all you need." I had so many reasons to thank the girl I would have considered a simple peasant under different circumstances. In my old life, our paths would never cross. The Brute would have never allowed her at the dinner table. In all honesty, I would have never found common ground if not for my predicament. I cringe at the thought the Brute and I have anything in common.

I was scared but relieved to see the doctor. Mina had one day off per week, but Mrs. Bina was out of town, and Mr. Bina needed her to work. She couldn't accompany me, so I went alone.

I drove past the clinic several times as the building looked like an old gymnasium. It did not look like the doctor offices I am accustomed to visiting back home. The parking lot was made of gravel; there were no white lines outlining individual spaces. Cars are parked in no particular pattern. Though I had an appointment, the line to check in with the receptionist extended out the door to the sidewalk.

I sit in the overcrowded waiting area feeling more alone, afraid and uncertain than I did the night I left home. None of the patients look like me. I am the only Pakistani in the building. I am also the only patient sitting alone. The others are accompanied by doting husbands, boyfriends or supportive mothers.

I sat with the patient information sheet in my lap trying to answer the questions as best I could. The form had been copied so many times the text was lopsided.

After sitting in soiled chairs for over an hour, I was finally able to see the doctor. I am accustomed to women doctors who look like me. When an elderly white man with a Santa Claus beard greeted me, I was reluctant and considered leaving. The exam room was outdated. The dull and dingy paint in the exam room was beginning to chip away. Large black nobs and buttons stick out on teal green diagnostic machines. There was no touch monitors in the entire room. The doctor tells jokes that I do not understand to break the ice as he placed the cold stethoscope on my stomach. I was excited when I heard the baby's heartbeat for the first time; however, my happiness was short lived. The realization I would endure the experience alone became apparent when I could not answer questions on the paternal health questionnaire. I had not realized the magnitude of my decision. I have seen many women, mostly black, pass through the store with children and no sign of a man. They made parenting look easy.

The alarm sounds off. I am finally able to get out of bed and place my feet on the floor. An intense pain travels from my right side down to my thigh. The doctor says it is sciatica and common in pregnant women. He permits taking over the counter pain medicine, but I will not risk anything happening to this baby. I endure the pain, limp to the bathroom, and wash my face. I sniff my armpits. I need a shower, but a sponge bath will have to suffice. I straighten up the house and take baby steps to the door. I manage to get in the car and drive the twenty-minute ride that seems like an hour because the route from my house to work is a two-lane highway with buildings several miles apart. As I turn off the main road into the lopsided parking lot filled with potholes, I notice the parking lot has more cars than usual.

Mina stands beside her cleaning cart on the side of the building out of view of the main office. I sit in my car for several minutes and observe her strange behavior. She constantly looks over her shoulder while cleaning the same spot on the window. She alternates cleaning the window and moving a worn-out broom back and forth along the walkway. She periodically stops the phantom cleaning and peruses the parking lot. She allows the broom to fall on the floor and begins to clean the outside of the soft drink machine. She waves her hand frantically to get my attention as I exit the car. I close the door of the secondhand car she allowed me to purchase and register in her name for a small fee and walk with extreme caution to the soft drink machine where Mina is fully engaged in fictitious cleaning. I notice a cut on her lip and a dark circle around her eye.

"What happened? Why are all of these cars here?"

"Mr. Bina's family is moving here to help with his businesses. He is getting suspicious." She places her finger to her lip and instructs me to quiet my voice. "Mr. Bina keeps asking questions about your family." Mr. Bina is the owner of the hotel as well as several slum properties in the small town. When I first arrived, Mina introduced me to his wife who gave me a job and agreed to pay cash for cleaning the rooms and the rat and roach infested restaurant next to the hotel. "I told him your husband is home now. He wants to meet him."

"Did Mr. Bina hit you? Did he do this to your face?" I embrace her face with both hands.

"No worries, he punches like a girl." She removes my hands from her face. "Don't go inside." She grabs hold to my arm so tight I cannot move. Her affect is familiar. I see my mother's eyes in her eyes. It is a defeated look, the result of allowing someone to drain all your power. I take her suggestion seriously.

"I will not go inside." He owes me for one week's pay; he can have it. The fear and concern in Mina's eyes are real.

"You should not come back."

"Saturday coming is your day off." My voice cracks as I fight back the tears. "Call me and I will meet you."

"That will be nice." She pushes me away and escorts me to my car. Mina has become a good friend, more like the sister I never had. She prepares traditional foods for me to eat, makes teas for me to drink, for a small fee, to ensure my baby will be healthy.

I leave the hotel and drive the back roads home. I do not feel well and did not feel like working anyway. I drive around aimlessly until I spot a convenience store that looks almost identical to the Brute's store on Central Drive. I park the car. As I enter the store, a tall, slim Sikh greets me with a bright smile. He is nothing like the Brute. People freely walk about the store. I walk to the back of the store to the freezer, choose a pint of Black Walnut ice cream, and bring it to the counter.

"Hello, young lady." His smile is contagious. "The little one wants ice cream." His eyes fall to my bulging stomach.

"Hello." I touch my stomach. "Yes, he is a greedy one."

"It appears that it will not be long now." He smiles. "Is this the first child?"

"Yes."

"You and your husband are very blessed. That will be $2.89, my dear." He places my ice cream in a black plastic bag without me asking for one. The brute never offers a bag. A customer could have two handfuls of loose candy and have to request a bag. Depending on his mood, if a child is unaccompanied by an adult and requests a bag, he will instruct the child to stuff the candy in their pockets. I remove the money from my purse, pass it to the clerk, grab my bag, and leave.

I am not ready to go home, so I engage in what I read is called nesting. I stop at the thrift store I pass daily on my travel to work. It is more of an open barn than a storefront. Old gasoline signs are nailed on the wall. Empty soft drink bottles are positioned on an old wooden table in no particular order. I walk up wobbly dry rotting steps into an open area filled with secondhand furniture, vintage clothing, and used kitchen ware. I browse the furniture section and find a second-hand white bassinette.

"That there is in good shape." An elderly man in faded overalls with brown crust in the corner of his mouth walks over and stands behind me looking over my shoulders. "It just came in yesterday." His southern accent is thick.

"How much?"

"Well," he scratches his head then looks at my protruding abdomen. "You can have it for fifty bucks."

"I will give forty-five."

"You got a deal." I pass him the money. He takes the money, walks away, and attends to an older woman entering the store. I would have thought the clerk would have called someone to assist in placing the item in the car, but he does not. It takes a lot of maneuvering, but I somehow manage to drag it out the store and get the bassinette in the back seat. I am tired and hungry. I finally arrive at the small cottage I rent for three-hundred dollars a month and turn the television to the news. The coverage of Panther's shooting has all but disappeared. It is as if he never existed. I second-guess my decision. I am overwhelmed, anxious, and have a host of feelings I cannot name. I don't know what made me believe I could pull this off. Prior to this desperate move, I never lived on my own.

I am vulnerable. Mina is my only fried. I fear she is like my mother, shackled to Duty and Tradition, but she is all I have right now.

The idle time I have as I wait for Saturday drives me crazy. I spend the days watching television and eating everything in sight. I would not be surprised if I gained ten pounds. I was anxious to see Mina. Her education is not formal, but she reads a lot and is savvy. She came to this country under the guise of a daughter to a pediatrician. I suspect she is cheap labor to Mr. Bina and probably a niece or cousin who did not score well on exams to enter a university. I once picked up her pay envelope by mistake and found a measly one hundred dollars inside.

"Is this all you are paid? You work over eighty hours per week!" When she was not cleaning, she worked the receptionist desk at night. "One hundred dollars is slave labor."

"This is not your concern." She grabbed the envelope and placed it in her pocket. Mina is very smart but enslaved to old fashion values. She is to marry next summer. I doubt she has ever met her groom.

I ring her phone for three days. She is probably too busy to answer my calls. She is most likely the only person cleaning the rooms and restaurants. Mr. Bina is cheap. He will most likely not hire someone to assist her. I call her Friday during her usual break time and am beyond happy when she answers my call.

"Tomorrow is your day off. Do you want to go for a drive with me?"

"Yes." The excitement in her voice is encouraging.

"I will meet you at the gas station down the street from the hotel." I am cautious. I have known Mina for over four months, but I don't feel comfortable entertaining her at my house. We have created a bond, but I don't trust subservient women. The right amount of pressure can make a submissive woman forget loyalty. "I will call you tomorrow." I quickly hang up the phone. My sciatic nerve is acting up again. My stomach is so tight I can feel my skin stretch. This baby has its own personality. It gets lively at night, and its kicks feel more like stomps.

I am asleep when I hear the phone ring. At first, I think I'm dreaming, but by the fourth ring, I am conscious "Hello."

"It's Mina." She speaks so softly I can barely hear her. "I will meet you down the street from the hotel."

"I will be there in twenty minutes." I quickly get dressed and wobble out the house to the car to meet her. I am so excited to see her I drive ten miles per hour over the speed limit. She stands at the gas station behind the telephone booth. I feel as if we are on a clandestine mission. I shift the transmission to park, run to her, and tightly embrace her.

"Did you tell your uncle where you are going?"

"No." She looks around carefully to ensure no one is following. "You don't have a husband." It was a statement and question mixed in one.

"Why are you asking?"

"My uncle suspects you are running away. I eavesdropped on his conversation with his brother visiting from Birmingham."

"Did you say anything?"

"No, of course not. We are friends. Remember? I was thinking maybe when you have your baby, I could come with you. I know you do not plan to stay here."

"No, I have no intention of staying here."

"Will you reunite with the father?"

"No, he was murdered."

"Did your parents...?" She inhales deeply and places her hand over her mouth.

"No, they did not have anything to do with it." I could go into detail of how Panther was murdered, but that would be too much. We drive Interstate 85 North straight to Atlanta. Once we reach Atlanta, I take the scenic route, so she can see the downtown skyline.

"I would love to live here. Perhaps, if I have to marry, my husband and I could make this place our home." I am uneasy when she speaks of her husband but encouraged as she has never used "if" when speaking of her nuptials. She becomes silent and engrossed in the view of the city. "This is where you are from?"

"Yes, born and raised." I exit Interstate 85 at Jimmy Carter Boulevard; after several miles, Jimmy Carter changes to Mountain Industrial then Harrison Road which crosses over Central Drive. I am amazed how life changes in a small amount of time. All the stores are bustling with activity except for the Brute's. The parking lot is empty. The grass is overgrown. There is a gathering of about eighty people across the street at the Korean store and on the sidewalk in front of the Brute's store. I park the car at the Korean store on the side farthest away from the Brute's store. I see White Junkie Boy standing under a tree talking to a group of day laborers. I motion for him to come close.

"Hi." I forgot his name and doubt if he would be okay with White Junkie Boy.

"How are you?" His eyes immediately land on my stomach. He extends his arms toward me as if he wants to touch it. His dirty nails and knuckles stand out against his white skin. Small blisters sit between his fingers. I step away. "How have you been? I have not seen you around since the funeral. Are you okay?" His tone is fatherly or at least what I imagine a fatherly tone would be.

"I am fine."

"Jean-Jacques told me about the baby." His eyes become glassy. "He was happy, scared but happy." He nervously chuckles.

"Yes." I rub my hand over my stomach. Mina stands away taking it all in. "What is all of this about?"

"People are still angry. Everyone loved Jean-Jacques. Nuri is paying people for photos or videos of Jean-Jacques and the police officer that shot him. He thinks he can put something together to clear Jean-Jacques' name."

"Nuri?"

"The black guy with the suit and bowtie."

"Jermaine?" I can't believe my eyes. "Is that Jermaine?"

"He calls himself Nuri. He changed his name." Someone calls to White Junkie Boy. He turns and walks away.

"Hey," I call to him. "Don't tell anyone I was here."

Chapter 22
Josh

Thoughts bounce off my brain like a ping pong ball. I need a sack of my special medicine to slow everything down. Running out of the medicine is scary. Needing the medicine and not being able to immediately get it is excruciating. When I first started using, I was in control. It was cool and almost fun, but things quickly spiraled out of control. I use when I don't want to, and even when I want to use, it does not work like it used to. I have gone three days without my medicine, but the withdrawals are once again taking a toll. I am not doing well managing Monster. I try to fight through the cravings. Sometimes I win, but most of the time, I lose. I am making progress. I have been working with the day laborers to earn money but also use the time as an opportunity to leave the scene and get away from Central Drive.

I had to do something to break the cycle. I was in a grip so bad I stopped leaving the neighborhood, set up camp, and stopped going home. Working with the day laborers is an opportunity to do something different and earn a little money. I jumped on the back of a construction truck for the first time two weeks ago. I was the only white boy in the mix of six Mexicans. My heart rate increased, and my temperature quickly rose. I was slightly paranoid. Anxiety took over once we turned right on Memorial Drive. I became overwhelmed and fearful when I realized I was actually leaving Central Drive. I stood while the truck was moving with the intention of jumping out. I did not factor the truck was traveling at least 45 miles per hour, and I would have most likely burst my head wide open.

"We don't bite, amigo." One of the workers grabbed my shirt and pulled me back to a sitting position. I was not uncomfortable being the only white person in a truck full of Mexicans. I panicked and became anxious because leaving Central Drive meant leaving the suppliers of my medicine.

By the time we exited Interstate 285 to Interstate 20, my heart rate began to stabilize. I was calm and relaxed by the time we reached our destination, an old warehouse under renovation to create a live, work, play community. It was a floor demolition and installation job in South Atlanta. The labor was pure physical. The contractor had one commercial grade, gasoline powered Jack Hammer for himself. The Mexicans and I used Jack Hammers powered by human muscle. I was surprised I had not lost my athleticism and could keep up with the Mexicans who are notorious on Central Drive for their ability to perform manual labor. I worked hard and kept up all morning, but by noon, the withdrawals were kicking my ass. The contractor became furious that I spent so much time in the bathroom. At the end of the day, he paid the other workers $125 and paid me $100. I didn't argue about the difference in pay. I was grateful for the experience.

It felt good behaving like a responsible adult for the day. I made it through the cravings but well aware the real fight will begin when I am dropped off at the store on the corner of Harrison Road and Central Drive. If I go to the apartment, I will have to share the money with Simone. In less than an hour, I will be broke and on the grind again. I opt to hang out on the corner and sleep on the bus stop bench. It was an uncomfortable sleep, but better than the alternative.

I am usually passed out or sitting around other people in abandoned apartments, scraping residue from discarded foil or spoons at night. I am not usually out late and surprised to see that even in the wee hours of the morning, people were still pounding the pavement on Central Drive. Some of these people I had never seen before. The dealers loiter in front of the store waiting for customers. Cars from northern counties cruised up and down Central Drive until they spot their familiar dealer. A black Mercedes and white BMW with New York tags grabbed my attention as they parked on the side of the Pakistani store. The drivers exited their cars and casually walked across the street to the Korean store.

When I first landed on Central Drive, the Mexicans had the black tar on lock, and the blacks owned the crack cocaine market. Most of the crack addicts are gone. Where they went? I don't know. There are a few, but most have disappeared. Many of the black dealers have gone bankrupt. The County Marshall attaches dispossessory notices on their doors every other month, and their fancy cars are getting repossessed daily. Every day, long bed tow trucks cruise the neighborhood looking for cars the owners try to hide.

Many of the black drug dealers became angry at the Mexicans who created a lucrative market with their high quality, cheap heroin. The financial disparities created a lot of tension and caused many gun battles. However, the current political climate is slowly balancing the drug market. The black drug dealers should thank the new political agenda that focuses on deportation of illegals. The Mexicans have been forced to share the business. The immigration raids shake a lot of them, so the Mexicans have allowed the black dealers to have the streets at night. At sundown, Miguel and his cohorts are nowhere to be found.

My heart is filled with gratitude when I open my eyes and see the sun rise and know I made it through the night. I grab my backpack, throw it on my shoulder, and walk across the street to the Korean store. The Pakistani store no longer opens early. The protestors have almost run him out of business. I purchase a white T-shirt and an overpriced bar of soap. I cross the street and go behind the Pakistani store, clean up, then run back across the street, stand with the Mexicans, and wait for work with the other day laborers.

"You." The tile contractor I worked for yesterday stops me from boarding the truck. He points directly at me; disdain covers his face. "No way."

"Boss, I was not feeling well yesterday. Give me another shot. I really need the money. I am better now."

"No way."

"I will work for 25.00 less than you pay the amigos." He pauses for several seconds then uses hand gestures to signal permission to board the truck. The truth is the few hours away from Central Drive motivate me to keep trying to kick this viscous habit. I mostly listen, but sometimes join in conversations about wives, politics, and sports. Conversing with people about family and children feels weird. I have forgotten what it is like to have normal conversation.

Today, instead of eating at the site, we walk across the street and purchase burgers. In my past life, I was accustomed to dining in five-star restaurants with quality cut meats. A burger joint would not excite me, but for the past year, my addiction consumed everything. I am so low I feel as if I am not good enough to be in this greasy burger joint.

After lunch, I go back to work feeling fucked up as I think about the mess I have made of my life. It's been three days since I used. The medicine relieves the physical pain but also numbs my emotions. I feel everything and feel like a zero. I have not seen my wife or children. I forgot what my baby looks like. I am the screw up my mother always knew I was, which is why she spent so much time and money covering my fuck ups.

I am engulfed in my work when Julio taps my shoulder. "Quitting time. Pack it up."

"You did well today." The contractor shakes my hand. "I have another job next week. If you are around, let's make this money." The contractor pays all of us $150. I was expecting $125. I take my money and add it to the small stack I already have. My stomach begins to boil, at the sight of the cash. My sweat glands are working overtime. I have purposely stayed away from Simone and the crew, but right now, she is occupying my mind. I have money. She will pretend to be angry, but she will let me in if I have cash. The contractor drops us off at the corner. The Mexicans walk to their respective apartments. I stop at the Korean Store and purchase two beers and a bottle of water. As I leave the store, I pass five bucks to a young white kid who looks to be about seventeen years old. His hair is greasy, his clothes are covered with stains, and he wreaks of urine and unwashed body parts. He does not go inside the store; instead, he stands in the same position, and continues to collect donations for his self-destruction fund.

I walk behind the store, squeeze through an opening in the fence, and walk past a row of abandoned apartments to Simone's new abandominium. I knock on the door. The smell of old chicken grease mixed with the smell of an unflushed toilet hits like a ton of bricks when she opens the door. The water company has probably turned the water off and taken the meter, so the water can't be illegally turned on.

"Where have you been?" She has lost weight in a little over a week. The whites of her eyes are yellowing. "If you want to come in, you have to pay your way." Simone usually charges one hundred bucks per week for each room as if she has a legal lease. This is another abandoned apartment she has broken into and paid someone to illegally turn on the power. She has new thrown out furniture to replace the old thrown out furniture she has to leave behind every time she is forced to move.

"I have money."

"Where you get money? Wifey put you back on?" She knows I do not like for her to speak of my wife. She is throwing daggers to trigger me.

"No, I have been working."

"I heard." I pass her a twenty. "I hear you been on the corner protesting, too." She laughs.

"What they did to that boy was foul." I leave her in the living room, step over passed out bodies, and go to a back room. I remove the bottle of water from my bag, remove my gear from my pocket, and place everything on the dingy mattress positioned in the middle of the floor. My entire body shakes at the sight of the gear and the anticipation of the relief once I get the medicine in my veins. I wrap the tourniquet tight around my arm. I place the medicine and a couple of drops of water on a spoon, heat it with a lighter and was getting ready to syphon the medicine in the needle when I hear a small army of footsteps run past the window. I slowly stand, peep out of the window, and see several officers protected with bulletproof vest and combat gear run past the rear gate behind the retaining wall toward the front of the building. I grab my gear, throw it in my bag, unlock the window, and ease it open.

"The cops are coming!" I nudge the guy passed out next to me with my feet. I hear a loud bang and ear-piercing screams from people in the front of the apartment. The guy quickly pulls himself together as someone in the front of the apartment yells, "Cops." We jump out of the window, climb the retaining wall, jump the fence, and sprint in opposite directions. I sprint like I did as a young man on the football field. I turn the corner to Central Drive and run into a small army of officers.

"On the ground! On the ground!" I fall to the ground, lay spread eagle with my face on the broken sidewalk. The officer notices the tourniquet still tied on my arm. He searches my pockets, removes foil, a burned spoon, and three baggies of heroin. "You are under arrest for violation of a Georgia controlled substance."

"This shit ain't mine!" The officer bends

forward in a fit of laughter as he pulls rubber gloves over his hands, unties the tourniquet from my arm, and places it in a plastic bag. He grabs my shoulders, helps me to my feet, and leads me to the front of the apartment building. I stand on the side of a police van next to six other men. One by one, we are loaded into the white van. The officer orders us to sit on hard metal seats before placing cuffs around our ankles and connecting the cuffs to iron hooks at the bottom of the van. I look out the window and see the police lead a line of people including two women and several children from an abandoned apartment across the street to a black van with dark, tinted windows.

An officer closes the back of the van then walks around to the passenger side. The van's engine roars loud then cuts off. The driver taps the accelerator three times and turns the ignition again. The van jerks as the driver shifts the gear from park to drive. I am shaken. Paranoia sets in at the roar of the van's engine. The van travels north on Central Drive. We tumble off the seats and over each other as the van comes to a quick stop to prevent running over a group of protestors standing in the middle of the crosswalk. "Look out the window! Look at the phone!" The protestors surround the van and videotape the faces of everyone. I look out the back window and observe a line of people with their hands cuffed behind their backs. Simone is the first in line. She bends forward, crying hysterically. She is on paper and has missed several appointments with her probation officer. This violation will most likely land her in prison.

Protestors slowly leave the crosswalk and allow the van to proceed. The crowd carries signs that read *"No More Butter!"* Only now the signs are professionally printed instead of handwritten.

I alternate between relief and anxiety as we pass the protestors. The van turns left onto Harrison Road in route the county jail. By the time we reach the jail, I slowly gain acceptance. I begin to look at my predicament as an opportunity as I stand in line to be processed into the jail.

"Will you make bond?" The detention officer's voice is flat and void of emotion. He sits at an old desk with an outdated bubble back computer monitor and asks the same question to all the detainees.

"No," I answer as I look at the tall metal door with the humongous locks.

"Follow the green arrows." I follow the green arrows to a hallway with three cubicles. An androgynous officer greets me. I don't know whether I should say "Yes, Ma'am, or yes, Sir." I glance at the officer's chest and pelvic area and still can't determine if the officer is male or female.

"Undress and place your clothes in this bag." The officer passes a brown paper bag. "When you are done, place the bag on the table." I undress and place my clothes in the paper bag. The officer steps behind me. "Bend forward, spread your buttocks, and cough." I spread my cheeks and cough as instructed. "Sir, unless you want an anal exam, you will need to cough harder." The detention officer removes a wrinkled latex glove from a box. My heart rate doubles. Perspiration drips down the side of my face when the officer pops the glove against his or her wrist. I cough so hard it feels as if my tonsils will detach and fly out my mouth. "That is better. Follow the red line to the shower." She or he passes a large orange jumpsuit and a pair of hard, plastic, brown slides. I walk past five naked men, careful to keep my eyes on the floor, and take my place under a vacant showerhead. The hot water feels good on my skin. I have not been in a hot shower in a while. Bathing in a bucket or standing under cold water does not compare to hot water spraying out a showerhead.

I leave the shower and dry with a dingy white towel that feels like a Brillo pad against my skin, stand in line, and wait for the detention officer to assign a cell. There are no available beds. He passes me a thin plastic mat and assigns me to a corner on the floor. I sleep the entire first day after I am processed in the jail. I wake up, briefly leave my mat, and watch TV in the sitting area. The endless noise and lackluster conversation drown the sound from the television. After a fight breaks out and a few chairs are thrown, I leave the sitting area, go back to my cell, and lay on my assigned mat.

Thoughts of Rebecca and my kids occupy my mind. I am compelled to call, but the guilt I feel is overwhelming. I leave the cell and stand in line, pick up the handset, and place it back in the cradle three times before I finally get the nerve to make the call. I am not sure if she will accept it. I have not contributed to my household in forever; I feel like a zero making the collect call. The ringing stops. I hear Rebecca's crisp southern voice. The automated operator instructs her to press one to accept the call or two to decline. I pray she presses one. I did not bother to speak with Rebecca while free. Everything I needed and the people I needed to talk too were within walking distance. I am speechless when she accepts the collect call.

"How are you?" I hear the kids in the background and feel my voice crack.

"I am fine. I am getting ready to drop the

kids off at my mother's. I have a job interview today. In another week or so, I hope I will be teaching third grade." The joy in her voice comes through the phone. I am shocked that she has sought employment. Rebecca graduated from college with a degree in early childhood education but immediately stopped working after we married. She accompanied mother on her many social engagements which left little time for work.

"Wow, that is great."

"I have no choice. Our children have to eat." Guilt has my mouth glued shut. I feel like a minus zero for not providing for my family.

"Can I speak with the kids?"

"No." She pauses. I detect sympathy. "I don't feel like explaining your absence. Things are hard enough. Your mother is evicting us from the house. She has given me sixty days to vacate."

"What?" I can't believe my ears. "I will speak with her."

"Don't bother. I am sure I will get this job. One of my mother's sorority sister's daughter is the principal at the school. Are you taking care of yourself?" I am surprised she inquiries about my well-being.

"I am doing the best I can. I managed to stay clean for a few days, and then I fucked up."

"At least you are trying." She pauses. "So are we going to ignore this big elephant? Can we discuss why you are calling from jail?" We both laugh.

"There was a raid at the place I was staying. I got caught up in it. They found drugs on me."

"What did your mother say? What time is she coming to bail you out?"

"She is not coming. I did not call her. I am

going to sit this one out."

"That is a good start." I did not expect the compassion. I don't deserve it.

"Is it okay if I call sometimes? I am going to put up a fight this time." My voice cracks. "Wow, I have seen so much. I am so sorry. If I get the opportunity, I am going to make this up to you and the kids."

"Shush. Take care of yourself. The kids and I are good. Call me later. I have to get going or I am going to be late." She ends the call.

When I leave the phone area, other inmates are lining up for food trays. I told myself that I would not eat anything until I leave this place. The food smells stale and looks unsafe for human consumption. What is placed on the tray has no resemblance to food, but the hunger pangs are excruciating. I grab my tray, sit down at the table alone, and begin to eat my sandwich. Just as I open my mouth to take the first bite, it is snatched out my hand. The hard blow to my face takes me by surprise. My bottom lip gets caught on the edge of my teeth. The salty, iron taste of blood mixed with a small bite of the stale bologna sandwich makes my stomach turn. Darrell, as he is called, walks away confident there will be no repercussion. Perhaps he believes this athletic body is for show. Maybe he believes I am a white man in fear of his blackness. I have endured a lot of self-induced pain. He does not know the damage I have done to myself and the inner anger it has caused. He does not know I used to spar with the best boxer in the South.

I close my eyes and hear Jean-Jacques in my ear. Keep your hands up! Balance on your toes! Bob and weave! I see Jean-Jacques' smile, and it gives me life. Confident there will be no answer to his transgression; he has taken a third bite of my sandwich. He opens his mouth to take another, and instead of the sandwich, his mouth is filled with my fist. His head snaps backwards. By the time he knows what is happening, I am all over him, pounding his body with powerful left and right blows.

"Come on, man. It was just a sandwich. You are going to kill him over a sandwich?" Other inmates pull me away before the guards enter the pod.

"Don't fuck with me, bitch!" I yell. "Dude, I am not the one! Not to-motherfucking-day!" I walk away and go back to my cell, praying I can make it through Sunday night. Court is set for Monday where I will see a judge. I borrow paper and a pencil to write a letter to Rebecca. I have no intention of mailing the letter. At this point, my words most likely mean nothing to her.

. . .

"Line 'em up?" The guards call everyone with a Monday court date. Darrell stands in line in front of me. His lip is burst open, and his eyes are swollen. I am prepared to finish what he started should his ego get the best of him, and he decides to step to me again. When the bailiff calls my name, I expect to meet with the court appointed attorney. Instead, Mr. Greenspan, our family attorney, approaches the bench on my behalf.

"Hello, your honor. I will be entering a plea of No Lo on behalf of my client." He places his briefcase on the table. "Your honor, my client is from a very respectable family. He is addicted to opiates and would very much like to get treatment for his addiction." And just like that, I have a get out of jail card. I should go home to my mother's or a treatment center, yet even after the brief stay in jail, the magnetic pull to Central Drive is stronger than my common sense. The promise I made to Rebecca, who must have contacted my mother, means nothing. I borrow a few dollars from Mr. Greenspan, instructing him to add it to my mother's bill, walk to the corner, and wait for the next bus. My stomach begins to bubble as the bus travels down Memorial Drive. I become agitated and annoyed with the driver as the bus stops for passengers to board and exit the bus. I am standing at the door waiting for the door to open when the bus finally reaches my stop.

"Hey you." Nuri leaves his post on the sidewalk next to the Pakistani store as I exit the bus. The other owners are taking notice and have stopped the anonymous phone calls to the police to have the protestors removed.

"What's up?" We shake hands with one hand and embrace with the other. "I have not seen you around in a few days. We are having a meeting at the gym where Jean-Jacques trained."

"Why not use the restaurant again?"

"We need more space." He leans closer. "We have footage that makes us believe the Russian is a Russian. We are going to look at the footage and would like for you to come when we take our findings to the media. We believe your white privilege can be an asset." He laughs, but we both know he is serious.

"Why would you believe Vladimir is involved?"

"He is not involved in the murder of Boxing

Boy, but there is so much crime committed by these store owners. Somehow, they never get arrested. Us melanin kissed Gods are the only ones going to jail in this neighborhood. We have to trust our own."

"You did notice that I am white."

"Yeah, you a different kind of white. Your spirit is a little different than your Aryan brothers." His eyes travel from my greasy, uncut, and tangled hair to my run over shoes back to my puffy eyes. "You seem to be struggling with some of the same demons that affect many of us in this neighborhood."

Chapter 23
Benazir

The pain starts on the side of my right leg then travels upward to the side of my right buttock before settling in an excruciating cramp in the middle of my back. The doctor says the extra weight from an enormous baby is the culprit. I have gained sixty pounds, and most of it is baby weight. The doctor assures me the sciatica will go away once I have the baby and lose the weight.

Moving around eases the pain. I walk out the front door, stand on the porch, and admire the landscape filled with lush greenery and blooming flowers. I leave the porch and walk around the perimeter of the yard; the pain slowly goes away. I am surprised I never explored the spacious yard. My routine has been working and home with little activity in between. I make my way to an old metal, rusty chair that sits lopsided under a tall and thick pecan tree that must be at least a hundred years old. The long drooping branches provide ample shade from the sun.

Country life is peaceful, but I miss the city. There was never a dull moment on Central Drive. I meditate on the predicament I find myself, but it is far too late to second-guess my decision. I was so engulfed in the memory of my Panther that I did not properly think of the long-term consequences. This is so much more than I bargained for. I left everything I know. My only friend is a nice loyal peasant; if I were not in this situation, I would not entertain her beyond a passing salutation. I hate to admit the Brute was right. My life was privileged, and I had much to be grateful for.

My eyelids are heavy; I can't keep them open. The cool breeze and the sound of cars cutting through the wind is relaxing. I had fallen asleep when an intense pain jolts me awake. It begins as a dull cramp then escalates to a pain so intense it feels as if sharp knives pierce each side of my uterus. I grab hold to each side of the chair and pull myself to my feet. After a few minutes, the pain subsides. I leave the shaded space under the tree and walk back to the house. I reach down and pick one of the yellow lilies that line each side of the concrete walkway that extends from the front door to the curb and place it in front of my nose. I inhale deeply when another cramp travels from one side of my uterus to the other. It is so painful it stops me in my tracks.

I have read several books on childbirth, watched several videos, but nothing prepared me for the panic when warm liquid soaks my underpants then travels down my legs. No matter how tight I contract my Kegel muscle, the flow will not stop. Panic and despair creep in. I cannot remember the emergency plan I have practiced a thousand times to prepare for this moment. Fear and panic morph into anger. I wish my mother was here to share the experience with me, guide me through the process, and teach me all the things the books do not. Right now, I hate her as much as I hate the Brute.

I am spiraling into a dark space. I am

overcome with anger when I think of the white racist cop that took Panther away from me, leaving me to experience this alone. I remove the cell from my pocket and scroll through the contacts until I find the doctor's phone number. His answering service picks up the call on the second ring. The receptionist takes my name, phone number, and advises the doctor will call back in a few minutes.

I don't know what I expected, but this is not the answer I wanted to hear. I didn't want the doctor to come to my house, but simply taking a message and waiting on a return call seem too simple of a response for something as complex as having a baby. I am a bag of nerves as I wait for the doctor's call. The Nurse Practitioner responds instead of the doctor; she asks a series of questions. I try to conceal my annoyance as I was expecting to speak with my doctor. The Nurse Practitioner advises to come to the hospital when the contractions are five minutes apart.

I wobble to an oversized loveseat and turn on the television to pass time. I flip through the channels until I notice a familiar scene on the Atlanta local news. The large fathead of Panther in a boxing pose draws me in. I visited Panther's stepfather's gym a couple of times, and the colorful fathead of my Panther sticks out among black and white photographs of boxers who have trained at the gym. I increase the volume. Members of the boxing team stand behind Panther's stepfather, Jermaine who now calls himself Nuri, and White Junkie Boy who is dressed in a suit and tie but somehow still looks like a junkie.

The Brute watches the evening news nightly on a small television that sits next to the cash register. Unfortunately, I was forced to endure it with him, but this reporter is new to me. He appears past reporting age. His toupee is off-centered and sits awkward on top of his head. The lapel on his polyester jacket is wide and almost touch his shoulders. He asks a series of questions and places labels on my Panther that infuriate me. Thug, gang member, drugs are words that do not belong in the same sentence with Panther.

"The toxicology report states there was marijuana in his system." The elderly reporter sits back in his seat; his legs are crossed at his thighs.

"I don't believe that," Nuri quickly responds. "Boxing Boy didn't do drugs!"

"I can explain," White Junkie Boy interrupts. "Jean-Jacques would sometimes allow me to tag along and run with him as he trained." He laughs. "I could never keep up. That kid was full of stamina and power. A day or so before he was murdered, I was sitting behind the gas station smoking a joint. He was going through something with his girl."

"Girl, what girl?" the stepfather interrupts. White Junkie Boy raises his hand; the stepfather stops speaking, but the confused look remains on his face.

"He was going through something with his girl," White Junkie Boy continues. "He took the joint from my hand. He took one puff and coughed so hard I was surprised his lungs did not blow out of his mouth. He was not a drug user." The stepfather shifts in his chair, looking at White Junkie Boy like he wants to kill him. "It is my fault. I should have stopped him. He was not a drug user. Period."

"Sir," the reporter addresses Panther's stepfather, "it is public record that you have served a lengthy prison sentence for..."

"Excuse me," Nuri interrupts; the scowl on

his face is intimidating, "Mr. Riley is not on trial. He is one of many victims in this case. When I decided to give you the story, I explicitly instructed all questions would be related to Boxing Boy's murder. You agreed. This family has been through enough." Nuri opens his laptop; the camera pans to the screen. Rows of video clips and thumbnails cover the entire screen. "We are going to stay focused on the subject that brought us here. These are images and videos of the rogue cop who killed Boxing Boy committing rogue cop crimes against the people in the community." He presses play; a video of the police officer striking a young black male who looks to be no older than sixteen on the legs several times with a metal rod. "Pay close attention around the one-minute timestamp." The gym is completely quiet. Everyone is focused on Nuri's computer. It is obvious he has studied the footage. At one minute and ten seconds, the video shows the officer, now known as Rogue to the community, toss a metal rod to the ground. He slams the boy's limp body against the car with one hand and uses the other to remove the contents from his pockets. He scans the Korean store parking lot and quickly stuffs the contents in his pocket. Another video shows what appear to be young girls stopping in the middle of the Central Drive and bending forward to shake their backside to the beat of background music. Rogue is in the far corner on the side of the Korean store beating a young male as a female stands with her hands cuffed behind her back a few feet away screaming for him to stop. The girls dance, laugh, and appear oblivious to the violation filmed in the background. "This dirty cop believes he can come to our community and do whatever he pleases. Notice he did not arrest anyone."

"Mr. Nuri, have you taken these videos to the police?"

"No, Sir, we have no faith in the police." Nuri folds his arms across his chest. "We have to gather more evidence. And we need independent media and independent reporters like you to help us bring this rogue cop's behavior to light. We will clear Jean-Jacques' name. The Pakistani on the corner where the murder happened has video footage. He will not release the film footage to us. He supports the police against his own interests. We have virtually run him out of business. He is holding on by a thread, and if he does not cooperate soon, we are going to cut the thread." He looks into the camera. "I need all of the storeowners to look at their surveillance videos. If you have given videos to the police, we need to know that, too. The footage in this computer is the tip of an iceberg. Some very interesting video footage has come into our possession. We will reveal more at another time."

"Mr. Nuri, you don't deny the area is crime infested." The reporter removes a piece a paper from his notebook. "The number of arrests on Central Drive is incredible, and the number of young Black men convicted of crimes..." He raises his shoulders. "You can see for yourself." He attempts to pass Nuri a piece of paper.

"Sir," Nuri pushes the paper away, "I live on Central Drive. I don't need your statistics. I have a bird's-eye view of what happens in our community." He looks dead in the camera. "You are right. There is a lot of crime, but the real criminals are behind the scenes. The arrests and convictions are another story. Many people in our community go to prison and have not committed crimes that are prison worthy. They simply cannot afford legal representation." Nuri removes a notepad from his pocket. "Check out the District Attorney's stats. How many trials has she brought before the court? She does not put defendants on trial. She backs them against the wall and threatens them with lengthy prison sentences if they go to trial and are found guilty." He looks at the camera. "What this D.A. does is nothing shy of extortion. This system is rigged, and you know it. The prosecutors know it, and the judges know, too, but that free prison labor makes everyone turn their heads." He laughs. "I would love to see some of these prosecutors' and judges' investment portfolios. I wonder how many have stock in commercial prisons." He locks eyes with the reporter. "There is more footage out there. I am offering one thousand dollars for each video I can use to prove that Jean-Jacques, our beloved Boxing Boy, is not a murderer."

"Mr. Nuri," the camera pans from the reporter to Nuri, "where do you get the money to finance such an endeavor?"

"Sir, we have benefactors that believe in what we are doing."

"Mr. Nuri, what do you suppose is being covered up?"

"I am not quite sure, but best believe we aim to clear Jean-Jacques' name and bring the rogue cop to justice." He looks away from the camera. "Not this time. They will not kill one of us and get away with it. Not this time."

I turn the television off as the pain becomes intense. I have lost track of the minutes between contractions. I feel a strong urge to push but remember reading premature pushing can rupture the uterus. I grab my bag, leave the house, and wobble to the car. The pressure on my vagina makes it uncomfortable to sit. I panic when I realize I have waited too long and call 911.

"Good afternoon 911. What is your emergency?" I want to scream fuck the emergency and get someone out here but manage to keep my composure.

"I am having a baby. I don't think I can drive to the hospital." I grab tight to the steering wheel to get through a contraction. The breathing techniques in the videos are useless. Instead of breathing, I scream to the top of my lungs.

"Is your husband available?"

"I don't have one." I somehow manage to remember my address and scream it into the phone.

"Help is on the way. I will stay on the phone with you until county emergency arrives."

I sit on the front seat and alternate between the urge to push and enduring the pain. It seems as if it is taking hours before I hear a siren. I look over the seat and see red flashing lights approaching the house. I have never been so happy to see another human being when I see the female technician jump out the ambulance before it completely stops. She escorts me to the ambulance and immediately helps me onto the gurney. She removes scissors and cuts away my pants and throws a white sheet over my legs.

"Hurry, guys!" She lifts the sheet and takes a quick look between my thighs. "We may not make it to the hospital." They turn the lights on and drive so fast it feels like we are flying. The technician calls the hospital while holding my hand. "This is EMT#310. We have an impatient baby that wants out now!" She continues to hold my hand. "Breathe, Momma." Within a few minutes, we arrive at the hospital emergency.

The EMTs roll me out of the van and through the emergency door to the delivery room. The doctor and nurses are waiting and ready. They don't wait for my personal doctor to arrive. Instead, the emergency room doctor lifts the sheet and takes a quick look and yells, "The baby's head is in the birth canal!" The doctor positions himself between my thighs and screams, "Push!" I grab my knees and push with every muscle in my body.

"Stop!" I lay back. I feel pressure as the doctor manipulates my opening to assist the baby's exit from the birth canal.

"Push!" This time, the nurse pushes my back forward. I grab my knees and push again. I feel my vagina spread as the baby's head pushes through. I push three more times, and my baby has fully entered the world. "You have a beautiful baby boy." The doctor cuts the cord and places the baby close to my face, so I can see the dark brown blob with a head full of jet-black hair. His cry is more of a roar than the soft vibrations of a baby. I wait for the feeling of euphoria I read about in the many childbirth books I purchased; the euphoric feeling never comes. I smile with the nurse, but I feel odd, off balance and lost. I am not happy; instead, I feel burdened.

"Mom, we have to clean the baby up, get blood work, and tag him." Her smile is bright. "We will bring him right back to you."

"It is okay. You can keep him in the back until I am ready to go home. I am very tired and want to sleep."

"Honey," her smile disappears, "you must get used to the baby's schedule. Have you called your family?" Her smile is bright again. "Are they on their way?"

"No, no one is coming." I turn my head, close my eyes, and wait for sleep to come.

Chapter 24
Myrtle

I flip through television channels while waiting for the evening news. Commercials have taken over all the channels. I leave the living room and go to the kitchen for a glass of tea. I rush back when I hear the introductory music that sounds like typewriter keys hitting the platen at rapid speed. The headlines are the best part of the news. Barbara Bell, my favorite anchor, is beautiful. She looks more like an A-list actress than a news anchor. Her hair and makeup are always flawless. The camera man always captures her best side. She looks straight into the camera. Her affect is flat as she announces a special investigation report. The camera pans to a side-by-side picture of Barbara Bell at the news desk on one side and a gathering of several men moving around a gym on the other. I lean closer to hear the headlines. I quickly grab my glasses. I rub my forearm to ensure I am awake, alive, and not dreaming. It is Jermaine, but it does not look like the Jermaine we know. He is sitting with Lance Leslie, an award-winning anchorman who retired several years ago.

The screen with Barbara Bell in the newsroom disappears. I have to look three times to be sure it is Jermaine. The black suit appears tailored to fit his thin frame. The colorful bow tie blends well with the suit and accentuates his beautiful brown skin. The messy braids are gone and replaced with a neat, precise, and close haircut. His face is much slimmer; his sculptured cheekbones are more pronounced. After introducing Jermaine who he calls Nuri, a picture of the dead thug who shot Chandler appears on the television screen followed by a picture of Whit.

Jermaine or Nuri as he is now calling himself has been protesting daily on the corner on behalf of the misfit who killed Chandler. He should be ashamed; Chandler helped many of the black young men in the community who were headed down the wrong path. Jermaine is one of those Chandler helped. Chandler arrested Jermaine more times than I can count for public drunkenness, disorderly conduct, and various minor drug violations. Chandler was so kind that after he placed him in the back of the car, he would take him to his mother's house so she would know where he was. Chandler would beg Betty to let him stay in jail for a few days to teach him a lesson, but she never did. As soon as a bond was set, Betty would be at the jail, cash in hand, waiting to bond him out.

When I first saw Jermaine on the corner protesting, I thought he was running some type of scam. Bums and drug addicts often hold signs on the corner claiming homelessness and begging for food. Every once in a while, a small child will stand next to the adult as a prop to pull on heart strings. I was shocked when I did not see a bucket of some sort in Jermaine's hands requesting donations.

A couple of weeks after Chandler's murder, I was returning home after running errands. I turned on Central Drive from Harrison Road, and I saw a crowd congregate along the sidewalk in front of the convenience store owned by the Pakistani. The crowd was a mixture of school aged children and young adults. My window was up though it was warm outside, a precaution in the event one of the hoodlums attempted to jump in my car. The criminals are so brazening they will steal your car while you are in it. I removed my foot from the accelerator and crept along. The voice sounded like Jermaine only more articulate. I turned into the parking lot, parked in front of the store, and observed the spectacle.

"Am I next? Should I tell my mother to set aside money for a black dress?" His eyes were filled with fury. His voice cracked with emotion.

"Hell no! Fuck that shit!" The anger from the crowd frightened me.

"Will it be you, brother? Will your son be the next unarmed black male murdered by this rogue cop?"

"Fuck with mine, they will see what time it is!" A tall male with a construction hat on top of his head, a tool bag in one hand, and a tall beer can in the other yelled over the crowd. He stood next to what appeared to be a preschool aged boy carrying a book bag. He reminded me of a cartoon character, as he bobbed his head to every syllable that came from his mouth.

"That's just it, brother." The crowd began to part as the speaker made his way to the construction worker. "Brother, you are Boxing Boy; your son is Boxing Boy. They only see this color," he pulls up his sleeve and points to his arm, "this color has no value to them. We all know many of us do messed up stuff out here in these streets and are due for some spiritual retribution. I raise my hand as a former menace to our neighborhood. I was a problem, but that boy represented hope many of us never had, or if we had it, we lost it."

His voice came nearer. I rolled down the window so I could hear. I near lost my breath when me and Jermaine made eye contact, and he behaved as if I were a stranger. I have known him all his life but seeing him without a beer in his hand and dressed respectably in a Sunday suit was too much to take in at once.

"It's time we demand justice for Boxing Boy and for all of us! Let's get Boxing Boy his due process."

The crowd threw their fists in the air, and yelled, "We want justice" as he passed out flyers.

We made eye contact again, but there was something about the energy that made me uncomfortable. I quickly made my way out the parking lot and rushed home.

I am anxious. Hives pop up all over my skin. This Breaking News has yet to begin, and I instinctively know it is not good. I have not seen Whit in almost a week. He was supposed to stop by on Monday. It is Friday. I have called him every day. In the beginning, I called every hour; the calls were routed to his voicemail. I am overcome with emotion when I see his picture on television.

I feel like a fool. I ignored all the signs. They were apparent, but I was flattered by the attention. I am ashamed at my judgment. I loaned him twenty thousand dollars. My bank account is almost at zero. I had to rush to the bank last week and make a quick deposit to prevent an overdraft. Loaning him money was not intentional. He is smooth. Each time I gave him a loan, he paid the money back, and somehow, he ended up with what he paid back plus more. He is an officer of the court for God's sake. I simply did not expect this type of behavior. Initially, I made excuses for his sudden lack of communication and unreturned phone calls. I blamed the ex-wife. I told myself maybe she had Whit arrested for child support or missed alimony payments. He has been struggling. He has been looking sickly lately. His eyes are always glassy, lids always red, and he has frequent nose bleeds. The criminal element that he confronts daily is getting worse. He was recently attacked by neighborhood thugs. According to Whit, the thugs took him by surprise, held him down, and burned his face.

I believed I was helping him by loaning him money to pay his child support. He painted a picture of a vengeful ex-wife determined to terrorize him forever for a failed marriage. I thought Whit was a victim. He presented a mild and caring persona. In my mind, a woman would have to be an idiot to leave a man like Whit. He presented me with a dilemma, and I volunteered to solve it. Each time I loaned him money, he said he would repay. The first loan was for five thousand dollars, but somehow the loan amounts kept increasing. It was out of the ordinary the way it happened. One evening, I was watching television in the sitting room when I heard the doorbell.

"Hey you." I smiled. I could barely contain my excitement. He removed a bottle of wine from his coat. "I thought you may want to have a glass with me."

"Sure, I would love to." I was taken aback and didn't know how to take the attention. Is this a date or a neighborly gesture? I am sixty-seven years old, but I can tell when someone is flirting with me. I think, *what could he possibly want with me?* "Come on in. Let me get some glasses. Where is your car?"

"I parked down the street at the corner store. I wouldn't want people talking. There is too much going on." He smiled. "I see you have a new haircut."

"You noticed?" I rubbed my fingers through my new short pixie cut.

"New hair color, too?"

"How do you like it?" I turned around to give him a 360-degree view. "I am told it makes me look years younger." I lie; Whit was the only person who had commented on my new hairstyle. I sashayed into the kitchen, hoping he noticed the slow and deliberate movement of my hips.

"You look beautiful as always." He was sitting comfortably on the sofa when I returned. He took the glasses from my hand, opened the bottle of wine, and poured until each glass was half full. "Are you dating? Do you have someone steady in your life?" His smile was wide, and his eyes appeared hopeful.

"Me?" I smiled. "Oh gosh no. My husband died several years ago." In the most seductive way I could, I crossed my legs, ran my fingers through my hair, and leaned back into the sofa. "I have been on a few dates." I am lying; I have not been on any dates. "I just have not found the right fella." My smile is wide. I bat my eyes seductively.

"You think maybe you have not been looking in the right places?" He slid closer. He placed his hand on my thigh and gently squeezed. He looked into my eyes then down at my legs, I followed his hands with my eyes as they moved from my knees to my thighs. I instinctively parted my legs, and he softly massaged my inner thighs. My heart rate increased as he massaged what my deceased husband used to call his special little button. I leaned back deeper in the sofa and opened my thighs wider. I was happy my arthritis didn't act up as I moved my hips to the circular motion of his fingers. He rolled on top of me. I traced the roundness of his shoulders and the outline of his toned and tanned arms with my hands. His body felt hard and strong.

"I really like you." He looked deep into my eyes. "I don't want to do anything disrespectful."

"Oh, honey," I used my tongue to push my top dentures back in place. "Don't be silly." I pulled his face to mine and continued to spread kisses all his face. He slid my pants over my hips and down to my ankles, and slowly massaged my opening with his fingers. He stepped away and pushed his pants and underwear down past his hips. I admired his patience; it took a while for my body to open and accept him.

He was probably twenty years younger than me, but I met him thrust to thrust. My heart began to flutter. My lower extremities felt as if a million butterflies had taken flight. I had not experienced sexual pleasure with another human in over twenty years. After several minutes, he collapsed on top of me. His face was flushed, and his breathing was labored. I was happy, more like surprised, I could still please a man. He rolled off me to the next cushion and poured another glass of wine for the both of us. "I hope I didn't take advantage of you."

"God no." I took the wine glass from his hand. "I am grateful to know I am still alive. I thought that part of me had long died." We both laughed; his disposition quickly changed from jovial to somber. "What's wrong, honey?"

"Oh, nothing." He leaned closer and kissed me. "You have been so good to me."

"Is your ex-wife harassing you again?"

"I don't know what to do. I pay the child support as best as I can. Thanks to you, I have finally gotten caught up and now she is threatening me with garnishment because I am behind on the alimony. I offered her two grand. That is all I have after paying you the five thousand I owe you. I can barely pay my rent."

"How much do you need?" I found myself getting angry at his ex-wife though I had never met her.

"I can't ask you to loan me anymore money. I am fifteen grand behind. If she does not take the two grand, she will simply have to garnish my wages. When I lose my job, she will not get any money."

"No such thing." I stood, reached down, and pulled my pants up. He followed me upstairs where I removed my check book and wrote a check for fifteen thousand dollars. I passed the check to him, as he climbed into my bed.

"Thank you so much, honey. I will pay you back. Do you mind if I stay the night?"

"Of course, I would love the company." I quickly opened my lingerie drawer, removing a nice negligee I had never had an occasion to wear. I took it with me into the bathroom where I showered then grabbed a plush spa towel and patted myself dry to keep my skin moist. I sprayed perfume and pressed an extra pump down there in the event he wanted to make love again when he woke up. This was the first night in over twenty years that I did not sleep alone. Leaving the bathroom, I found him smiling as I walked toward the bed. He raised the covers, and I slid underneath them. I fell asleep with his arms wrapped around me.

When I woke up, the sun had already set. A sticky note lay next to my pillow.

Thanks for the loan. I will pay you back ASAP.

I smiled when I saw tiny hearts next to his name. I walked downstairs and found the envelope with the five grand he repaid gone.

I try to shake the memory from my mind. I sit in front of the television watching Jermaine; he is surrounded by several people. The white boy next to him is a neighborhood bum who walks aimlessly around Central Drive, but he is cleaned up. He is one of a few young white kids stuck in the neighborhood. They arrive in nice fancy cars and the top-of-the-line designer clothes. Within a few months, the cars are gone, and they are walking while the drug dealers drive their cars.

The white bum looks very professional. His voice is authoritative. His words are sophisticated. He exudes confidence. The reporter asks questions about the shooting that took place four maybe five months ago. I am surprised people are still talking about it. People get shot all the time in our neighborhood; I don't understand the big deal about this shooting. The camera pans to Jermaine's computer. The footage is grainy and distorted, but there is no doubt the officer is Whit. The bald head and broad shoulders are a dead giveaway. He stands with his weapon drawn and pointed at two young black kids standing in front of his unmarked police car; their feet are spread apart. Their hands are on the hood of the car. He removes something from one of the kids' pockets, quickly looks around, and places the contents in his pocket. He places his gun in the holster on his hip, slams their heads into the hood of the car, shoves them to the ground, and steps over them like trash in the street. I use my hand to wipe the tears away and tell myself to breathe deeply to stop my heart from racing.

Jermaine taps his laptop; videos of young girls dancing provocatively in the street are displayed on the screen. The girls are laughing and appear oblivious to Whit beating a teenage boy with a long black object behind them. "This is not all." Jermaine taps the pause button on the computer and looks straight in the cameras. "This rogue cop is not in our community to protect and serve." He turns away from the camera and presses the play button. Seconds pass and footage of the Korean store parking lot filled to capacity with high end cars appear on his laptop. "For many, this appears to be nothing, but everyone in our neighborhood knows what goes on in the back of the store in the wee hours in the morning. This is Rogue cop. It is one in the morning. This store turns into a high stakes gambling casino and only God knows what else. The gambling stakes are rumored to be in the millions. You will not see anyone from the community in this room. These businesses are fronts for illegal activity."

"So, Mr. Nuri." The reporter's face is expressionless. His voice is void of emotion. He gets straight to the point. "What do you think happened?" I think to myself, Stop calling him Nuri; his name is Jermaine.

"I know what did not happen. Boxing boy is lefthanded. Everyone, especially those in the boxing community, knows he is lefthanded. Rogue cop is messy and didn't do his homework. The gun was planted on his right side. He did not shoot anyone. We will prove Rogue cop shot and killed Boxing Boy and Detective Chandler."

"Why? What would be the motive?"

"I don't know. We are still going through footage." He looks into the camera. "I want all of the store owners to pay close attention to what has happened to the Pakistani store owner. We want the truth, and we want it now. If we don't get the truth, we will shut down all of the businesses on the corner of Central Drive until we do."

Chapter 25
Benazir

I can't take care of this baby. The crying for no apparent reason drives me crazy. I feed him two ounces of formula every two hours as the nurse instructed, but he is always hungry. I change his diaper immediately after he soils it, yet he kicks, screams, and moves his body erratically making a simple task, such as changing a soiled diaper, an event. Nothing is good enough for him. He sleeps all day and stays up practically all night. He knows he is driving me crazy. I lay him next to me and keep the lights on at night, so I can sleep. He somehow knows when I close my eyes and begins to scream to the top of his lungs. He immediately stops crying when I open my eyes. His cry is annoying; he does not have the soft cry of a newborn baby; it is deep like an oboe.

Last night, while bathing him, he peed in my face. I detected a slight smile as I screamed with urine dripping down my face. I was comatose with anger; I allowed myself to act out a fantasy that has played in my mind since the day I bought him home. Our eyes were locked. He began that god-awful cry but quickly stopped when I removed my hand from the back of his head and released him in the water. He slowly sank to the bottom. I placed my hand on his chest, slowly pushed him under the water, and held him down. The water covered his eyes, mouth, nose, and forehead. His arms and legs moved rapidly with a force I did not expect to come from a baby. His resistance slowly weakened. Bubbles floated from his nose and mouth to the top of the water. I quickly regained my senses and became overwhelmed with fear. I lifted him out of the water and softly patted his back to help him cough the water out of his lungs. He cried for a couple of minutes but nowhere near as long as usual. He looked straight into my eyes as if he was reading my mind. I dried him, put on his pajamas, and placed him in his bed. He normally cries and screams for several minutes when I lay him down, but he just lay in his bassinette and follows my every move with his eyes. I don't think this baby likes me, and I am ashamed to say the feeling is mutual.

I am the worst mother on the planet. Looking at this baby brings me to tears. I am overwhelmed with despair and remorse. This is so much more than I bargained for. I have dark skin but a different kind of dark skin. When I first saw him, my hope of passing him for a Punjabi, Muhajir, or Sindhi all disappeared. Panther has strong genes. Khoudir looks like a round, dark blob with a mass of jet black loosely curled hair. He has Panther's features. He will not pass for any of the dark-skinned Pakistani ethnic groups. His features are clearly of African descent.

The sun is up. He decides it is time to sleep. I feel like prodding and poking him to keep him awake, so he can know how it feels to have sleep interrupted. I am happy he is quiet; I dare not wake him. I honestly thought of leaving him in the hospital but had faith that I would get used to him. My faith is waning.

The staff did everything to make me comfortable; however, I dreaded each and every time the nurse came into my room with the baby. Caitlyn Smith, the day nurse, truly got on my nerves.

"Have you called anyone, sweetie?" She stood next to the bed rubbing my arm as she checked my blood pressure. "Where is your family?" Her Southern accent was strong.

"I don't have one." I turned away, thinking she would leave.

"Well, sugar, unless you are giving birth to baby Jesus, there has to be someone." She giggled. "It kind of takes two." She held up two fingers in front of her bright toothy smile.

"My husband is away in school, and my family is out of the country. My mother will be here next week." I smiled. I was sure my story did not add up, but I hope it was enough to make her go away.

"Well, dear, how will you get home?" She continued to rub my hand. "The doctor will release you in a day or two. What about the baby's car seat?"

"Car seat?"

"Yes, Sugar, we cannot allow you to leave with the little one without a car seat." I didn't think of that. I read several books to prepare for this baby but did not recall reading a car seat is mandatory for the baby to leave the hospital.

"I will have my co-worker bring my things. I can order a car seat, and have it delivered here, or I can leave him here until the car seat arrives."

"Sugar, you are funny." She bent forward, laughing so hard she held tight to her stomach. I was annoyed that she thought I was comical. "Don't worry, sweetie. I will take care of that for you." She tapped my hand and before leaving said, "I will get a car seat for the baby."

I am unstable; I can't believe these people allow me to be alone with this baby. Either they didn't care, or I am good at hiding my insanity. However, they began to appear uneasy as they pushed me in the wheelchair to the waiting taxi.

"Sugar, are you sure there is no one we can call?"

"Yes, I am fine. My husband is studying for exams. My mother will fly in next week." The nurses assisted me in the taxi and secured the baby in the car seat. Before waving goodbye, one of the nurses placed a card in my hand. I turned it over and found the number to County Mental Health.

I walk to his bassinette. He lies on his back and appears peaceful in his sleep. Images of the blue pillow that lies next to him on top of his face flash through my mind. God, I wish I would have simply left him at the hospital. I remove the pillow from his bassinette and throw it in the garbage.

I quietly go through the bags in my closet, careful not to wake him. I remove the videos I took from the store and place them, one at a time, in the DVD player. The first few videos are disgusting, cheaply made porno flicks starring some of the young neighborhood girls who barely appear to be out of their teens. Others are videos of neighborhood thieves placing items in their pockets and leaving the store without paying. I view several videos before I find something interesting. The footage is clear. I don't recognize the surroundings, but it appears to be a back office in one of the stores but not our store. Several men have converged in a narrow hall; they shake hands and greet one another as if there was significant time since they were in each other's presence. They walk down a narrow hall that leads into a spacious room. The Brute is obviously the person making the video, as I hear his voice but do not see his face.

He along with several gentlemen including the police officer that killed Panther sit around a long mahogany table. Young girls in skimpy clothing walk around with drinks and thin lines of white powder on a platter. "We have all made a lot of money in this neighborhood. This Chandler is fucking shit up." An olive-skinned Middle Eastern man with short dark hair walks in front of the camera. He looks at the cop that killed Panther. "We are paying you a lot of cash to keep us informed." He opens a notebook, removes his calculator, and presses a series of numbers. "Last year alone, we paid you over one hundred thousand dollars to protect our interests." He holds the calculator close to the officer's face.

"Yes Jack, and I appreciate everything, but I had nothing to do with Detective Chandler's transfer. These monkeys wanted him here; he grew up in the neighborhood. They believe he is a God." He throws his hands up. "If you guys would have given the Negros a piece of the pie in the beginning, none of this would have happened. You all have to admit the violence has gotten out of hand." He stops one of all most naked girls. She extends the tray with the white lines of powder. He passes bills to her and bends forward and sniffs the white powder on the tray through a rolled-up dollar bill. "Fuck, they want him to run for political office. They have raised a lot of money for a potential campaign for county sheriff."

"He is fucking up our money! The monkeys are providing information on all of the dealers on Central Drive to Detective Chandler." A slightly overweight man with dark, curly hair who appears to be Turkish hits the table hard with his fist. "Our suppliers are losing their cool."

"You are right, Jack. He set us back with the drug bust a few months back. The news reports the bust netted two million dollars and 100 kilos of heroin, but our connections say they lost four million dollars and 200 kilos of heroin." An older, bald male with a gray beard joins the discussion. He toasts his glass with a clean-cut younger male with dark hair who appears to be Hispanic. I can't tell if he is Mexican, El Salvadorian, or Guatemalan; he brings a shot glass to his mouth and throws his head backwards.

"Where is the rest of the product? What you bet dirty cops took the two million unaccounted for and supplied the monkeys with our product?" He stares at Officer Whitley. "There is a black dude and white girl who recently set up shop down the street, and I hear the West End is now heavy in the game." He hits the table. "What do you bet they are selling our shit?"

"We are going to be under scrutiny and out of business like the crack dealers. Someone is greedy and lacing a good product with a deadly additive that is killing people." The Hispanic shakes his head as if he is disagreeing with his own conclusion.

"To keep peace, we have to let a few of the blacks in the game." A young Asian chimed in.

"The monkeys don't play by the rules. We tried working with them. They cut the product and mix it with God only knows. The rich white kid found at the bus stop with a needle in his arm a few months back bought a lot of attention. Usually no one cares about junkies, but he was a college kid making high marks. His parents made his death breaking news, blamed the school, the neighborhood, and everyone but the junkie. Their inquiry connected the dots to four more overdoses and one near fatality. All the sudden, law enforcement led by that goodie two shoes cop acts as if there is a pandemic. If the junkie gets their shit and move on, we are good. Our guys don't offer credit or borrow their cars. The blacks develop personal relationships, borrow cars, and sleep with the women. You can't mix business with pleasure."

"You guys are in the wrong business." The Russian pours a round of drinks to everyone.

"Thanks, Vlad." I am shocked when I hear the Brute thanking the Russian for a drink. He has always maintained he does not drink alcohol.

"The drug game is old," the Russian continues, "and there are too many risks. It is time to elevate business to less riskier endeavors with high returns."

"If you would do your fucking job," a burley white guy slaps Officer Whitley on the back of his head. "We would not have all of this heat."

"I did not know Chandler would take the job. I had no idea his wife would be okay with him coming back here. She was the reason he left the neighborhood in the first place."

A distinguished, young, dark-skinned male who looks to be of East African descent chimes, "Go easy on the popo. It's not his fault. The thing is this new junkie is not poor white trailer trash. This new breed drives late model sports cars with alumni tags from major universities. We don't need rich white kids coming down here getting a fix and getting robbed or these young white girls getting stuck down here with these black guys. It is bringing too much attention to Central Drive." He swallows his shot. "This gambling thing you have, Vladimir, is impressive. I have some people on the East Coast who are willing to invest."

"I have several college football and basketball players willing to throw a game for a couple of thousands of dollars while we make millions." Vladimir sips from his glass then places it back on the table. "I have my eyes on a winner." His voice is filled with excitement. "I reached out to the mother. I am telling you there is a black kid in the neighborhood who is a beast in the boxing ring. We can place bets on him and make a killing. If we get him on our side, we can also place bets against him and make a killing."

"Is he on board?"

"No, his mother's boyfriend or husband trains him. The rumor is his natural father is dead. She is protective. They won't let anyone near him, but I am still working on it."

"We need Chandler gone!" The Turk waves his hand in the air. He is not impressed with Vladimir's gambling enterprise. "Gambling, selling cocaine, weed none of our businesses are safe with Chandler around." The one referred to as Jack opens an envelope and pours the contents in the shot glass, uses his finger to mix it, and swallows. It must be strong as he stands, shakes his head, and beats his chest before sitting back in his chair. "What is Chandler's price?"

"He does not have a price." The police officer who killed Panther responded.

"All cops have a price. I have never met one who did not favor green over blue."

"Not this one." The killer cop placed his glass on the table and leaned back in the chair.

"We have been able to build fortunes here. We have paid college tuition for many family members," the Korean says in broken English as he hits the backside of one of the girls who walks past him. "We have to protect our investments. It was you who underestimated this community." The Korean's round face is filled with anger as he points to the cop who killed Panther.

"It took you a long time to get transferred so you could oversee this operation; we want something done about Chandler immediately. Central Drive is the ideal location to supply those small northeast towns. Our boys can drive down and move the product to the northeast with ease."

"We want Chandler gone!" the Korean yells before placing a black duffle bag on the table. He removes a stack of bills and passes them to the cop. "We trust you will come up with a solution very soon."

Chapter 26
Marie

The neighborhood boy stands about an inch from my daughter in the threshold of the front door. His smile is wide. His eyes are flirty as he speaks in a very low volume. I listen to their conversation as I slowly walk to the kitchen. The only audible word is *"Surprise."* The clean-cut young man who used to be one of many neighborhood bums is smitten with my daughter. She moves her body subtly seductively; her smile is bright. Her eyes lighten at every word that leaves his mouth. It is obvious the attraction is mutual. I startle her when I leave the kitchen and enter the living room. She quickly glances over her shoulder. Our eyes lock; I look away and walk back to the kitchen. I stand by the corner of the refrigerator where I can easily see her, but she can't see me. She speaks in a soft tone and says, "I will watch. I wish we could watch together."

"Me, too." His smile widens. "I have to go. I have to meet with the sponsor to tie things up." They stand at the door and stare into each other's eyes. She stands on her toes. He bends forward, kisses her forehead, and steps away.

"Bye, Nuri." The words flow out her mouth

like a song.

I am on route back to my room when I hear him say, "Bye Jazz." I want to interrupt. She never allows anyone to call her Jazz. He slowly walks backwards away from the door. She stands in the threshold long after Nuri has left then slowly closes the door. She turns and props against the door.

I go back to my bedroom where I lay in bed and try to sleep without a sleeping aid. I am restless. Sleep will not come. I leave the bedroom and walk past the living room to the kitchen. She has moved the chair from the dining room and placed it directly in front of the television. I don't understand the necessity for this closeness to the television. It is a fifty-inch, flat panel and positioned on the wall for easy viewing no matter one's position in the living or dining rooms.

"Why are you so close to the television?"

She jumps out her seat. Her affect is a strange mixture of fear and surprise. She fumbles with the remote. It flips in the air, lands hard on the floor, and slides across the newly stained hardwood floors. She quickly leaves her chair to retrieve it and surfs to channel two, then channel five, and lastly to channel eleven. *"Breaking News"* headlines all the local channels. She turns the television off and attempts to leave the living room with the remote in her hand. I pry the remote from her hand as she passes and turn the television back on.

The District Attorney stands proud with the Chief of Police on one side and the mayor on the other. The murderer stands proudly behind the D.A. and Chief of Police in solidarity with a small army of uniform and plain clothes law enforcement officers. She is dressed to impress in a black suit that perfectly fits her toned body. Her jewelry is simple yet classy; diamond studs in each ear and a large diamond ring on her finger reflects the sun. Her hair is perfect. Her makeup is flawless, and she looks as if she enlisted an A-list Hollywood makeup artist. "Condolences, justifiable force, no charges filed, weapon, toxicology..." flow from her mouth with ease but are jumbled in my brain. A life-size black and white photograph of my son after a boxing match sits lopsided on an old easel on the woman's left side. The altered photograph makes my son appear angry, menacing, and much older. He is dressed in his favorite gray hoodie he believed bought him luck in the boxing ring. A bright full-color picture of Detective Chandler dressed in his detective uniform sits perfectly straight on a bright new easel on her right side.

"No, Mommy, you don't' need to see any more of this. You don't need to listen to anymore of the lies." My daughter tries to pry the remote from my hand. I tap her shoulder with one hand while I hold tight to the remote with the other. I stare deep into her eyes, raise my brows, and convey the message, you had best let go of this remote without words leaving my mouth. She releases the remote and backs away without saying a word. The She Devil stands confident with lies flowing from her mouth like an erupting volcano.

My entire body aches. The pain begins in my head then travels down to the back of my neck. Depleted of energy, I sit on the sofa; my daughter sits beside me.

I can barely move my arms as the D.A. reads the results of the toxicology report. "Cannabis," she deliberately says the word slow and enunciates each syllable to perfection. How can this be true? Jean-Jacques was a professional athlete dedicated to his craft; he would never use drugs. A flood of tears finally begins to flow from my eyes. I can barely keep my head together. Maybe she is right. Maybe I am wrong about the man I love. Maybe I am wrong about my son. If he used drugs, he would have gotten them at the gym. His entire life was boxing and that gym. Why would Jikki allow such a thing?

"This should be a wakeup call." She speaks with authority of the ills of the community I call home. "We have to invest in our youth." A picture of my son in his hoodie stands as her poster child for the disenfranchised black youth in our community. Disenfranchisement was not Jean-Jacques' narrative. She looks to her right at the Reverend. "Reverend Manchester, who is the pastor of the Holy Saints Church, a mainstay in the community is stepping up to the plate." She smiles. "Reverend, would you like to speak?" He smiles, pops his collar, and proceeds to the podium.

"To God be the glory." He looks toward the sky and then directly at the audience. "We know that only God can make something good out of this terrible tragedy." He removes his handkerchief from his pocket and wipes spittle from the corners of his mouth. "My wife and I..." The camera pans to the pastor's wife who sits in the first of three rows of folding chairs with a large brooch on the right side of her chest that matches the large hat that sits perfectly on the top of her heavenly head. Her legs are crossed at the ankles; she appears perfectly saintly. "We have been in the community for a while. We know the people. We can all agree that it is past time we do something about our youth."

He stops speaking and scans the small audience as if he is standing in the pulpit as opposed to the top of the marble courthouse steps in front of news reporters. "This young man..." He points to the picture of my son. The television signal scrambles. A dark blue screen replaces the news. The words *"Signal Lost"* suddenly bounces up and down the television screen. I check the cable connection then sit back down when the signal returns. "He did not have to lose his way. We could have caught him. This young man..." The reverend points to the picture that looks like a mugshot of my son again. "This young man lost his life because he decided to take another life. We can't do anything about this young man, but we can try to save others." He clears his throat, looks toward the sky, and scans the audience. "I will be running for county commissioner in the upcoming election." He raises his head, straightens his jacket, and stares into the camera. "It is time we work with law enforcement and take back our communities. The hoodlums have taken..."

The television blacks out again *"Signal Lost"* bounces from the top to the bottom of the television.

I stand then slowly sit down when pink balloons tied to a white balcony with chipping paint float in the air. The sound of children laughing with adult music in the background draws me closer to the television. A long banner taped to the balcony reads *"Happy Birthday Shericka."* Children with colorful hats on top of their heads run around in circles chasing one another; their innocent laughter sounds like a beautiful melody. Adult voices playfully yell, "Smile" over rap music with vile lyrics. The video pans to another group of children jumping in a bouncy house. An adult in the background yells for the children to jump higher. The footage is filmed from a balcony of one of the apartments on the side of the Pakistani's store with the camera pointing down.

I am confused. My daughter and I lock eyes; our mouths are wide open. We raise our shoulders simultaneously and turn our attention back to the television. I move closer to the television to get a better look at the footage behind the bouncy house. Three bodies run in a straight line past the front of the Pakistani's store to the side where a black chain link fence separates the store from the apartment complex where the birthday celebration is in full party mode. The fence, thin trees, and overgrown vegetation block most of their bodies, but the top of their shoulder to the top of their heads are clearly visible. One of the runners is Jean-Jacques. Officer Whitley's bald head stands out; he runs behind Jean-Jacques with Detective Chandler following suit. My daughter and I move closer to the television.

Jean-Jacques stops running as he reached the black chain link fence. The children continue jumping in the bouncy house, appearing totally oblivious to the events behind them. Jean-Jacques grabs the top of the fence and begins to pull himself up, as if he were going to jump over it. Officer Whitley's head moves closer. Jean-Jacques suddenly stops, lowers himself to the ground, and turns in the direction of Officer Whitley. His hands are held high above his head. The top of the fence that separates the Pakistani store from the apartment stands slightly below Jean-Jacques' shoulders. My daughter grabs tight to my arm. I cover my mouth with my free hand. The officer advances toward Jean-Jacques, and an unusually loud gunshot followed by a bright spark paralyzes us. Jean-Jacques' head quickly falls from the footage. The officer quickly turns as Chandler steps closer. The second gunshot is so loud my daughter and I both jump out of our chairs. Chandler's head drops from the footage. The children's high-pierced screams interrupt a few seconds of complete silence. They fall over one another as they run away from the bouncy house. Officer Whitley advances in the direction toward the fence where Jean-Jacques dropped from the footage. His head disappears. The footage begins to shake as if an earthquake has taken place then blackens. The sound of adults cursing fades out. My daughter and I look at one another; both of our mouths are hung open. I am crying and laughing at the same time.

"Nuri said he had a surprise for me." She smiles with tears flowing from her eyes. "I have to call him."

The knock on the door startles us. I am stuck to the sofa. I cannot move. My daughter manages to unlock her eyes from mine and answer the door. My tall black king stands in the threshold. He steps inside. Tears stream down his face like a fast-flowing river.

"Did you see it?" He uses his left hand to wipe the tears away. "Did you see it?"

"They lied. They smeared his name. Why would they do that?" He steps closer. I leap from the sofa. "Je vous aime Jean-Jacques. Je t'aime ma fille. Je vous aime Jikki," I scream, "I love you, Jean-Jacques, I love you, my daughter, I love you, Jikki." I step close to him. I feel a soft movement in my left side. I step back, and Jikki opens his jacket.

"What is this?"

"This is Khoudir." He removes a light blue coverlet. A dark-skinned bright-eyed baby with a mass of hair looks directly into my eyes. I have seen these eyes before on my beloved Michel. I have seen this exact same nose on Jean-Jacques. The blanket drops to the floor. I cover my mouth.

"The Pakistani girl and a young girl she said was her cousin came to the gym. She was a mess. She gave me the baby. He removes paperwork from his pocket and passes it to me. "This is the birth certificate." He smiles. "This is Jean- Jacques' baby."

"What? How?" I unsnap the baby sling, remove it from Jikki's shoulder, and reach for the baby. His body fits perfectly in my arms. The television blanks again. The mayor is now speaking. The district attorney sits in the background. Someone walks behind the mayor and passes the D.A. a cell phone. She holds the phone close to her face. She looks at the phone as if she has seen a ghost. She covers her mouth and quickly places the phone on her lap.

Chapter 27
Jefferson Thomas

I usually spend my time glued to law books. I left my cell early this morning and set up camp in the television room. I use money to create alliances willing to do battle with anyone who stands between me and the television today. Nothing can keep me from the news today. The noise in this place is crazy. Most of the time, I block it out, but today, the conversations about nothing are working my nerves.

Deez Hands and his entourage of dummies sit in front of the television. It's 5:53. The news starts at six o'clock. Seven minutes to go; I hope I don't have to lay hands on Deez Hands again. I imagine he believes his entourage will take me; I have no intention of finding out. It is 5:57. I walk to the television and stand next to the controls.

"Jake, did your girl get the money she needed to take care of her business? Are the kids okay? Tuition paid?"

"Yeah man, good looking out."

"Terry, your mom cool?" He raises his thumbs.

"Y'all commissary straight this month?" Everyone in the television room nods except Deez Hands and his make-believe entourage. I turn the channel, and as I suspect, Deez Hands and his dummies who actually believes he is a rapper because he has a two second verse on one song on an independent mix tape rush toward the television. They quickly back down when the true thugs and lifers stand and surround them ready for battle.

"Now that we have an understanding, I only need to watch television for a few minutes, and you can have it." I look around to ensure there are no objections. I stand anxiously waiting for the commercial to end. My heart races to the sound of the news introduction. The sexy news anchor introduces herself followed by her Caucasian male co-anchor. *"Breaking News"* is highlighted, the camera pans to the county steps in front of the courthouse.

One would think she is a class A act. On the exterior, she is polished. Her suits are tailored to fit perfectly. Her hair is cut to precision, not one single strand is out of place. She is not exceptionally beautiful, but when you add all her assets together, she can be perceived as stunning. She is confident on stage as she shakes hands and engages in small talk with the Mayor and the Chief of Police before they are officially on the air.

The friendly smile disappears as she walks to the podium. She is the District Attorney, crime fighter extraordinaire. She stands between the Mayor and Chief of Police. A black and white picture of a young black male in a hoodie is positioned on her left, and the deceased, decorative officer serves as the backdrop on her right. She provides background on the incident that left an officer and a neighborhood teen dead and shares the testimony from neighbors who allege they witnessed the justifiable shooting of Jean-Jacques Gomez. She commends the officers' fine work. I can only imagine what the family is thinking as she announces her findings. I pray they wait and do not leave their television with anger. Joy will soon come.

"The Mayor, the Chief of Police, and I put one hundred percent of our faith in this officer and those on the force who do a good job no matter the danger in protecting our communities." I lean closer as she introduces a minister from the community. Other inmates look at me as if I am crazy as I cannot contain my laughter when he announced he is running for commissioner. She has found a new patsy. I wish there was a fast forward button. The minister's presentation is tiresome. The footage scrambles, and white letters that read *"Signal Lost"* bounce from the top to the bottom of the blue television screen. When the signal unscrambles, I stand and get nervous when the screen goes black then returns to coverage of "Breaking News Press Conference."

I sit in my chair when *"Signal Lost"* returns and pans up and down the television screen. Footage of pink balloons floating in the air and children with birthday hats sitting lopsided on their heads replaces the news conference. The sound of children laughing as they jump in bouncy house mixed with adult gangster rap with no bleeping of the curse words is out of place. Pink balloons and a banner wishing *"Shericka"* a happy birthday decorate the landscape. The party attendees are oblivious to the activity on the other side of the black chain link fence.

Three males, one wearing a gray hoodie over his head, one bald white male, and one black male run at a rapid speed past a convenience store until they reach a black chain link fence. The hoodie falls off the younger male's head as he jumps on the fence and pulls himself up. The officer stands behind him. The teen lowers himself to the ground and slowly turns around with his hands held high in the air. Adults laughing as they film a children's birthday party are clueless to the crime they are inadvertently filming until the sound of gunfire erupts. Children begin to scream and fall on top of each other as they leave the bouncy house and run into the apartment building for safety. The runner with the hoodie instantly drops from the footage. The bald white male quickly turns around, walks a step or two, and faces the black officer. A few seconds later, screams are heard after a second and louder gunshot. The third runner falls out of the film footage. The white male walks towards the fence. He disappears from the footage. A few minutes later, other officers arrive on the scene.

The television signal unscrambles with the mayor speaking. The D.A. has taken a seat with other city officials behind the podium. A uniform officer steps behind the mayor, stands next to the D.A., whispers into her ear, and passes her a phone. It seems as if her body begins to shake. Her hand covers her mouth. She quickly regains her composure. She stands with a fake smile as the audience applauds.

"Madam District Attorney, do you have any closing remarks?" She does not speak. She manages to keep the fake smile, waves her hand, and leaves, as reporters swarm with their microphones extended in her direction.

The noise in the prison breakroom returns.

"What the fuck did we just see?"

"Brothers, you have witnessed a get out of jail free card for anyone who was arrested by Officer

Whitley." I stand. "If any of you are in this prison due to an arrest made by Officer Whitley, today is your lucky day. In a few days, lawyers will be trying to find you."

I leave the sitting area and stand for thirty minutes in line waiting to use the payphone.

"Katsa."

"How are you, brother?"

"You did a fine job, Katsa."

"I don't understand how this will help you."

"It won't. The corrupt cop never sent me to jail." I laugh. "I can do these last two years with ease just knowing it will not be too much longer before I get out of this prison."

"I will be shutting down shop. When you get out, you know where to find me."

"Yeah, you and Theresa will be in some cave, or climbing a mountain who knows. Tell Theresa I will make this up to her."

"Theresa is fine. She knows she holds the key to my heart. She understands the business."

"Keep my money safe."

"You bet, brother."

"Oh, have you found the other bitch that placed me here?"

"Still working on that one. The Russian she ran off with had just as many connections as you." I hear a slight giggle.

"Had?"

"Theresa took care of him for you" He laughs. "She still has this thing for spilling blood. Trust, it will not be long before I find her. I am the master at what I do."

www.ingramcontent.com/pod-product-compliance
Lightning Source LLC
Chambersburg PA
CBHW021304250626
47155CB00002B/374